It's Not My Wedding (But I'm in Charge)

Books by Sharon Naylor

IT'S MY WEDDING TOO

IT'S NOT MY WEDDING
(BUT I'M IN CHARGE)

Published by Kensington Publishing Corporation

It's Not My Wedding (But I'm in Charge)

Sharon Naylor

KENSINGTON BOOKS
http://www.kensingtonbooks.com

KENSINGTON BOOKS are published by

Kensington Publishing Corp.
850 Third Avenue
New York, NY 10022

All Kensington titles, imprints and distributed lines are available at special quantity discounts for bulk purchases for sales promotion, premiums, fund raising, educational or institutional use.

Special book excerpts or customized printings can also be created to fit specific needs. For details, write or phone the office of the Kensington Special Sales Manager: Kensington Publishing Corp., 850 Third Avenue, New York, NY 10022. Attn. Special Sales Department. Phone: 1-800-221-2647.

Kensington and the K logo Reg. U.S. Pat. & TM Off.

ISBN-13: 978-0-7582-1437-9
ISBN-10: 0-7582-1437-5

First Kensington Trade Paperback Printing: April 2007
10 9 8 7 6 5 4 3 2

Printed in the United States of America

It's Not My Wedding
(But I'm in Charge)

Chapter 1

I am walking down Madison Avenue with a check for ten million dollars in my pocket.

It was there. I had slid my hand into my bag, spreading the billfold of my wallet to feel for its rough serrated edge, about a hundred times in six blocks. I could feel it. It was warm somehow, like it was heating up the thirty-one dollars in cash I had right next to it. Each time I touched it, it felt hotter and hotter.

You kind of lose your mind when you have ten million dollars in your bag, or maybe that's just me. With each step of my boot heels on the puddled, slushy sidewalk, I had another separate fantasy about the ten mil I'd been entrusted with for a twelve-block walk to the bank.

What if I just hop down to Atlantic City and put it all on red at the roulette table? Just slap that little sage green check right there on the red circle while a crowd of amazed senior citizens and hard-core gambling addicts with dark bags under their eyes gathers around me and peers over my shoulder. Someone would call the six o'clock news, and they'd have a hot Italian camera guy covering my ballsy move. "Woman Puts $10 Mil On Red." I'd double my money and stay in Trump's personal suite for the week. With the hot camera guy.

Or, *What if I just walked into Tiffany right now and showed them the check? Would eight smiling Stepford jewel supermodels float out from the back room with champagne and strawberries, ushering me into a private suite where I could try on the diamonds Jennifer Aniston wore to the Oscars?*

What if I could cash it in twenties, take it home, and roll around naked in it for a while? I've always wanted to do that.

I was walking with a lascivious smile on my face, all but petting the side of my purse, and people were looking at me strangely. *Am I giving off a vibe that I have a ten-million-dollar check in my bag? Is that guy checking me out because he KNOWS, or because he's just checking me out? Am I going to get mugged here? Am I going to wind up in a police precinct answering a detective's raised-eyebrow questions on why I'd be so stupid as to walk down the streets of New York City with a check larger than the amount in most armored cars? I'd wind up on the six o'clock news: "Idiot Woman Makes Herself a Walking Target—$10 Million Gone Like That." They'd use an animated graphic of fingers snapping and a flurry of dollar bills floating away into the air.*

I am losing my mind.

Four more blocks until I reach the bank, deposit it into the account, and return to a place of sanity. I was practically running now. *Get this thing out of my purse.*

I was, and was not, surprised that my boss entrusted the check to me. Zoe Brandenberg had . . . moments. Moments of clarity, and moments she called the "purple-plum veil of haze." Even when describing her depression, she had to accessorize it well. She was, after all, the reigning contessa of wedding planning. She was the wedding coordinator to the stars at the highest stratospheres, the ones who spent six figures on their wedding cakes alone and commissioned artisans from Morocco to weave them custom rugs for the outside doorway to the church. These were the elite, celebrities who breathed different air than we did, since they paid about one hundred thousand dollars a month for someone to show up with pink metal cannisters of O2 to plug into specially designed outlets in their homes. *But I'm getting ahead of myself.*

Zoe Brandenberg was *the* name in celebrity and royal weddings. Dakota Fanning had her prereserved, and the twin grandchildren of the Queen of the Netherlands already had a date chosen for them . . . and they were in preschool. Zoe would be sixty-five when their weddings rolled around. But that was her demand level. As the ads said, *If it's not a Zoe wedding, it's not a wedding at all.* We in her back room, of course, had much fun with her commercials. *If it's not a Zoe wedding, it's a blowy wedding.* We'd been breathing too many hot glue vapors, it seemed sometimes.

I might be in the back room, but I was Zoe's right-hand woman. I was her "Number Two Woman," she said, and I'd never been comfortable with how that sounded sometimes. Especially when Zoe was on a manic high, reinserting pearl pushpins into the center of roses in *concentric circles* rather than spirals. "Mylie! You're my Number Two! Put down your jacket and help me concentric these!" She could go for days on end, and with me as her right hand, I sometimes didn't see daylight for three days. For her average four-million-dollar wedding, that was a lot of pearl pushpins to redesign in the centers of barely bloomed roses.

Everyone asked me if I liked Zoe Brandenberg, and I honestly didn't quite know what to say. As a boss, she was demanding, but you got to understand the logic behind the lunacy. When she was up, she was on fire, and she created magic. It truly was amazing how she preenvisioned color schemes and could make an orange theme actually work without looking like a Syracuse University homecoming dance. When she was done with it, it looked like the vibrant oranges and yellows and reds of a dramatic sunset in Hawaii. She made orange sexy and smoldering. She made purple rev up your libido. And I don't even want to tell you what her reds did. Her happy clients said she shared the same palette as Mother Nature, with all the same creative force. These were actresses. They were paid to be dramatic. While I wouldn't get quite so powers-of-the-universe about it, I had to say that Zoe was a genius. And like most geniuses, her mind was . . . complex.

Do I like Zoe? Absolutely. She could be shrill and obsessive, Type A-plus, haunted and maniacal about invitation fonts, but she was never rude. When she got tired, her hands shook. Her eyeballs darted from side to side. And she'd occasionally burst into tears when she couldn't get the leatherleaf ferns to arch just right. She once threw her Jimmy Choos at an ice sculpture because the facial expressions of the two doves looked pained, not enraptured. And I was always there to place my hand on her back, whisper a secret message into her ear, and lead her back to her spa room for some rest. She had a spa room in her design studio. White reclining couches, a Zen water fountain, vases of gardenias brought in fresh daily. And a Lalique tray of Godiva chocolates, raspberry-filled starfish. I guided her there with a light touch on her elbow, since she didn't need to be helped, as gentle and as loving as a daughter putting her on-the-verge-of-dementia elderly mother to bed.

Zoe appreciated my tenderness, apparently. She raised my pay by ten thousand dollars each time I rescued her from a particularly bad downward spiral. And she slept with her lips in a slight childlike smile, her face softer like she'd grown ten years younger. "Thank you, Mylie. You're my angel," she said each time. "You're my hands."

And I stayed up through the night to rearrange pearl pushpins in concentric circles just as she would want it. I bundled up in a parka, climbed into the deep freezer, and chiseled out just the right facial expressions on the ice sculpture doves, first trying out my own enraptured expressions in a mirror to get the lip lines just right, and Zoe slept like a cherub while I *shushed* the night cleaning crew and found just the right font for the monogrammed napkins.

I dated someone once who tried to analyze me. He said I saw Zoe as a replacement mother figure, that I was trying to please her, to become her. I took my toothbrush home from his place and laughed with the cabdriver about it on my way back to my place. That was what I got for trying to meet a guy on-line. I wasn't going to waste my time or ruin a perfectly good mojito by trying to explain, "No, I'm learning from her. I have the same genius. I'm just learning from her. And she's a person who needs a little kindness once in a while."

"And how much did you say you get for this kindness? An extra ten thousand dollars?" My snakey former date clucked his tongue and still didn't manage to dislodge the tooth-clinging parsley he had popped to help out his breath (which, by the way, did not work). "You, my dear, are taking advantage of a floundering old woman whose passion is driving her mad."

The guy's one-man, one-act play had just been canceled in the city. He wore black and saw everything through a telescope of bitterness, too far removed from reality to see anything clearly and with his own purple-plum veil of despair. He should have paid me ten thousand dollars just for putting up with him for five dates. But I digress . . .

Zoe Brandenberg. She was a genius. She trusted me. And she said I "have it." *I'm sticking with her.*

That was why I was walking a ten-million-dollar check to the bank and depositing it, with blue ink still wet on my hands from signing a CIA-level, four-inch-thick confidentiality agreement with the celebrity bride and groom who have come to us—sorry, to Zoe—to create *The Wedding of the*

Millennium. I haven't met the two stars yet, although I have had very vivid sex dreams about the groom-to-be in the past. Their associates showed up with the confidentiality agreements in locked black leather briefcases. They even brought their own pens, and held out their catcher's-mitt-sized, meaty hands to get the pens back. According to the terms of the confidentiality agreement, Zoe and I were to be the sole designers. No support staff at all. If any word leaked out at all about the plans for this ten-million-dollar celebrity wedding heavenly extravaganza, the henchmen would return to harvest my eggs, my ovaries, my spleen, my kidneys, and my corneas with plastic pudding spoons and no morphine.

We called this a Zip It job. Talk to no one. Put nothing in writing. No e-mails. Use only a scrambled-line cell phone. Jennifer Garner would play me in the movie, I decided one night while waiting for the subway. National security was not this tight. We had spy gear for planning weddings. I really could use one of those black leather jumpsuits Jen Garner wears on screen. And I'd need a code name.

It was while considering what my code name should be that I reached the bank and pushed through the heavy rotating doors with a *whoosh*, suddenly walking with the high, confident step of a runway model (only not as horselike), working it, secretly hearing the theme music to *Mission Impossible* in my head. With my black hair braided tightly back, diamond earrings in my ears, black stiletto knee-high boots, and freshly red lips, I stepped up to the counter and used a voice that wasn't my own. I went throatier, sexier. It was how Jennifer Garner would have delivered the line in the movie of my life: "I'd like to make a deposit."

Chapter 2

I would get five percent of the ten million.
When the wedding was over.

I wasn't a math major, so it did take me a minute or two to move the decimal point and figure it out, but that certainly was enough money to roll around in naked when the time came. And it was enough to furnish my dream apartment entirely with everything in the Williams Sonoma catalog. Well, most things. I wasn't wild about the white lamps with the yellow polka dots. I was thinking more of a chocolate-colored palette . . . rich, deep cocoa browns, champagne pales, bronze accents, hints of pink here and there . . . no, wait, scratch the pink and replace it with cinnamon.

I should be focusing on the cabernet-colored calla lily bouquets I was making right now, pairing them by the arch of their petals, the curve of their thick pale green stems, the delicate ways they nestled together, but instead I was in two places at once. Normally, I could shut out the outside world and focus on the task at hand. I was in the back workspace, chilly from the cool temperature we kept it at to benefit the flowers, and it was 5:00 A.M. We had a wedding today. An ambassador's daughter and an oil magnate's son. All of their flowers must be the color of her childhood bedroom, a pinkish purplish red. She was unable to produce a color swatch for us, so we had to fly to Belgium and find her childhood home, knock on the door, and ask the current owners if we could look at the upstairs bedroom to get a color match. Zoe's French was perfection, and of course we had no trouble getting in the door. Or scraping off two coats of midnight blue wall paint to see the pinkish purplish red beneath. The owner of the house recognized Zoe from the *Oprah* show, so we could have gotten the paint sample and helped ourselves to everything in their refrigerator if we had wanted to. Plus their VCR. I was amazed at how doors literally opened for Zoe. She had a name. Her face was known. She was an icon.

"How are the bouquets coming?" Renata pushed the heavy door closed and pulled a sweatshirt over her head. She lost most of the baby weight in record time, but still insisted that she needed bulky outfits, even when she wasn't in a refrigerated workspace.

"If I could focus, they'd be done by now." I sighed, sounding way more whiny than I'd intended to.

Renata was the only other employee of Zoe's who was in on the secret that we were doing the ten-million-dollar celebrity wedding. She was the backup in case I got hit by a bus. *I swear. It's in the confidentiality agreement.* She knew we were going to be working on it, but she wasn't in on any details. A deal was a deal.

"Then focus." She winked, her violet eyes the main reason why Zoe hired her in the first place. That and her six years of experience at the New York Botanical Gardens. But Zoe said her eyes were the exact color of a sunrise she once saw in the Arizona desert, the rich purple outline of cliffs in the distance.

We worked in silence, wrapping the bridesmaids' bouquets with lengths of pinkish purplish red silk ribbon, affixing a circular cork bottom to the stems, and then origami-folding the ribbon into an intricate closing pattern, sealed with a crystal charm at the bottom. For the one larger white calla grouping, we use a diamond pin that the bride could take off of her bouquet and wear in the future to all of the cotillions and oil magnate estate parties, dinners at the White House, and alumni gatherings at Harvard. We always added a little something that could be kept for the future. From the bouquet, from the veil, from anything. This time, it was a diamond brooch the size of a silver dollar and worth about fifty thousand of them.

These kinds of things still took my breath away.

I hoped I'd never lose my ability to see the beauty in each detail, each accent. I hoped it would never get old and boring for me to see the perfect arch of a calla lily's petal, the shine of a Swarovski crystal, the tiny little rainbow in the tiniest corner of a diamond as it caught the sunlight just right. The smell of gardenias, and how it always reminded me of my grandmother, who would have been so proud to see the work I do.

"Nice," Renata whispered as she fastened the last charm to the last bridesmaid's bouquet. She stepped over to the wall— which was actually a giant dry erase board—and crossed off "Make bridesmaids' bouquets" and "make bride's bouquets" from our dwindling To-Do list. Without a word or a moment to absorb our accomplishment, we moved right to the boutonnieres. Lily of the valley for the groom, mini ranunculus for the groomsmen. No one was doing baby roses for the men anymore. Although they would probably come back in style a month from now. Things moved quickly on the market. Usually when Zoe said so.

"So tell me . . . have you met him yet?" Renata smiled, her dimple denting her smooth cheek. She was thirty-five but looked twenty-two. I was thirty-five and looked thirty-four. I'd take it, having seen some brides who were thirty-five but looked forty-five from too much hard living.

"Who?"

"*The* guy."

I rolled my eyes. *Get off my back, woman.*

"Still doing Match.com?" she tried. As most happily married new moms did to their single friends.

"No, turned it off." I didn't lift my eyes away from the tender droops of lily of the valley that I was now matching together like puzzle pieces. Most people would just bunch them like a handful of parsley, but I knew Zoe's microscopic view. She'd light it on fire if the edges didn't match well, the flowers not falling well.

"Bored?"

"Bored."

Renata nodded. "Gotcha."

An ex-boyfriend of mine, one of the many that I stayed friends with over the years, once told me over a cold Bud at a steakhouse, "It's easy for mediocre people to find each other, Mylie. They have so much in common because the middle ground is so flat. But if you have something special about you, it's just going to take a little longer." He was, of course, including himself in Club Mediocre (and, I assumed, the nineteen-year-old he started dating after me), but his insight was spot-on. "And you are not so pathetic as to wish to be mediocre," he said, patting my leg where he had once kissed it not too many months earlier.

I then asked him why so many guys insisted on leaving the bathroom door open when they went to pee. What was *that* all about?

"Fear of being trapped," he said. "Run from those guys."

So I have now added a new rule to my arsenal of dating musts: never date a guy who peed with the door open. It was a long list.

"Where are you?" Renata's voice drifted into my reverie.

"Just remembering something," I whispered, actually sounding a little bit embarrassed.

"No, I'm looking for the glue gun." She laughed, tossing a

handful of lily of the valley at my face so that it landed and stuck in my hair. Which was exactly the moment that Zoe walked in.

She wore a white suit—pretty risky in our notoriously stain-happy environment here—her blond hair done up in a perfect chignon with a single stephanotis tucked into the curl, diamond teardrop earrings, and pale pink lipstick. That was one of the signs I read to gauge her mood. Was her lipstick on well? When she was ultramanic or ultradepressed, or heading in either direction, it was the lipstick that told the tale first. She was fine today.

"Two more hours," Zoe sang, waving her manicured fingers (and a giant diamond ring on her right ring finger) and practically dancing into the room.

Hm, maybe I should check that lipstick line a little more closely.

"How are my little elves doing?" She picked the lilies of the valley out of my hair and set them in a neat pile on the table, patting my arm in the international sign for *it's okay*.

"Excellent, Zoe." I nodded, hands now on my hips, scanning the table to assess our work. She zipped her gaze to the Wall of Progress and nodded as well.

"Spectacular," she said. Her new favorite word. *Fabulous* was out of style.

"Think the weather will hold up for them?" I nodded toward the window. Menacing clouds threatened their no-tent outside garden wedding. It was dark and eerie out there, the sun never really having a chance to shine at this early hour.

"The clouds tend to part for our clients." Zoe winked, and I knew she was going to use that line on the oil magnate and the ambassador in just a little while. And she was mostly correct. We'd had only two complete rain washouts in the years that I'd been here, and only one fire. Working with Zoe had a ninety-nine percent protection from the elements clause. "Mylie, I need you ready to fly in four hours."

I blinked. "Ready to fly?"

"We're going to Hawaii," she sang, and danced out of the room.

I turned to Renata, whose frown of disappointment turned quickly into a half smile. She wasn't the jealous type, but she could use a vacation in Hawaii more than I could, with a colicky new baby and a husband who was not quite used to sharing his wife's breasts with anyone else. She had two babies on her hands right now. And a burn from the hot glue glob she just dropped on her pinky.

Chapter 3

Did I mention I love my job?

Practically singing in the cab on the way to the airport, my carry-on stuffed to the groaning point because Zoe didn't ever allow baggage to be checked when we flew to Naples or Orlando, Cairo or Morocco, Monte Carlo or Vegas. I had enough frequent flier miles to get to Jupiter and back, but no time to use them.

I met Zoe in the First Class VIP lounge. She was sipping a mimosa and chatting with a silver-haired gentleman who was trying very hard to hide his wedding ring. The arthritis wouldn't allow him to slide it off and drop it into his pocket as he had probably done for decades before now. I smiled at the man and stepped between them, my shoulder telling him to go find a flight attendant to chat with.

"Mylie, my dear, you're right on time." Zoe drained her mimosa and mouthed a silent "thank you" for my interference with the Old Cad. "I hope you brought a suit."

Does she mean work suit or bathing suit?

"We're meeting with some clients as soon as we arrive, so be ready to change on the plane." Her lack of details—and Zoe *always* got into details—told me immediately that these were *the* special clients. The ten-million-dollar clients. I blushed just thinking about the groom. "And no blushing."

* * *

Granted, the rest rooms in first class were larger than in coach, but was still hard to pull on panty hose in there.

Zoe was a nervous flier. She popped Xanax like Pez and considered herself above the no-drinking-while-on-meds rule. While most people would turn into stammering, drooling morons after so much ingestion, Zoe was always fine. Bright-eyed. Eloquent. Charming.

I was not so well acquainted with prescription drugs or liquor, so while I was a nervous flier as well, I had to take a pass on the help. Instead, I fidget and shift, certain to be catching the eye of whatever air marshal had already pegged me as a Person of Interest. If they would just pump a low dose of nitrous oxide into the cabins of planes, everyone would be very happy during their flights. It would be hugs all around and utter bliss when the dried-up sandwiches and pretzel packs came out. They wouldn't have to show an in-flight movie because everyone would be staring into space and smiling, or looking at something shiny, or saying, "I love you, man," to the business traveler next to them. And the kids would not kick the seats in front of them.

I smile to myself as the captain announces our descent. I'd already changed into my light blue suit, wrestled on my stockings, and forced on my strappy heels, even though my feet had swollen from the flight. My toes looked like little sausages, which I hoped would not be noticed by the superstars I was about to meet. My mouth was dry already. I wasn't normally nervous meeting celebrities. I'd met them all. But I'd never expected to meet one that I'd dreamed of taking a bath with, among other things.

"Ready to go?" Zoe turned to me, chipper and pink-cheeked, ready to step into the biggest deal of her lifetime. And mine. Her confidence was contagious, and I was smiling as well. We had two very important clients waiting for us.

And the plane touched down in Hawaii. We had arrived.

Chapter 4

Celia Tyranova (called "Supernova" when she first splashed into the movie business as the industry's final answer to the question "Who is the next Julia Roberts?") and Christopher "Kick" Lyons were inside the resort. Not much other than that would ever be able to distract my attention from how blue the sky was in Hawaii, how azure the ocean, how red the reds of the hibiscus flowers dotting the long drive up to the fountain at the front of the resort. But I could have been driving up to a maximum security prison and still been enchanted with the idea "They're inside!" I would allow myself the distance between here and the sliding glass doors at the entrance to be a giggling, star-struck idiot. Then I would be all business.

Our driver pulled to the front doors, and the valets knew to step away from the limousine. The driver would open the door for us.

Zoe and I had long ago mastered the art of stepping out of a limousine without flashing your underwear (in my case, a thong) to the crowd of people who appeared out of nowhere to gawk at who was about to get out of the stretch black limo. It was a quick swing and a firm first step. Fast as anything, smooth and graceful, as much in the hips as in the legs. We practiced when I first started working with her, due to an unfortunate paparazzi photo featuring my sliver of red panties quite visible in the background of a celebrity shot. Not that anyone noticed. I was not the movie star in the picture whose mascara was running black down her cheeks after a public fight with her professional baseball player boyfriend, but there I was in the background. And Zoe *did* notice. She pointed it out to me with a magnifying glass and a scowl on her face.

This time, I got it right. The swing and the step, the hips and the leg. No flash of thong at all. And I was all business with my black sunglasses, my hair slicked back in a tight ponytail, my suit free of wrinkles, and the diamond tennis bracelet Zoe lent me for these meetings sparkling in the sun. All around us were the vacationers in their swim trunks and bright floral sarongs, or their tennis whites or day-of-golf green Izod shirts, craning their necks and whispering "Who is that?" and I always hear Zoe's name. I was invisible, of course, but I kind of liked it that way.

First things first. We were *frisked*.

Two enormous security guards whose arms were as big as my thighs patted us down from our necks, down our shoulders and arms, our waists, our stomachs, hips, bottoms (that one's just for fun, I'm sure), and down our legs. They checked our shoes, which I found out later was to look for tiny microphones or bugs that we might have installed in our heels, or that someone else may have placed on us. They took our cell phones away, promising to give them back when we were done. Camera phones were not to be risked.

They checked our earrings, presumably for bugs, although I distinctly got the feeling that one of the security guards was looking for flaws in our diamonds. He nodded, impressed, and I gave him a look that was part annoyance and part amusement.

They asked me to remove my ponytail clasp, and they ran their fingers through my hair. Zoe's chignon was not disas-

sembled, though, even though it looked like she had a defi-
nite microphone in her updo. I half-expected them to pull out
a speculum, but they trusted us with our orifices. Thank
God.

"Pull your shirt to the side." One of them stood with his
hands on his hips, feet a distance apart, like a cop trying to
make himself look wider and thus more intimidating.

"My shirt?" I blinked.

"We just need to see the bra straps . . . in case of wires,"
the cop wannabe said without blinking. Having no choice,
and not wanting to wind up at the end of some bar somewhere whining that my resistance to showing my bra strap to
a semi-Neanderthal cost me my job and my opportunity to
meet Kick and Supernova, I pulled on my jacket to reveal my
bra straps. Of course, not to be messed with, I revealed the
whole cup and modeled it, stepping from side to side like I
was modeling for a camera. Zoe suppressed a smirk and then
showed her own wide, white bra straps. No cup.

It didn't stop with a bra check. Now, we went hi-tech.

They pulled out an ominously glowing blue pad and asked
us in little more than grunts to press our thumbs against it
and hold it for three seconds. "Done." They nodded when
the little blue pad beeped for each of us. "Fingerprints," one
explained. "All we need is the thumb." I choked back a smart
comment about their need for an opposable one, as these men
took their responsibilities very seriously. Who knew what
their confidentiality agreement contained?

Next, they took out what looked like a thin silver pen and
shined a red light into our eyes. "Oh, my," Zoe remarked,
fluttering her thick black lashes and stepping back. We'd just
had a retina scan, and I hoped my blue contact lenses had not
rendered me null and void in Identity Central. I sometimes
wore the green ones. *Will I not be able to access my life when
my eyes are green instead of blue?*

"Stop the smirk," Zoe whispered to me. I had forgotten,

for a micromoment, to be professional. *Yes, please do take every kind of scan of me possible. I'll need a mammogram in about five years, so let's get that going right now, okay? Bone density scan, anyone?* "Mylie, I'm serious," Zoe warned, and for a moment I felt like a scolded little schoolgirl caught talking in class. She fixed my ponytail to make it straight, and we were then allowed to turn the corner on the penthouse floor and walk into a rarified atmosphere. *When that door opens, everything has officially begun.*

I swallowed, readying my smile, smoothing my skirt, calm and steady.

I checked Zoe's lipstick. Fine.

We were ready to go.

The door opened before we even knocked.

I wondered if there was some kind of sensor inside, as hi-tech as we'd been scanned here in the hallway. No one seemed to have radioed in our arrival, as the security guards were watching us from three feet away, squinting, breathing through their mouths.

A thin blond woman wearing a headset opened the door, talking to the headset, not to us. "Yes . . . yes . . . yes . . . no . . . ," she said in an English accent, and I wondered if this was British phone sex or if she was ordering a pizza, accepting the veggies and rejecting the pepperoni. Finally, the answer came: "She'll talk to *Vogue* now, but she won't talk to *W* until November." Ah, the Over-Exposure Police. Dole out the interviews.

She waved us in, and we stepped onto an almost too soft carpet, our heels sinking in. An Oriental rug centered an octagonal table, on top of which was an ice blue vase filled with white lilies. *I wonder if that's standard room décor, or if the stars have presented a list of "Must Have's" like Mariah Carey with her Cristal.* The walls were a cool light blue with white sconces turned on, even though it was daytime.

We were led through a white-carpeted living room, with all white couches and a silver ice bucket cooling an uncorked bottle of wine. And a collection of Mounds bar wrappers left on the coffee table. Before the thought of any kind of eBay auction seriously entered my mind—I was in line for way more cash than the three hundred dollars I'd get for Kick Lyons's Mounds bar wrappers—I followed the still *yes*-ing assistant to a sliding glass door that opened to a dream of a view. Nothing but ocean all the way around. Clear blue ocean with not even a sailboat marring the horizon. Complete privacy. Palm fronds dancing in the delicious ocean breeze. A massive pool with a bubbling hot tub. A bar made of large white stones, set atop with ice blue tumblers and dishes of macadamias, white flowers in a matching ice blue vase. And across the pool, the only place they could be: a large steel frame draped with white netting. Celia was sunbathing topless just outside the shade of her cabana. Kick was not there.

Celia heard the clicks of our heels on the poolside stones and quickly wrapped a sarong across her chest. We'd all seen her breasts in her last three movies, so it wasn't a big deal, but I was pleased that she covered them up for business meetings. Through the netting, we could see her stand, step into flip-flops, and smooth her hand over her hair.

The netting parted with a graceful reach of her arm, and she walked toward us. For a second, it was as if she was not real. Like I was looking at a cardboard cutout of her. But time caught up to my sense of reality, and she was a glowing, gorgeous redhead with that signature smile and the most perfectly arched eyebrows I'd ever seen. I was instantly self-conscious of my own.

"Hello!" She stepped forward, smelling of cocoa butter and jasmine, and hugged Zoe first, then me, quickly, but a real hug. Not an air hug.

"Celia, hello." Zoe didn't bother with the Ms. Tyranova

thing. She went right for the instant familiarity. "May I introduce my assistant, Mylie Ford?"

As if she would say no.

Celia hugged me again, her green eyes warm and friendly.
"Mylie . . . that's an interesting name. . . ."

I took a breath to begin sharing the story of my name, but
Zoe jumped in. "Yes, and funny we should be telling you
here in Hawaii! Mylie was named after the female romantic
interest in the Elvis movie *Blue Hawaii.*" Zoe nodded, proud
of her FYI.

"*Really?*" Celia blinked. "I *loved* that movie. They filmed
it at the Coco Palms."

I smiled. My parents had conceived me at the Coco Palms
hotel. Maybe I'd share that little FYI with her a little later
than within the first two minutes of meeting her.

"So you're Hawaiian-bred?" Celia asked with a nudge to
my arm, and I realized I hadn't even spoken to her yet. Had
I? I'd better come up with something witty and memorable.
Something none of her other fans would ever have said. But
she beat me, looked at me strangely. "Does she speak?"

Zoe burst into laughter, and I quivered out a smile . . . and
probably a hibiscus red blush. "Yes, hello, Celia," I finally
managed, praying the red would drain out of my face.

"Ah, she does speak." Celia grabbed my hands and shook
them, like a girlhood friend on the playground. "I thought
we'd gone a step too far with the security . . . that Zoe had
hired a mute." She giggled and wrinkled her nose. "That's
one tactic we hadn't considered."

Zoe and I laughed, as did the British blonde, who appeared
out of nowhere with a tray of pink lemonade in footed tumblers. And Mounds bars. Seemed our girl Celia had a personal
favorite.

"Did you bring your swimsuits?" Celia asked, placing her
hand—the ring hand—on my shoulder. Of course, I had to

look. I'd seen the picture in *InStyle Weddings*, a zoom that I now saw didn't even begin to capture the facets of her spectacular Asscher cut. "I have only an hour, and I really wanted to get in the pool."

She wants to take a meeting in the pool? That's a new one.

"Unfortunately, our luggage is back at our resort already." Zoe frowned, even though I knew she'd rather die than take a meeting in a skirted swimsuit. "But feel free . . ." Zoe rather presumptuously swept her hand outward to give Celia permission to step into her own swimming pool. It was the first flicker I saw in Celia's eyes, followed by a narrowing and a furrow in her brow. Just for a second, but it was there. Zoe was off her game . . . we had found her Achilles' heel: how she looked in a bathing suit. This was a woman who would take a meeting while skydiving with a celebrity. She'd done it before.

"I'll join you, Celia." I overstepped my bounds and pulled from my purse a tiny black bikini. Never fly to an island with your bikini in your luggage. For exactly these kinds of situations . . . *Well, maybe not exactly this kind of situation, but you get my point.*

The British Yes Woman smiled a message to me—*good save*—and waved me to follow her back inside. I almost didn't want to leave a flustered Zoe with Celia, but I knew I could quick-change before Zoe did any more unknowing damage to our deal. Sorry, *her* deal.

"I'm Angelique," said the British blonde and held out her tiny, child-sized hand in a surprisingly firm handshake.

"Mylie."

"We're all very excited about the wedding, and we know you'll do a superb job of it." Angelique smiled a whitened smile and slid open the heavy glass doors leading back inside.

"We're just thrilled." I nodded. "We're looking forward to seeing what Celia and Kick have in mind."

Angelique rolled her eyes. *Whoa. What was that?*

"Well, I can tell you that they want everything to be the best . . . as they deserve."

"We wouldn't do it any other way," I promised. "Whatever they want, they'll get it."

Angelique nodded, looking from room to room just as I was . . . looking for *him*.

We passed a fabulously decked out kitchen with silver, top-of-the-line appliances for the chefs to use, a tropical gardenesque bathroom with a glass-door shower and flickering candles in hurricane lamps, a spare bedroom with lavender bedding, a spare bedroom with deep blue bedding and a wispy canopy, a spare bedroom with all white bedding and a canopy. *Geez, how many bedrooms are in this place?*

"Mr. Lyons doesn't appear to be here." Angelique looked markedly disappointed. "I wanted you to meet him straight off."

I mustered every ounce of professional distancing. "Well, I'm sure we'll meet him soon enough."

We walked on down the hall in silence, just us girls completely bummed out. Elvis had left the building.

"There you are!" Celia was already in the water, leaning against the wall, poised like a glamour cat, while Zoe sat in a white chair at the edge of the pool, holding a piña colada, already with pink lipstick stains on the top of the straw. I walked toward them in my black bikini, barefoot, and kept my sunglasses on as I slipped into the bathwater-warm pool. Zoe nodded a silent thank-you to me for being a real team player. Truth was, I just wanted to get out of those stockings and into a bathing suit. I wanted to get in that water. Taking a dip with Celia Tyranova wasn't even going to register until later.

"Oh, it's beautiful," I practically moaned, and Celia laughed.

"Good, you're a real person," she said. "I like that."

And I knew just what she meant. I couldn't even imagine what Celia's life must be like with people all stuttery and nervous in her presence. She seemed like the kind of girl who loved flannel pajama bottoms and eating ice cream out of the carton. Her smile was real, her breasts appeared to be real, and she just had that magical something that put you at ease with her right away, like you'd known her forever. Not everyone had that gift. Some people you still felt a distance from even months later. You seemed to know them less and less as time went by. Celia Tyranova was not like those people.

"Mylie, we were just discussing the guest list," Zoe filled me in, nodding.

Celia beamed, so I knew her number was stratospheric. Five hundred would be a low estimate. "And the magic number is . . . ?" I smiled at Celia, who all but giggled at the excitement of it all. They were all the same, the brides. Bright and cheery and dreamy at first, but about four months in, all veiny-templed and pouty and angry at any semblance of limitation to their plans. The richest ones wanted everything for free, and thus were the most stressed-out. Celia, again, was not like those people. At least, I hoped not.

"Nine hundred and twenty-four." She clapped. Only royal weddings in Brunei had a larger guest list.

"Wow." I laughed. "Impressive."

"Isn't it?" Celia was just delighted. "We wanted to keep it small and simple." She winked and splashed me on the chin. I stepped back, surprised by her childlike play and her friendliness. I almost splashed her back, when . . .

"Well, well, well," came a familiar voice from behind us. A male voice. *His* voice.

"Kick!" Celia twisted around and in one fluid motion lifted herself out of the pool and excitedly embraced the shirtless Kick Lyons. He wore orange bathing trunks, which only he could pull off. With those abs, he could pull off lemon yellow with pink daisies and still be the most virile thing alive. My mouth went dry, and I tried not to be too obvious about checking him out. Those abs were amazing, I must say. Not trusting me at all, and rightly so, Zoe stood up from her chair and blocked me from his vision.

"Kick, I'm Zoe Brandenberg, and I'll be helping to create your wedding celebration." From the back, I watched Zoe accept a kiss on the cheek from the man of the hour. He held her hand for a few seconds longer than normal, his other hand moving to . . . her *hip*.

"And this is Mylie." Celia motioned with her hand, causing Kick to lean around Zoe to take a look at me wading in his pool.

"I'm helping out," I said, then immediately recoiled. *Idiot!* "Nice to meet you, Mr. Lyons." Was that my voice? It sounded all high-pitched and tinny. Celia laughed. She noticed it, too. It must happen all the time.

"I'll save your kiss for later." Kick winked at me, and Celia just wrinkled her nose and smiled at me. A don't-mind-him kind of shake of her head. That must happen all the time, too.

I could have come back with so many different responses but thought wiser of it. I am a professional, after all. In a bikini. Checking out the client's abs.

"So, it looks like you girls have a lot to talk about, so I'll just—" Kick tried to make his escape, leave the wedding planning to the ladies, but Zoe would have none of it.

"Nonsense, Mr. Lyons, your input is most important to us." Zoe attempted to draw him in, and he instinctively drew away. Jerked his arm away is more like it.

Wow, he's kind of an ass.

Celia looked a little bit annoyed with him, too, but tried to hide it under a wavery smile. "Kick . . . ," she warned.

"Not now, honey." He kissed her on the lips, and she melted. "I have an hour off before I have to meet with the vultures, and

I want to just shut everything off here for a while. Okay?"
Only it came out as a very patronizing *k?* I'm surprised he
didn't pet her on the head and toss her a crunchy treat. She
slouched, deflated, her eyes cast down.

So much for an inside view of a fabulous celebrity partnership. The guy had already turned me cold. He wasn't what I
expected. I guess I expected him to be more like her . . .
warm and friendly, the couple next door. What I saw instead
was the high school jock manipulating the class sweetheart.

"All right," Celia sighed. "But we'll get to you later."

"I'm sure you will . . ." He winked, as if he hadn't been in-
appropriate enough to her already. He strutted off, baboon-
like, and made sure we all heard him sigh in relaxation as he
lay back on a lounge chair, popped in his iPod earphones,
and drummed his hands on his chest.

"Sorry about that." Celia turned back to us and looked
downcast as she lowered herself back into the pool with me.
I patted her on the arm and whispered some comfort about
grooms taking a while to warm up. She shrugged, already
past it, and then was soon beaming about the grounds of her
California wine country estate as the ideal location for her
wedding. We'd be flying there from here tomorrow morning
and staying for two days. Which meant Renata was in *big*
trouble back at the office.

Chapter 5

"**I** so don't like him," I grumbled as the limousine rolled away from the resort, our cell phones having been returned to us upon our quick and uncomfortable exit. Celia had definitely cut our meeting short when her oh-so-charming fiancé strutted out to sunbathe. Yes, she beamed about her Sonoma estate and about her wishes for it to "rain gardenias" in the sculpture garden, but with each one of Kick's outbursts as he sang along with the music in his ear, she grew smaller and smaller, that twinkle in her eye dimming down, retreating into herself.

Zoe patted my leg. "He's just not what you expected, that's all, darling."

Yes, she does talk to me like she's my mother.

"He's so . . ."

Zoe pushed the button to raise the privacy shield between us and the driver. Drivers, it seemed, are notorious for their loose lips to the tabloids. I'd heard they could make tens of thousands on top of their measly driving fees. That was how the tabs got that shot of the mascara-running movie star in mid-breakup (and my red underwear).

"Mylie . . . don't read into anything," Zoe warned, pulling out her cell for the dreaded call to Renata. Ren would *not* be happy about this. "Ren, darling? I have some unfortunate news for you."

We all knew what that meant . . . extreme overtime.

"Mylie and I will be away for an extra two days." No details were to be given out via cell phone. *They track terrorists and celebrity wedding planners that way.* "So . . . yes . . . yes . . . you have to take over the Montgomery wedding. Yes. All of it."

I could only imagine Renata's face . . . beet red with anger. She had a baby at home, and her unfortunate working partnership with us—not to mention being cut out of the six-figure commission we would each be getting for this wedding—meant she had to carry all the weight back at the office. I wish she'd demand a raise, or the entirety of commission for that one, but she never asked. Never. She just smiled and said she could do it.

"You want what?" Zoe coughed, gripping her seat belt and leaning a little bit forward as she spoke.

Or does she?

"Oh, darling, that would be impossible . . ."

"Give it to her, Zoe," I suggested in a whisper and with a nudge, not even knowing what exactly Renata had asked for. "She deserves a break."

"Ren, darling, it's just . . . But I'll be in attendance at the wedding." Zoe fought for her own chunk of the pie. Granted, it was her name that brought it in, but it was Renata making all the arrangements, making all the calls, doing the legwork. It was Renata who wouldn't get to see her baby for the next three days.

"Zoe, don't be a bitch." Only I can talk to her that way, since she did ask me for some help with social cues. She did request that I tell her when she was being a bitch. Of course, she was highly medicated at the time.

Zoe covered the phone mouthpiece and glared at me. "Behave!"

I turned my head away and looked out the window. There, in the distance, were sailboats and jet skis, people on their vacations, suntanned and oblivious to their lives back home, to their bosses back home, the mortgage, the To-Do list. I needed a rest, too. Just a few hours out on a sailboat . . .

"All right, Ren," I heard Zoe give in, and when I turned my head, Zoe looked hurt and scared by my seeming frustration with her. I was just looking at the sailboats and dreaming, not turning my back on her forever. "I'll give you sixty percent of the Montgomery."

She was silent for a moment, and I imagined Renata doing her victory dance in the office, with her little tiny steps and way-out-of-date arm movements, hips jutting back and forth. She'd done it! She finally found her spine again after that epidural.

"And thank you for all of your good work, Renata," Zoe complimented her genuinely. "When I get back, we'll talk about a raise as well."

Wow.

Zoe clicked the phone shut and winked at me. "She's a good one, that Renata," she said. "I'm glad she finally took a stand."

I smiled, amazed. Zoe had *wanted* Renata to fight for her rights. *I'm impressed.*

"Now, you were saying that you don't approve of Mr. Lyons . . ." Zoe drew on our former conversation, but after seeing how shrewd she could be, I decided to just let it go. Or she'd figure out the whole sex dreams thing. Which I was sure I would not have again. He wasn't good enough for Celia . . . or for me.

Zoe gave me the rest of the afternoon off, since we were slated to spend the day with Celia and Kick and were shown the door about six hours earlier than expected. And with only a guest list tally and the location set up, there wasn't much we could do from here. We had half a day's vacation on their dime. Zoe wanted to take a nap. I headed for the pool after slipping back into my damp black bikini, a black and white sarong, and flip-flops. I took my hair out of its severe ponytail, appreciating the waves the tropical air created, and readied myself for the downtime I so desperately craved.

The elevator glided down slowly, a little too slowly—6 . . . 5 . . . 4 . . . 3 . . . 2 . . . 1 . . . L.

With a whoosh, the mirrored doors opened, and I stepped out into the lobby with its open-air arrangement, fountains in the center, birds flying through, no walls to keep the rain and weather out. Chipper bellhops greeted me with a tip of the hat, and my walk toward the pool area was a little too brisk. I wondered if the hotel staff could tell which day of vacation you were on by how quickly and stiffly you walked through the lobby. I was obviously a first-day kind of person. I needed to get out there too badly. Too anxious. In too much of a rush.

The path burned hot through my sandals as I followed its winding scope through a veritable rain forest of trees and flowering bushes, past a koi pond, a wishing fountain with hundreds of shiny copper pennies at the bottom. And, I noticed, someone had thrown in a ten-dollar bill. *Must have been a big wish*. Around the next bend, a waterfall spilling over rocks, white-crested at the bottom. Right there, my shoulders came down a little bit. What was it about waterfalls that did that?

I could smell the cocoa butter, the sunblock, the ocean air. My shoulders relaxed a bit more.

The path delivered me to poolside, a sparkling clean enormous pool that wound in rounded arches, a bridge over the narrow parts, and a sign directing to the topless beach. Bored-looking lifeguards in red shorts slumped in their chairs, twirling their whistles around their fingers. Bartenders in bright whites handed out jewel-colored frozen drinks to eager hands reaching for them, both at the on-land bar and at the swim-up bar. It was only a matter of seconds, I knew, before I'd have one in my hand.

I dropped my towel on the first available lounge chair and tunnel visioned my way into the water and right to the swim-up bar. Again, my first-day expression gave me away.

"Just arrive?" the bartender said in an Australian accent.

"That obvious, huh?" I laughed.

"You have an intensity about you." He nodded. "Dark circles under the eyes . . ."

Wait, I thought bartenders are supposed to be cheerful and flatter you. Where is my "Aloha?"

"Don't worry, miss. We'll take care of that. . . ." And without another look at my hideous, dark-bagged eyes, he made me a bright blue drink and moved away. Was I that scary? That much in need of some relaxation?

"He's a real charmer, isn't he?" From two seats away, a man leaned in to get my attention. And he was the kind of man you actually *did* want to lean in for your attention, not a pasty conventioneer with a handlebar moustache. No, this guy was clean cut, attractive, the lean kind of well-built that said "I look good, but I don't try too hard. My body is not my career."

"That's one way to get me to pound this one and order another one." I smiled.

"I guess he has his methods." The man shrugged. "I'd have started with a compliment."

I smiled, noticing the man's blue eyes. *Yes, you would have.*

"I'm Bryan." He held out his hand for a shake, and I took it.

"Mylie. Nice to meet you." I'm not normally the coquettish type, but I did notice my hand raking through my hair in signature flirt style.

"Mylie. Interesting name."

I nodded, choosing not to share the whole Coco Palms and Elvis-inspired conception story just yet.

"Are you here on business or vacation?" he asked, moving a seat closer to me without invitation. With the ice-cold rum moving over my tongue and my eyes practically rolling back into my head from the pleasure of it, I really didn't mind him making his move. I was just glad he didn't say "business or pleasure," because I really hate cliched pickup lines.

"Business," I said, then coughed a little, remembering that massive confidentiality agreement I'd signed. Say nothing to anyone.

"Ah, me as well," he said. "But we'll just leave that aside. I don't like the interrogation, the whole what-do-you-do? kind of thing. People need to be more original than that."

Interesting. We share a dislike of cliches. Keep going, Bryan.

And like that, my drink was gone. Charming Australian Bartender appeared with another one without my having to ask. I must have still looked like I needed a few.

"So I've been amusing myself with watching the people around the pool." Bryan nodded toward a cluster of overly made-up women in their fifties in tiny bikinis, full faces of makeup, dangling earrings, necklaces, bracelets, and high heels. "The desperate wives' club," he said. "Lionesses, really. It's like watching the Discovery Channel."

I laughed out loud, having made the same observation at the community pool back home. They were quite pathetic, actually. Hunting all the lifeguards and single fathers, looking to upgrade, all of them either divorced or looking for payback from their cheating husbands. They planted themselves where they knew the object of their lust was headed, then made painfully pitiful small talk about how good the sun felt on their stomachs. As mine turned from the absurdity of it.

"Do they think that's attractive?" Bryan shook his head as we both watched a particularly desperate blonde with an almost too small face for the size of her head making a very big deal about bending over in a mini bikini to pick up the towel she just happened to have dropped in front of a gathering of businessmen. She didn't even notice that they were laughing at her. She just tottered away in her high heels to tell her friends how much those men all wanted her. She'd make up a few details to make herself seem less pathetic and then point out how much she was in the mood for a younger man. Who could be trained. Unlike her husband.

"I'm sure it works for them." I tried to be diplomatic.

"Yes, with a man whose self-esteem is even lower than theirs, I imagine it would." Bryan laughed.

"Wow, you're judgmental!"

"I'm observant. Big difference."

I nodded, intrigued. "So what else have you observed at this pool?"

Bryan rubbed his fresh-shaven chin. "I'm just so stunned with the lionesses today that I haven't noticed very much else. Yet. Oooh, wait . . . look!" He nodded toward the lionesses, five of them sunning themselves with baby oil, too brown, posing in their lounge chairs in unnatural positions to make their cellulite show less. A pair of pretty young blond women just entered the pool area. And they noticed.

Bryan immediately launched into his Discovery Channel announcer voice, Australian like the crocodile guy, in a stage whisper. "As the younger females enter the Serengeti, the older females have taken notice."

I laughed. He did a good impression of the crocodile guy.

"Sensing no threat, the younger females fearlessly stake their claim on the prime hunting ground."

The young women, no older than twenty, grabbed two lounge chairs right by the edge of the pool. Every man with a pulse noticed.

"The older females are immediately alarmed by their presence. . . ."

The women in the half circle of desperation were frowning, hands on hips, making snide comments about the young women's bodies, mocking them in a very juvenile and obvious way. This was fun to watch, even more fun to observe through Bryan's eyes. I thought men never noticed these things . . .

"Here we see posturing, the pacing of the lioness . . ."

True, one of them was actually pacing. Because the group of businessmen had noticed the two younger females. And was preparing to send drinks over.

"Ah, the male has made his intentions known," Bryan continued with that signature overenthusiasm and breathless delivery. "The older females are in a frenzy, sensing their feeding ground to be a thing of the past. Will the older female make a move? Will she move in between the males of the species and the certain replacements?"

Sure enough, as Bryan predicted, two of the older lionesses stood, stepped out of their stilettos, and walked over to the group of businessmen, sitting uninvited on the lounge chair next to them. The men looked nonplussed, irritated at the brazen display of territorial insecurity. One of the men tried to be a nice guy, make some small talk and guide them away, but the other men were concerned about the impression made on the two younger females. Who had noticed and thought the men beneath them through sheer affiliation with the lionesses. Guilt by proximity.

Knowing better, the two younger women grabbed up their towels and headed toward the beach without a second glance toward the businessmen. "Ooooh." Bryan snapped out of crocodile guy mode and became himself again. "Nice move, girls. You don't want any part of that."

I raised an eyebrow. "You're on the prey's side?"

"I like to see how smart women handle themselves around dumb women."

I blinked, never having heard that from anyone before.

"Women are quite vicious to one another," Bryan said. "You wouldn't believe what I've seen in my years."

I let my straw pause against my tongue. Who was this guy? Where were these observations coming from? And what did he do for a living that he was so knowledgeable about how territorial desperate women could be?

The businessmen picked up their towels and gear, said a halfhearted farewell to the posing lionesses, and headed back into the resort. They wouldn't have much luck following the young women to the beach, so it was time to retire. The lionesses had ruined their chances, tainting them by their very presence. Instead of admiration, the lionesses got glares of hatred instead. And they weren't smart enough to tell the difference. Even better, some small child in a little yellow bathing suit and hat yelled out, "Mommy, why are those old women in bikinis?"

Bryan and I practically spat out our sips of drinks.

Ignoring the innocence (and honesty) of youth, the lionesses then turned their attention to the lifeguards. Surely, they'd have better luck there. And as Bryan and I observed over drink number four and an invitation for dinner, the lifeguard boys accepted room keys. *Ah, that's life by poolside. Seems like even on vacation, some people are doing a lot of work.*

Chapter 6

"So, you never said why you're on the island for business."

I smirked, still feeling the tickle of the flower behind my ear. Bryan had placed it there when we met at the bar, having just plucked it from a tree somewhere, probably.

"Ah, you said you prefer more originality than that." I raised an eyebrow, taking another bite of my ahi and reaching for my glass of wine. They had served the white wine in a red-wine glass, my professional instinct had noticed and then blew the unwelcome thought away like a bubble.

He smiled. He had a dimple in his cheek. Why did I not notice that before? Normally, I was quite observant, but I guess he had me looking the other way for most of our afternoon at the swim-up bar.

"True, true." He blushed. "I don't have a routine for things like this," he said shyly.

"Things like what?" I drew him out, playing not so much coy as more self-protective. He was a man I met at a swim-up bar at a resort, after all. While I saw no tan line where a wedding ring should be, you just never knew.

He sighed, running his hand through his hair. "Like a date. I didn't expect to be on a date."

I beamed, loving how shy and on just the right side of unpolished he was. The man was not a player! "Well . . . surprise!" I wrinkled my nose at him.

"There you have it."

"There you have it," I repeated, taking a nice, healthy swallow from my wineglass. Careful, of course, not to drink too much. I was a woman with secrets. And I was also a lightweight. I was still feeling those four frozen drinks from the pool, even though the last two were more juice than rum. Australian Bartender must have a system for preventing sloppy drunks from having to be dragged out of the water. The lifeguards had better things to do with their time.

Bryan and I sat at the edge of the open-air restaurant, with a stone wall containing sprouting tropical plants right at the edge of our table, a sweetly scented breeze making the fronds dance and wave at us. Daring and unafraid birds darted in, perched on a stem to watch us, tilting their heads and waiting for us to say something interesting. Just past them, even in the darkness, the unmistakable sound of the ocean's surf rolled in a steady heartbeat. This was heaven.

Bryan and I ate in mostly silence. Not blind date silence, not end-of-the-relationship silence, but the kind of comfortable silence of long-together couples who communicated more with their eyes and with the raise of an eyebrow, a silent appreciation without the need to fill the space between them with words. Amazing, I thought, to feel that with a man I just met, whose last name I didn't even know. It was the first time, in a long time, that I didn't feel the need to pull details from the man across the table from me. Somehow I knew they would come in good time.

"So what are we getting for dessert?" Bryan smoothed his shirt down in front of him, then folded his hands on the table. I was stuffed from my tuna and whipped potatoes—no carb wimp here—but when an intriguing man wanted to share a dessert . . .

"What's good here?" I asked, finally needing to rub the

itch away from the flower over my ear. Why was this thing so annoying?

"In desserts?" He winked, and I smiled, getting that cheek ache from too much grinning in a short period of time. "I highly recommend the oversized cream puff with mango buttercream."

The mention of buttercream sent a little shiver down my spine. That's right. A reminder of my job. I'd be talking about buttercream for hours at Celia Tyranova's wine country estate tomorrow. "Sounds delicious." I nodded, stopping myself from launching into a did-you-know speech about how the mangoes from India were far tastier than from anyplace in the world. We did a wedding there once, and the fresh fruit from the marketplaces was just unbelievable.

"Now, we have a choice here . . . ," Bryan started, looking a little uncomfortable and shifting in his chair, and I immediately assumed he meant we should look at the dessert menu first. Before I protested with my love of mangoes and buttercream, he went on. "We could go for a walk on the beach, and I could try to figure out the perfect moment to lean in for a kiss . . ."

Gulp.

"Or we can skip the romantic vacation pickup cliches and just exchange cards, continue this on the mainland where it has a chance." He ended his statement with an uptone, like a question. Then he cleared his throat, looked down at his hands for a moment, and then immediately looked into my eyes. I almost understood the power Kick had over Celia with his eyes, but Bryan was not a colossal jerk. So this made more sense. The spell I was under, the jaw dropper, the this-is-really-happening buzz rendered me speechless.

I sat back in my chair. This was too much to absorb, and it had happened out of nowhere. Maybe Renata was right when she said it'll happen when you're not looking for it. I instinctively ran my hand through my hair, and knocked that itchy flower right off my head. It bounced off my wineglass and landed on the white tablecloth in front of me. "Um . . . ," I said. I'm very eloquent.

"Shocked or considering?" Bryan formed a sexy little half smile, and I wondered if it was flattery that he found me above the stereotypical walk in the moonlight. Or a very suave way of disentanglement. "Or both?"

"Cards," I said, straightening. "Let's exchange cards."

Chapter 7

"So how's the groom?" Renata knew to speak in code, untrustworthy as cell phones were. We hadn't yet been handed our little black, scrambled-line cell phones by Celia and Kick's crack security guards. Renata had probably been sleepless for hours, waiting for my report on Kick Lyons's real-life persona.

"Unimpressive," I yawned. The mango buttercream sugar crash mixed with the worn-out wine buzz had me draggy. I pulled the surprisingly soft hotel room bedsheets over my legs and leaned back into my pillows. I had a 7:00 A.M. flight to Sonoma in the morning and needed to look well-rested, so my check-in call to Renata would be brief. She was, as expected, breast-feeding at the moment.

"Really?" she squealed, then immediately apologized to her baby for the outburst.

"He's kind of a jerk." I stifled a yawn.

"Like an arrogant, center-of-the-world jerk, or flirting-with-you-right-in-front-of-the-bride jerk?" Again, no first names allowed on the cell phone.

"Yes."

"Wow," Renata said, and I loved the little touch of Rhode Island accent she still had after so many years in the city. It came out as *wahw*. "It's not surprising, though."

"No, not surprising at all," I lied. Secretly, I had been hoping for the warmest, most wonderful man in the world, who adored Celia and brought her a drink by the pool, placed his hand on the small of her back, being merely cordial to any other woman in the area. I wanted him to treat her the way he did in front of the cameras on those red carpets, all looking into her eyes, their hands clasped. Every body language expert in the world had analyzed their relationship as the real thing just because their hips touched almost constantly and he held his head at the same angle as hers.

"So what's the bride like?" Renata asked, then *sh . . . sh . . . sh*'d her baby as he began to whimper a little.

"She's terrific, like someone we would hang out with." I nodded, though she couldn't see me. "Zoe says you'll be there on the wedding day, so you'll find out."

Renata let out a yelp, and her baby immediately screamed a piercing wail, nothing that could be calmed. This was a wall shaker. Renata panicked, being so new to the whole thing. "Shit! Oh, sorry! James, Momma's sorry!" I had to smile a little at how she apologized to a three-month-old. "Mylie, I . . . I gotta go! Have a good time at . . . oh, never mind. Just have a good time." She hung up noisily and clumsily to tend to her howling baby, who undoubtedly thought his peaceful, serene mother was on fire. I imagined her pacing with the baby in her arms, begging the child to stop wailing, and her husband Pete running down the stairs to save someone's life. All because Renata would be in attendance at the Wedding of the Millennium, as they called it.

I didn't even get a chance to tell her about Bryan. Or to find out how the Montgomery wedding was coming along without us. Or to ask if that shipment of burgundy organza had arrived. Or if the printers had sent over the proofs for Ambassador Shelton's invitations. Or if the Ecuadorian roses were on the second and third shelf of the refrigerator unit instead of the top shelf where they would freeze.

Just trust . . . came the message as I pulled the sheets up higher over my chest. I often had to remind myself not to get swirled into a vortex of worrying. Zoe's micromanaging ways were contagious, after all. I was definitely more detail-centric than I used to be, I assessed. I had been trained well, and I absorbed the rest. But I was still wise enough to know when to let go of the details. Well, some of them.

With the French doors open to the patio, the ocean surf sound just a faint whisper in the distance, I fell into the deepest sleep and dreamed of sunflower fields as far as the eye could see. And I had a flower tucked behind one ear . . . that didn't itch.

Chapter 8

God, I love wine country.

I loved the drive, the way the trees seemed greener than anyplace else in creation, the rich and earthy smell of the air, how you could tell that so much was growing all around you. You could feel it in your cells. Like it was such a healthy place. It was so unlike home, with cracked pavement and glass windows, everything hard and lifeless. People moved more slowly here, drove more slowly here, taking everything in. Your pulse slowed, your breathing slowed. It might be more relaxing than the islands.

As Zoe and I drove in a rented Range Rover, the day after arriving in Sonoma, through the winding streets of Sonoma toward Celia's estate, I looked around as much as possible while I was behind the wheel. Horse farms on hillsides with perfect white gates keeping the prize ponies from the rest of the herd, endless fields of vineyard in various states of readiness, grape clusters sparkling with dew, dangling like red and purple earrings toward the deep brown earth. Tour bus tourists with sun visors and wrinkled maps in their hands, drunkenly trying to find their way to the next tasting along the road, ankles clashing as they nearly trip and laugh their heads off with their shrieks echoing through the vista. Overhead in the seamless blue sky, hot air balloons in bright colors—pink, red, green, orange, paisley, and striped—floated in the air, the passengers too small to see from here, just little bursts of flame appearing over their heads from time to time. Gulfstreams and Cessnas zipped by occasionally, high above the balloons, of course, carrying some very important person to some very important place without the hassles of these bumpy roads and all of the beauty along them. And Victorian bed and breakfasts dotted the landscape with intricately swirled wooden details at the roof and windows, in pink, yellow, and orange colors like cotton candy, wraparound porches with cushioned rocking chairs in lines, rose gardens and trellises, stone driveways, and certainly histories if not hauntings of their own.

Enterprising children set up water stands along the streets, selling bottles of Dasani for five dollars a pop, knowing that parched, wine-soaked tourists would part with their cash for a sip of a palate cleanser. Smart kids, I thought, remembering my own budding entrepreneur days when I sold pretzels made of Pillsbury Crescent dough door-to-door in my neighborhood. The cheese and chocolate varieties were hot sellers, I remembered.

Around a tree-lined curve, I slowed for a pair of riders on horseback, a fat picnic basket secured to the back of one saddle. Honeymooners, I could tell, from the way they looked at each other. And inexperienced on horseback from the way their horses pulled at their too-tight reins. The couple leaned over for a quick kiss, the groom extending an arm to right his bride's position in her saddle. He was protective of her. Nice to see.

Zoe was not a bossy passenger. She wasn't the type to air step on the brake when you were going too fast. She didn't tell me to watch out for the horses. She was always in a zone while driving. Her mind turned off during long car trips, and she cared nothing for how she got to a place, just as long as she arrived on time. The clock was her nemesis. She glanced at her wristwatch and nodded, silently satisfied with our pace, then leaned back into the seat and closed her eyes.

I wish I could turn the radio on. This is scenery that calls for Sheryl Crow or Rob Thomas. I wish I could take my hair down from this chignon and let it fly around in the open-window breeze. But I was primped and buttoned up, wearing a suit when I'd rather be in jeans and a red tank top, barefoot in that inviting earth out there.

The bed and breakfasts started dwindling, farther and farther apart, and the estates began. High stone walls. Tall hedge lines. Brass plaques that announce Seven Sisters and Augustine Fields. It reminded me of *Gone With the Wind,* the way the estates were named, which was right when we passed a sign for an estate called Gone With the Wine. I checked my Mapquest directions, hoping that wasn't Celia's estate. If it was, surely the unimpressive Kick Lyons had named it.

I'd get no peek at these grand homes, as most of them were securely set back miles from the road. Winding driveways must have led past golf course quality lawns, fountains, and guard shacks with Armani-wearing security guards. I wondered what it was like to live like this . . . having so much yet needing to keep most of the world out. I'd never want to be so rich. The proprietors of the bed and breakfasts were probably far happier people. No Maserati in the driveway, sure, but a regular flow of regular people with pictures of their grandchildren to show, passing the maple syrup to one another with a grin, sitting by the fireplace at night, down-home barbecues out back, and warm hugs from the chef in the morning. The ability to lay out in the hammock and watch the people walking or riding by on the street. Random hellos to strangers. Compliments on their golden retrievers' coats. Just being able to take a walk in the evening when the fireflies were out, even if to buy a five-dollar bottle of Dasani from the next generation of megabillionaires by the roadside. Celia couldn't do that without a disguise. Which made me a little bit sad for her.

"Oh . . . my . . ."

Even Zoe was knocked out of her zone by the gates at which we arrived. Majestic iron gates, in almost a liquid-looking swirl, with sun-reflecting spires on the top, revealed an actual view of the estate from the road. Two cocker spaniels—one black and one coffee-colored—romped on the other side of the fence, not at all the evil, snarling rottweiler guard dogs I would have expected. It was Celia's place. Low bushes in perfectly flat trim lined the path to her gated entrance, and, of course, the gates magically opened at our approach.

How do they do that? How do they know it's us? Had the little kids selling Dasani by the roadside radioed ahead to say we were coming?

It turned out the gates were not opening for our approach, but rather for Kick Lyons. He was making his escape. He pulled his Porsche up next to us, and I set my arm on the now-open window's edge.

"Good morning, ladies." He removed his sunglasses and flashed us a smile. Since he was part-owner of that ten-million-dollar check, I had to paste on a smile for him as well.

"Mr. Lyons . . . good morning," I said, and he immediately noticed the lack of passion (and lust) in my voice. He blinked. Twice. Was his usual spell not working? I was supposed to hand him my phone number by now, wasn't I? Or jump out of my car and flash him some thigh? I really didn't like the guy.

"Kick, darling, how *are* you?" Zoe leaned over and held

up a Queen Elizabeth wave, stiff at the wrist, fingers together. Being over fifty, she didn't even register with his lower brain.

"Mighty fine, ma'am," he said in a Southern accent, which baffled us both. Trying to be more charming? Disarm us with a good ol' boy persona? Little did he know that Zoe *hated* being called ma'am.

"Where are you off to?" I took over, holding up a thick sample book of invitation styles. "We have a lot of work to do."

Kick slid his glasses back on.

That's right . . . cover up those windows to the soul.

"Making a getaway?" I teased, and Zoe practically stabbed me in the hip with her finger. "Kidding, of course." I winked, and that cheered him up. He thought I was flirting with him, that I was just devastated at his departure. Off came the dark sunglasses again. He would honor me with a look at his eyes. What a prince.

"I'll be back in a half hour," he promised and revved his engine a little. It took all of my strength not to roll my eyes. "It'll probably take you that long to get started, once Celia gives you the tour of the house."

Judging from the size of the estate, it would take far longer than that to tour it. Unless they had a monorail system.

"We'll look forward to it, Kick." Zoe smiled warmly and motioned low with her hand for me to drive through the gates.

"Later!" he called and zipped out of the driveway at a sharp and dramatic angle, going way too fast for this relaxed wine country environment. *The locals must hate him.*

"Mylie, please," Zoe admonished me with narrowed eyes. "What is your dilemma?" She doesn't say "What is your problem," as that's too common.

"I don't like the guy." I shrugged.

"Well, learn to like him." Zoe shook her head, never having had this problem with me before. I've been disillusioned by movie stars before, turned off by the rude ones, stunned at the drug addicts, immediately repulsed by the ones who treated their kids like accessories or tools to get what they wanted. One even had a baby just because she wanted to be on the cover of *Fit Pregnancy* magazine. Then she turned the tow-headed baby over to an au pair and pretty much forgot about him. I don't go see her movies. Especially the ones where she plays a loving mother.

"He's so . . . smug," I confessed to Zoe. "There's just something about him that really turns my stomach."

Zoe turned my chin and looked into my eyes. "Darling, you had a sexual fantasy about him, didn't you?"

I nearly choked on my Dentyne Ice.

"No," I lied, and Zoe patted her lap, pleased with her uncanny skills. "You don't think he's a little bit callous?" I turned the subject away as I drove slowly up the hill, past dramatic fountains and thick, ancient trees, one of which had a beautiful, intricate birdhouse on it that said "Robin's Place" in baby blue lettering.

"He's a *child*, darling." Zoe shook her head. "A boy in a man's body. He has no *skills* other than acting, so that's what he does. Constantly."

"And you don't think Celia deserves better?" I heard myself whine, and I surprised myself with my unrealistic concern over the romantic welfare of a woman I didn't even really know.

Zoe laughed. "I don't know, darling, but that's really not our job."

True.

"So because I know that you can't fake liking someone if you don't, then I encourage you to find *something* you like about him for the sake of the next few months we'll be working with him," Zoe suggested, or rather, warned. "Your contempt is on naked display, and I cannot have that."

She was right. I had been transparent. And Kick did have the power to wipe us away with a wave of his hand, and *that* would get out in the press. That we'd been removed from the job. It was a very real threat, as fickle as celebrities could be. We'd been dismissed by an aging celebrity once just because *Zoe* was a threat to her self-esteem in being younger than she was. I was a living nightmare to her as well, so we had to go.

So, Zoe was right. I needed to learn to like Kick Lyons. I'd add that to my To-Do list.

The estate, up close, was just dreamlike. White arches in front gave it a semi-Greek look, but this was more Hearst Castle than Coliseum. The place stretched on and on in both directions, tall and bright white, with expansive rounded-top windows, impossibly intricate details over the tops of them in an almost Victorian manor style. Disney-perfect landscaping, the shrubs obsessively flat cut, not a spent flower to be seen on any of the hyacinth trees, a circle of lavender by the door. Before I could gawk any more, my car door opened, and a friendly, white-haired man in a dark suit smiled and reached for my hand.

"Good morning," he chippered, probably loving his job. "Miss Celia has asked me to escort you inside to the sitting room for champagne."

At nine in the morning. Nice.

Another dark-suited assistant appeared at Zoe's door, escorting her out by a gentlemanly handhold as well. We reached in to get our sample books but were waved off. The men would bring us all we needed from the car. Zoe looked nervously at her books and binders, worried about that pesky little security thing.

These men might not actually work for Celia, she was clearly thinking, so I jumped on it. "Thank you so much, gentlemen." I smiled, clasping my hands together at my stomach, which was in knots of anxiety. We couldn't blow the whole thing before we even got in the front door, suckered by imposters because they were wearing dark suits. "But Zoe and I need to assess which of these particular books we need. It will only take us a second."

From opposite ends of the car, Zoe and I leaned in and pretended to fumble through the sample books and her bag of fabric swatches. We must have looked very graceful with our butts sticking out of the car.

"Good, Mylie." Zoe approved of my interference, and I clearly saw the nervousness in her eyes. On instinct, I checked her lipstick.

Uh oh.

Armed with about forty pounds of sample books and bags, we stepped into Celia's home. I would tell Renata later that it was the color of champagne, my dream home palette with rich chocolate browns, deep comfy carpeting, and those touches of cinnamon color in the plentiful throw pillows and vases. A fireplace big enough to stand in owned the one wall, a baby grand piano owned a corner, and tall potted trees reached up toward the skylights with not one dry or browned leaf upon them.

A chocolate-colored couch reached in a *J* shape with a huge glass coffee table set before it, and, of course, there was nothing on the coffee table. Unlike mine at home that held magazines and cell phone bills, the *TV Guide,* and whatever jewelry I took off at the end of the day and forgot about. And empty Diet Coke cans.

"Miss Celia will be down in a moment." Our gentlemen guides departed, and we were left on our own. To admire the place.

"Wow," I said to Zoe, who was similarly impressed. Her eye trained on the bookshelves, leather-bound classics (of course) mixed with trashy beach reads. Some of our clients planned their libraries for show . . . Dickens, Melville, Hemingway, all to give an impression of being well read and well bred. Or they paid interior designers fifty thousand dollars to clean out the local Borders for books with all light blue covers, so they would look good as an accent to the room, so that everything would match. Never mind that they had titles in there like the *Gastroenterologist's Handbook* and the *Field Guide to Bass Fishing* . . . the colors matched.

Celia's bookshelf showed that she was a reader. Wait . . . I remembered my new goal: Celia and Kick's bookshelf showed that *they* were readers. I tried to imagine Kick poring through a literary classic, but all I could come up with was him giggling at the pictures in *National Geographic*. This was going to be harder than I thought.

A glint of sunlight reflected in a picture frame drew me away from the books. Celia and Kick's home display of photos peppered a wall and crowded a mahogany table, all in deep wood frames with light orange matting. Of course, there was the requisite shot from when they both appeared on *Oprah*, hand-holding shots on red carpets with Celia in a flame of an orange dress and Kick in a smooth tuxedo sporting the ultrablond hair from one of his summer blockbuster movies. Celia with her friend Reese Witherspoon, giggling at something. Celia and Kick with Denzel Washington, Celia and Kick with George Clooney and Matt Damon, Celia at what looked like a bridal shower, hugging a woman who looked like her sister—they had the same red hair and smile.

"This one's my favorite." Celia appeared behind me, widening her eyes as she pointed to a very funny picture of Tom Cruise trying to get their attention (and a photo op) and a very annoyed looking Kick leading Celia away quickly. A total blowoff. A sister picture placed in the frame next to it showed the fallout: Tom looking stunned and rejected, and Celia and Kick suppressing smiles.

I laughed out loud, and Celia leaned in for a hello kiss on the cheek. It was one of those awkward, wrong turn of the face hellos that I hoped we'd get better at. At least she wasn't an air kisser. She wasn't a fake.

"I was just admiring your book collection," Zoe said, a little too high-pitched, a little too quickly. The lipstick was a good indicator. Zoe was ready for a manic spiral up like a bottle rocket. I fumbled in my pocket for the spare Xanax I always keep on me and slipped it into Zoe's palm as Celia kissed her a quick hello as well. When Celia's head turned to me with a bounce of her red ponytail, Zoe gulped down the pill without a drink—then immediately grimaced and started smacking her lips from the bitter aftertaste of it, her tongue darting in and out like a lizard. Knowing well enough, Zoe turned and pretended to admire the books.

"You like them?" Celia smiled, tilting her head so that the ponytail fell over her shoulder like a cheerleader's. With one hand on her hip, and minus the actress one-foot-forward pose to look slimmer, Celia stood before her library. "My decorator keeps telling me to go monochromatic with them."

"No!" Zoe and I both yelped, wanting better for our Celia than a color-matched book collection.

"This is great . . . it really shows who you are," I said, almost grabbing for a book and realizing that the one in my direct line of reach was a bedside Kama Sutra. I hoped that was something from a swag bag at the Golden Globes or some party favor from a premiere. I pulled my hand back.

"We keep Kick's books in the other room." She nodded, having seen what I almost pulled from her collection, subtly defending his talents. "Motorcycle books, science fiction . . . He's a big fan of David Sedaris, actually. Reads all of his stuff."

Ah, so my contempt of her beloved had been noted. It seemed she was trying to puff him up in my eyes. I immediately felt a stab of shame, then looked to see if Zoe's pill had started to take effect. Her eyes were still darting around. She was adjusting Celia's photo frames to line up evenly. Just four more minutes and she'd be functional.

"Your book collection is great, Celia. Don't change a thing." I smiled, wondering if she had a copy of *He's Just Not That Into You* stashed in there anywhere.

"Well, would you like the grand tour?" Celia offered and waved us on to follow her as she moved quickly across the living room, barefoot on that cushy carpet, her floral skirt swishing around her knees, tan line showing on her shoulders as revealed by the racerback white tank top she wore. I'd later make the case to Zoe that we didn't have to dress like senators for our meetings with Celia. The girl liked to dress down. "Kick should be back soon," Celia sang.

Yeah, right.

"Oh, the champagne!" She remembered, stopping with her foot on the first tan-carpeted step leading to upstairs. "I completely forgot!"

"That's okay," Zoe said, wiping a little bit of lipstick from the corner of her mouth, coming back to balance. "No rush."

"I gave my inside staff the day off today," Celia thought aloud, waving us to follow her up the stairs. "So I apologize in advance for lunch. I'm not a very good chef."

She could hand us a couple of bags of Crunchy Chee-tos and it would be fine.

"Kick is the chef of the family," she continued as she and I waited for Zoe to reach the top of the stairs. She seemed a bit wobbly, having trouble with her heels on the carpet, and also eyeing the more personal collection of pictures set in square-set arrangements on the walls. All pictures of Kick and Celia off-duty, in jeans, bathing suits on vacation, with family, hugging nieces and nephews. "Mandarin sea bass, lemon chicken . . . He makes a great buffalo steak, too."

Zoe nudged me when she reached the top step, encouraging me to put an end to this palpable dislike of Kick. "Sounds great . . . ," I managed. "Mmmm, buffalo steak."

It came out slightly more sarcastic than I intended, and there, Celia had me.

She put both hands on my shoulders, turned me to face her, looked me right in the eye, smiled enormously, and said, "You had a sex dream about Kick, didn't you?"

Zoe almost fell backward down the stairs. If I'd had that champagne in my hand, I would have dropped it to the floor. I heard myself stammering, felt the red-hot rush to my cheeks. I was busted.

"I knew it," she said, hugging me against her. "We get as many people hating him as gushing over him, and it's usually the same thing."

"I'm . . . I'm . . ."

"Don't sweat it, sweetie," Celia assured me with a poke on my nose. "He makes a better second impression."

Little did she know that his second impression out at the gates was equally smarmy, but I was willing to give him another chance.

But for good measure, I slipped Zoe another Xanax, and she swallowed it right down.

We weren't shown the master bedroom, of course, probably a wise move on Celia's part having just discovered my fantasies about her fiancé. But the rest of the upstairs was phenomenal. A movie screening room done up with leather reclining chairs and the sound system bolstered by speakers in the cushions. A warming mechanism in the seat also topped the boundaries of hi-tech. A full wet bar in the screening room, a packed refrigerator, and a freezer full of Häagen-Dazs bars and Grey Goose vodka.

The guest suites—all fifteen of them—probably each had

their stories and histories, but both Zoe and I were enthralled by the fabrics, the curtains, canopies, bookshelf room dividers, sunken living rooms, views of the gardens, and plasma screen television sets in each room, most of which descended from the ceilings.

The bathrooms could have been spas, with whirlpool baths in every one, glass bowl sinks and fountain showerheads, Italian marble, and towel-warming bars. Little rose-shaped soaps and oversized floral arrangements on nearly every countertop.

I realized later that I had completely screwed myself out of seeing Celia's closet. All because of the sex dreams about Kick . . . or rather, how transparent I was about them. Of course, I vowed never to have another one again, but you knew how it was when you told yourself *not* to think about something, right? Exactly. The man haunted my dreams.

We took the glass elevator (an *elevator!*) down from the third floor to the basement, where they had an indoor pool, sauna, Jacuzzi, and game room. Pool tables, two lanes of bowling alley, and an indoor badminton/volleyball court with sand. All in the one cavernous room.

I want my birthday party here.

They had a laundry *wing* down there, too, and the servants' quarters, which we did not tour. I somehow doubted they would be like the basement apartments I had seen in New York City, all cramped and windowless. Each maid and butler probably had a Jacuzzi and plasma screen TV in their rooms as well.

Then there was the spa. Another wing of the house. A full gym, massage center, reflexology *room*, hair and nails center with HEPA-filtered air systems to keep the fumes down.

And a chapel.

"This was Kick's idea, since he can't exactly go to a real church." Celia smiled, looking directly at me. Zoe smiled, appreciating the small, dome-ceilinged room with a painted fresco of angels and saints, gold-gilted crosses, and a kneeling altar before a half circle of religious statues.

"He . . . he put in a chapel?" I exhaled, marveling at the place, at the unmistakable scent of mass incense, the artwork and architecture, the arches over the doors, the reverent silence.

"Yes," Celia breathed, knowing she now had me at a place where I saw some good in him. Zoe looked deer-in-headlights stunned as well. "He does have a good soul."

I nodded, glad to hear that he had *any* soul. I would have thought he had an entirely different altar somewhere in the house, with lambs and chickens lined up for sacrifices.

"He just doesn't make it public," Celia said, and I remembered the picture in their living room. "You haven't met the real him yet, Mylie. He doesn't show it to anyone who is under the 'work' umbrella."

I understood. Humbly.

"He doesn't bring attention to his charitable work either."

He does charitable work?

"He doesn't fly a camera crew out to a third world country with him so that he can get credit for being a 'good guy.'" Celia pressed her lips together. I wondered which of the famous bad boys she and Kick knew she was thinking of at that moment. I could name a dozen possibilities.

"He's just my Kick." She shrugged. "He's the best thing that ever happened to me." And she had a tear in her eye. All of those body language experts were spot-on accurate. Celia and Kick were the Real Deal. And they wanted a Real Deal wedding.

Now that we knew about Kick's deeper beliefs, we knew where we'd focus the wedding planning process. At the ceremony first. The mass, the words, the ritual. We now knew that Kick was one of those who considered the cake, the linens, and the flowers to be ultraunimportant when it came to wedding rites. No wonder he'd bolted upon our arrival. Without being here, he would be introduced to us more fully by the house tour.

"I see . . . ," I heard myself say, and then asked for a moment alone in the chapel. Celia and Zoe granted me that.

Chapter 9

I almost wanted to hug him when he walked in the room. Kick Lyons *did* have a soul.

"Ladies . . ." He tipped his baseball cap at us and greeted Celia with a hug and a kiss on the lips. Celia beamed, then looked immediately to me. I smiled and looked down into my lap, embarrassed. "Don't tell me . . . you finished everything already, and I missed the whole thing, right?"

"Oh, you'd be crushed, wouldn't you?" Celia laughed and playfully slapped the brim of his hat down over his eyes.

"Ah, you're right on time." Zoe stood and shook his hand, one hundred percent steady on her feet and ready to outshine both of them with her genius. She flipped open her laptop and earned a lifelong fan in Kick Lyons. The software buzzed and whirred, opening with a dreamy montage of photos of Kick and Celia, elegantly swirled words, and Chris Botti trumpet music.

"What's this?" Kick removed his hat and sat in front of the screen, mesmerized.

"I'm designing your CD-ROM invitations." Zoe half smiled, not focusing at all on him but rather on the intricacies of the screen shots. She squinted at some miniscule element that wasn't quite right, the tone or contrast, the arch of the lettering, perhaps?

"Very cool," Kick approved.

"We can't chance your invitations to a professional printer, so we're making them ourselves," Zoe assured her ten-million-dollar clients.

That means I will be burning over nine hundred CD-ROMs at some point in the near future. I gulped.

"Wow, when did you do this?" Celia leaned over Kick, wrapped her arms around his shoulders, and blinked at the screen, both of them marveling at the invitation suddenly morphing into beautiful, light blue pages with a security code to access the flight and hotel details for the guests. "Nice!"

"When we were in Hawaii," Zoe said, her hand on her hip, assessing their faces for approval.

So while I was pounding drinks with Bryan at the swim-up bar, and while I was eating a mango buttercream-filled cream puff with Bryan over dinner, Zoe was hard at work upstairs in her room. No gold star for me that day.

Zoe tapped in the security code, and the screen filled with pictures of the hotel suites, virtual tours available of each so that guests could "move" through each room and see the accommodations before booking them, the fireplace living rooms, canopy bedrooms, spa bathrooms, Rande Gerber's restaurant nearby, the nightclub, nearby wineries' tasting rooms, and grape-filled arbors. Flight numbers were marked as 000, since Zoe didn't have that information yet, and would key it in at the last second. Same with the actual wedding date and place. She had filled in fake information for now, in case someone stole her laptop. I knew that she'd be sleeping with it under her pillow every night until the wedding.

"Now, let's fine-tune it." Zoe pulled up a chair to get to work, and Kick immediately jumped up and offered her his directly-in-front chair. She thanked him. Together, they switched background colors, tweaked the contrast, changed the font to a more masculine block lettering at Kick's request and Celia's okay, then chose a different music track from the Chris Botti

CD. (Zoe had seen the Botti CD on a counter in their resort in Hawaii. She had an eagle eye like that.) She airbrushed a stray curl away from Celia's forehead and eliminated a bra line from Celia's shirt like the most practiced *Glamour* magazine cover shot graphic designer.

Kick wanted his hair darkened a little bit. Done.

Celia wanted her skirt longer. Done.

Kick wanted the light blue background turned to a more Sonoma-appropriate burgundy. Done.

Zoe didn't mind the instruction, or the changes made to her hard-earned work. These were her clients. She wanted them to be happy. She wanted them to be in control. So if it meant scrapping everything she'd created, she would do it.

"Can we add a message from us?" Celia suggested. "I've seen that on people's personalized wedding Web sites . . . and we can't have that."

"Sure." Zoe placed her hand on Celia's arm, acting more like the anything-you-want-dear mother of the bride than most actual mothers of brides that we've seen. "Mylie . . . ," she addressed me, taking my attention away from the curve of Kick's forearm. "The camera, please."

"Now?" Celia squeaked. "Give me a minute . . ." Clapping, she ran out of the room and up the stairs as noisily as a child. Headed right for her hair and makeup center.

I dug through Zoe's bag and pulled out the digital camera she'd just upgraded to. Zoe knew her technology. She always had the latest gadgets, which impressed the life out of the grooms.

"Nice." Kick nodded and reached for me to hand it to him. I did. He looked through the lens and trained it on me. The green light kicked on. He was filming me. "Aaaaand, *action!*" he shouted with a smile, pointing at me.

Zoe smiled. The kids were bonding.

I was determined to impress him. So I looked side to side, cautiously, overacting in a way that would make Jim Carrey look toned down. "Shhhhhh . . ." I put my finger to my lips. "I'm on secret assignment. I have been sworn to say nothing, absolutely nothing, to anyone about anything, anytime, anywhere."

Kick giggled. "Ah, but we have ways of making you talk!"

"Never!" I laughed a diabolical laugh.

"Wow, you suck at this." Kick nearly doubled over, yet still kept the camera on me. Zoe, typing at the laptop, just laughed, shaking her head. "Tell me about yourself, Mylie," he said, his free eye squinted closed.

It wasn't the time for another diabolical laugh, so I became real. "What do you want to know?"

He thought for a second. He could ask where I lived, what my favorite TV shows were, or . . . "Why the change in your opinion of me?"

Zoe stopped typing. Held her breath.

"What do you mean?"

"Oh, please . . . an hour ago you practically spat venom when you talked to me," Kick said, then pulled the camera away from his face to use the display screen to track me. He looked me right in the eyes. "And now, you've softened."

I wanted to hate him again right then, but I respected his directness. He had every right to ask.

"I had the wrong idea of you," I confessed, and he hit the zoom button to come in closer, catch the nuances in my eyes.

"And what idea was that?" he led.

Behind him, Zoe was moving her lips silently, probably praying that I'd make something up . . . or faint. But this was going to be a relationship of honesty. Risk or not.

"That you were an arrogant ego case who didn't treat Celia the way she deserved to be treated." There.

He almost dropped the camera. His shocked expression, like I'd just slapped him, slowly grew out of frozen to a wide smile.

Zoe couldn't see that from her angle. She just dropped her face into her hands, seeing the ten-million-dollar wedding fading away. *As well as my employment.*

The camera was still trained on me, the green light still on. I blinked a few times, felt a twitch by my lip, but held my position. It was an Integrity Posture.

"Zoe?" he said, not taking his eyes off me.

Here it comes.

"Mr. Lyons, I am so sorry!" Zoe began, but he cut her off with the wave of his hand.

"No, don't apologize," Kick said without looking at her. "That's the first time I've heard anything so direct and honest."

What?!

"Most people just say what they think I want to hear." He nodded, and his smile grew wider. "So when someone is bold-faced honest with me, it's a welcome change."

I swallowed. Was I still going to get fired? There had to be a *But* coming.

"You're right, Mylie," he said. "I was a jerk that day. Just saw some tabloid thing and I was really pissed off." He turned off the camera and set it down on the table. "I hate it when they target Celia that way. And I wasn't feeling very social when I met you both. I just wanted to check out for a few minutes before I let Celia know what that rag said about her."

Things are not always as they seem.

"I'm sorry," I whispered, wanting to hug him. He was not acting.

"It's all right." He waved it away. "Your answer just threw me a little . . . You were looking out for Celia."

Wow, he really does love her.

"I admire that," he said.

"You admire what?" Celia came bounding in the room, in

a pink top with a sheer pink overjacket, her lips perfectly glossed, her hair out of the ponytail and wavy over her shoulders. She was camera ready.

He smiled at her. Stood. "Baby, you definitely hired the right people," he said, and even she was taken aback. Zoe looked from one of us to the other, silent, not knowing how in the world a scene that looked as if it was going so catastrophically bad could turn around and be so fate sealingly right.

Chapter 10

"*I know I'm supposed to wait three days, but I thought I'd try you.*"

The voice mail message was from Bryan. I breathed a sigh of relief. Most men who saw my business card and found out that I worked in the wedding planning business went running for the next bullet train out of town.

I still didn't know what he did for a living. His card had just his name and a New York City address (perfect), his phone, cell, and pager.

Renata held it between her fingers, turning it over to see if anything was printed on the back, feeling the edges for the telltale mini serration marks that said he printed the business cards up himself on a home computer. Her first husband had cheated on her. She knew all of the tricks.

"He avoided talking about what he does for a living?" She raised an eyebrow.

"Hey, I hid what I do for a living," I reasoned.

"Because you have something to hide, girl."

"Oh, Ren." I rolled my eyes and collected up the finished boutonnieres for the Montgomery wedding, boxed them with mounds of bubble wrap between them and the pew décor flower arrangements—white callas with silk bows to be affixed to the candelabras.

"I'm just saying . . ."

I sighed and set into the favors. I had three hundred baggies of sugared almonds to fill. I loved it when people went classic and traditional. I popped one in my mouth and started counting out a dozen for each baggie.

"So are you going to call him back?" Renata asked tentatively, not looking up from the monogrammed napkins she was inspecting.

"Yes."

"Oh," she said, clearly disappointed.

"He's a good guy, Ren!" I surprised myself with my outburst. "He didn't even try to kiss me! He could have gone for the vacation seduction, but didn't."

Renata nodded.

"What?" I was impatient with her. *Can't you just let me enjoy this? Someone knows what I do for a living, and they still want to go out with me. That doesn't happen often.*

"It's just . . . I have a guy who would be perfect for you."

Another one of Pete's work buddies, probably. Newly divorced, ready to give it another whirl. Having gone out for happy hour with them and their friends, I doubted there was a keeper in the bunch.

"Not now, Ren," I sighed. "I like this guy. You should have seen how cute he was when he put the flower in my hair." I went on and on about Bryan's charms, but they were lost on Renata. She was deeply absorbed in inspecting the stitches of the monogrammed napkins, finding an *N* among the *M*s. Happened every time.

"Hey," I said when he picked up the phone, hearing in his voice that Caller ID had announced me.

"Mylie!"

"Is this a good time?" I always started off with the consideration opener.

"Actually, I've just gotten a page and have to run, but can I call you back tonight?" He sounded hurried. My fault for calling during business hours.

"Sure, no problem." I swallowed hard.

"Great! I'll talk to you later . . . glad you called."

"Me, too."

"Okay . . . talk to you later." And he hung up.

Well, it wasn't a we'll-tell-the-kids-about-this-someday kind of conversation, but it was just a first attempt to connect. Tonight's conversation would be better, I knew. I could just tell.

"Mylie! It's Bryan. Sorry to have run like that earlier, but I got paged out to an important work call. Thought I'd try you in case you wedding people take a break at siesta time. Call me back."

"Bryan, it's Mylie. Sorry, I was delivering some things and left my cell in the car. Well, I'll talk to you tonight. I'll be in at nine."

I hung up and looked at Renata, who had a rotten little smile on her face.

"What?"

"Nothing."

"Finally!" He laughed. "We connect."

"Yes." I laughed, relieved.

"So are you all up to your ears in roses and ivy?" he joked.

I settled back into my couch, Diet Coke in hand with a pile of mini Mounds bars from Celia's house in a bowl on my stomach. "All right, all right, enough with the wedding talk."

"Probably scares a lot of guys, huh?"

I smiled. He was terrific. "Not you, though."

"Right. Not me. It's probably like working in a bakery. After a while, you don't crave the cupcakes anymore."

I was silent. Stunned. Normally, I tell people "It's like working in a bakery," only I follow it up with "After a while you don't crave the cannoli anymore."

"Yes . . . right . . . exactly," I stumbled. "So what do you do?"

"Ah, I guess I have to fess up now that your secret's out." He laughed. Where were these goose bumps coming from? "I'm in marketing," was all he said.

Great. A drug dealer.

"Marketing?"

"It's branding, actually. When a celebrity signs on for an endorsement deal, it's my job to make sure he or she is shown with the product," he explained. "Pretty boring stuff, actually."

"No, sounds fascinating." I unwrapped a Mounds bar, needing chocolate, hating that we had something very big in common and I couldn't even talk about it. Confidentiality. And a real concern that Celia and Kick's hounds had my phone bugged.

Instead, we talked about how the rest of his stay in Hawaii went, wondered whatever happened to the lionesses by the pool, and the conversation just flowed from there. To plans for dinner. Tomorrow night.

"I've been thinking about you all week, Mylie," he said. "There's something about you . . ."

"There's something about you, too," I breathed, loving how the hormone rush of initial attraction made even the corniest lines sound like poetry.

We said good night, and I danced around the living room in my T-shirt and underwear, fuzzy socks and ponytail holder, looking forward to the electricity of a first kiss tomorrow night.

Chapter 11

It was 8:59. I was going to be late for my date with Bryan. In high heels and a black wrap dress, I ran down the street to Ouest, the in-the-news French restaurant he had suggested. I wasn't one of those who thought so importantly of myself as to make the man wait for me. I wasn't the fashionably late kind, or the unreliable kind.

Turned out . . . he was . . . a little bit.

He wasn't there either. I took a seat at the bar, ordered myself a gin and tonic. We had had so much wine at Celia and Kick's estate that I wasn't in the mood for a Pinot for a long, long time. "Thank you," I said to the bartender, a short woman with Tang orange hair and a Cindy Crawford mole by her lip.

"You missed all the action," she said. "Jennifer Aniston was just in here . . . with a date."

I looked for signs of a paparazzi frenzy: broken bar stools, chandeliers swinging wildly from where those hawks dangled themselves to get a shot, other diners with black eyes from catching a thrown elbow, puddles of wine on the floor and smashed plates and a mush of food from a waiter's tray that had been knocked over. I felt for celebrities who were The Hunted. It couldn't be easy to live like that.

"The place looks pretty unscathed." I nodded, looking around, mostly for my date. We were supposed to meet at eight-thirty, but better he wasn't here for the celebrity sighting melee. The man of my dreams could have lost some teeth. *Wait, maybe he did.* I checked my cell phone, as much as I hated to be the girl at the bar who was obviously waiting for someone, nervously checking her voice mail for that horrible something-came-up message. As I punched in my numbers, I met glances with other patrons at the bar who had a smile in their eye: *she's been stood up.*

Message from Zoe.

Message from Zoe.

Message from Renata.

Message from Zoe.

Nothing from Bryan.

"A drink for the lady . . . Oh, you're all set."

Because he was standing right behind me, reaching a single yellow rose in florist-bought cellophane around my shoulders and before my eyes. I slapped my cell phone shut and swiveled in my seat to embrace him. As planned, the cut of my wrap dress revealed a very good percentage of my leg. Which he admired.

"How did I keep my hands off of you in Hawaii?" he half whispered, taking the seat next to me. And the warmth started at my toes and worked its way up. My eyelashes tingled.

"It's beautiful, thank you." I leaned over and kissed him on the cheek, with the flower held lightly in my hands. There would be no wasting the voltage of a first kiss—which should always be accompanied by the face touch, the head tilt, the slow approach—on a thank-you kiss at a bar.

"You're very welcome." He smiled. The bartender approached, looking far more surly than she had before. Maybe she had a rude customer. "Scotch and soda, please."

The bartender tossed her towel over her shoulder and set about making his drink.

"That's the reason I'm late," he said, pointing at the flower. "It took longer at the florist than I had expected."

The bartender paused a second in making his drink, then clasped her grip on the soda shooter, threw a straw into the glass, and plopped the drink down in front of him. She turned and walked away.

My eyes followed her, but came back quickly to Bryan as he complimented me on my dress. "Thank you." I blushed. Over his shoulder, I could see the bartender roll her eyes as she whispered to two of the waitresses, who seemed similarly displeased with my charming date.

That was never a good sign.

Perhaps Renata was right.

Guarded, I kept my arms folded on the bartop ledge. I adjusted my body angle slightly away from him, wasn't leaning in as he spoke about how he couldn't get a bag of Doritos featured prominently in a TV pilot. I was only half listening to him . . . All I was thinking was *Why do these women hate Bryan so much?*

His beeper went off. He gave me the just-a-sec finger, and I noticeably stiffened. *No one gives me the just-a-sec finger, buddy.*

"I have to make a call . . . it's work . . . but I'll be back in a second," he said, almost frantic to get outside with his cell phone. "Sorry."

As he scrambled out, looking side to side with one finger in his ear as he took the call, I drained my drink and headed over to the bartender and waitresses. "Ladies," I greeted them. They smiled, professionally and politely. "I couldn't help but notice that you seem to have a . . . dislike for my date."

One of them practically snorted.

"Help me out here," I begged them, looking back to the

front window, seeing Bryan pacing as he spoke, checking his watch. "What do I need to know about this guy?"

The bartender spoke first, the others chiming in. "He's a real snake. Run. Run now."

I opened my mouth to speak, but the others shared their takes in staccato phrases, not having much time to talk. The more they said, the less I heard. These were the words that registered as my mind turned fuzzy and my body weakened. . . .

". . . practically wrecked the place . . ."

". . . slept with me for tips on who comes in . . ."

". . . wanted me to call when a star comes in . . ."

". . . practically ran Jennifer out of here, saying the most awful things . . ."

". . . has no soul . . ."

". . . vulture . . ."

My jaw hung open. Bryan was a paparazzo. He hunted celebrities for money. Big game hunter.

My mind spun. *No wonder he was at the hotel in Hawaii. He knew Kick and Celia were there. He knows Zoe, as she's famous, too. He saw me get out of the limo with her. "There's something about you" is right. He's hunting me, too.*

"Sweetie, get away from that guy," the Tang-haired bartender said. "Don't worry about the tab. Just take off."

No. I was going to have dinner with Bryan. I had to see if he really had targeted me to get a scoop on Celia and Kick's wedding. *He doesn't know that I know.*

This is going to be good.

"Play along with me, ladies." I grew a devilish smile.

They looked stunned. Then grateful. They'd probably been waiting a long time for a woman to turn it all around on him.

He came back, apologizing, stuffing his cell phone into his pocket and checking his pager for good measure.

"Miss anything important?" I smiled sweetly.

"Nah, just missed a meeting is all," he answered, and I could sense him counting lost dollar signs in his mind. Being here with me, he had missed out on a prime picture-taking opportunity. Wonder where he had hidden his camera.

"Your table is ready," one of the waitresses said, smiling brightly and motioning for us to follow her. We took our seats.

Let the games begin.

"I just heard that Jennifer Aniston was in here," I marveled, a little too superficially, I thought, but Bryan was distracted.

"Really?" He took a sip of his drink, which had just been placed on our table by the bartender.

"I heard it was a real scene." I shook my head. "Can you imagine?"

"Yeah . . . terrible way to live," he dismissed it, wanting a quick subject change. "So how was your day?"

I was on the phone with Celia Tyranova all day. She's decided on her wedding gown, and Kick's decided on his tux. I'm one of four people on earth who know where and when this wedding will take place.

"Pretty interesting," I sang, buttering a piece of bread.

"Ah, any fancy weddings coming up?"

Please. Be more subtle.

"Several, actually."

"Really? Anyone I've heard of, since we're gossiping about celebrities tonight?"

"I doubt it."

I could see a bead of sweat breaking out over his eyebrow. That was how I knew. He was after the inside track on Kick and Celia's wedding.

And he thought he was smarter than me.

"It must be amazing to work on that level," he continued. "I've read that some of these celebrities spend a million dollars on their weddings."

That was where naïve little me was supposed to pipe up about the ten-million-dollar wedding I was working on.

"Money is money." I smiled, saying nothing and everything at the same time.

"Still . . . it has to be amazing to order, like, a fifty-thousand-dollar wedding cake for someone," he tried.

"I'll tell you what's amazing . . . ," I said seductively. He leaned in. "*Making* a fifty-thousand-dollar wedding cake. I watched a special on the Food Channel, all about sugar-paste flowers and marzipan flowers . . ." I went on and on and on about sugar paste and fondant and how the humidity affects the quality of the icing. My tactic was to send him into a boredom coma. He wanted details, he'd get details. "And the *fillings!* Coconut espresso mousse, passion fruit buttercream, key lime . . ." Again, I went on and on and on, sounding like that guy from *Forrest Gump* talking about shrimp.

"Hmmm, fascinating," he said and checked his pager for the twentieth time. He was missing calls all over the place. Losing tens of thousands of dollars by the minute in missed hunting opportunities. I considered my subterfuge to be an act of benevolence toward the celebrities I knew and loved. All two of them. If I could keep one paparazzo off the streets, my work here was done.

"You know"—I went for the jugular—"we've just hit it off *so* well, just so comfortable with each other, you know?" I flipped my hair in true bimbo-esque style. "That I can't help but think what *our* wedding cake would be like, you know?"

He went pale. "Yeah . . . really?" he said, that sweat on his brow becoming beadlike. Like his eyes. Funny how they looked black and cold to me now. That happened when the game was up. The eyes looked different.

"Yeah, I mean . . . it was just so *natural* when we met that of course you *have* to be my soul mate, you know?" I giggled,

acting drunk without being so. "So say it with me now. . . ."
I waited for him to start to form the words.

"Mango buttercream," we said together, and I leaned over
and kissed him on the cheek. "Sweetie."

He didn't run. I'd thought that would do it, but this guy
was made of steel. He was going to stick with me, no matter
what. Which told me that paparazzi photos for Celia and
Kick's wedding were going to be massively valuable. I could
get the guy to go to a sperm bank with me right now and im-
pregnate me "because it's just so right between us," and he
would do it. He wanted the advantages of knowing me that
badly.

The bartender and waitresses looked on, suppressing smirks.
They could see his face. Bone white. His hands clasped at his
seat edges, twitching with his fight or flight instincts. The man
in him wanted to run. The vulture in him said to stay in that
chair or else.

I went in for the kill. "My family is going to *love* you,
Bryan. And"—a giggle, a hair flip, a lean-in that revealed
cleavage—"we haven't even kissed yet."

He grabbed his glass and drank from it. Raised his hand
for another.

"Oh, you were so right, Renata." I called her from the car,
driving with about eighty-five percent focus to get home and
into my pajamas as soon as possible.

"He's married?" She sounded tired, was whispering. It
was feeding time.

"Worse."

"What could be worse?"

"For us? He's paparazzi."

She dropped the phone. I heard a very distant, "Oh, shit,"
before she picked it up again. "Does he know which events
you're doing?" Still, we had to be careful with the phone

lines, even though I had just handed my business card to the very same kind of shark that we had sworn our bodies, minds, souls, and earthly possessions to keep away from Celia and Kick's plans. And I had just invited him right into the middle of it.

"He probably does."

"Maybe he's just looking for other ones. Maybe he doesn't know what he has on the line."

I thought about that. He could have just been sniffing around for any celebrity news. But no. He was far too focused on the million-dollar figure. No one knew yet that it would be ten times that. "I think he knows."

"Oh, God, Mylie. This is terrible."

"If you say 'I told you so,' I am going to slap you," I warned, feeling a too-strong pulse in my temple. Tingling in my hands. *I can't parallel park in this condition!*

"You won't hear that from me," Renata promised, and I believed her. "Maybe it's really not as bad as it seems."

"Zoe is going to fire me," I whispered.

"No, no, that's not going to happen," Renata soothed. "Look at it this way . . . You found out now. You prevented him from getting anywhere near the wedding. His plan won't work."

True. He was busted.

"Just throw away his number," Renata warned, as if that would do any good. "And don't take his calls."

"I doubt he'd call me." I gave a nervous giggle. A *very* nervous giggle. As petrified as I was over Bryan being a threat to the wedding, I was equally amused by how I made the guy sweat tonight. I wasn't normally an insidious revenge freak. But this guy had it coming.

"What did you do about the good night kiss?" she asked.

"I gave him a *Godfather* kiss," I answered. "Keep your friends close and your enemies closer kind of thing."

"Good girl," Ren said, proud of me and my ability to think strategy in the midst of a blindsided fog. "That's a nice kiss-off."

"Oh, it's not a kiss-off. . . ."

"*What?!*" Renata coughed. I'd caught her in midsip of something. "You're going to stay in contact with him?"

"Yup."

"Oh, Mylie, please! You're not that desperate!"

"It's not desperation," I explained. "It's self-protection. If he does know that I'm working on the wedding, he's going to be all over us, and there's nothing we can do about it. I'd have to tell Zoe, and I'll get fired."

"I don't like where this is going. . . ."

"So my only option is to keep the guy on a leash so that I have access to him, throw him off the trail." *I am a genius.*

Renata was silent for a moment, considering if it would work. "Sounds like you're playing with fire. These guys do the job they do because they're devious by nature. You don't have a whole lot of experience with that, sweetie."

"I'm a fast learner." I laughed. "Besides," I held off saying *if this works*, "when I throw him off the trail, it throws all of his contacts off the trail, too. This could be the best thing for the couple." Meaning Celia and Kick, of course. No names allowed. At least I could manage that much.

Renata clucked her tongue. "This isn't for them," she accused. "Be honest. This is because the guy misled you. He's the proverbial last straw, and you want payback on him and his kind."

I hate it when Renata is right.

"Mylie, let it go. Don't play this game," Renata warned. "Just tell Zoe what happened and work it out with the couple's men. They can handle him. No one would blame you."

Actually, Celia would think it wasn't exactly funny that almost immediately after the retina scan, thumbprint, hair inspection and having our cell phones stripped, the first thing I did was hand my business card to a stranger at the resort pool who wouldn't tell me what he did for a living. No, I couldn't fess up to such stupidity.

I can handle this.

Chapter 12

"Mylie!" It was Zoe on the phone. By the tone of her voice, sounding like she hadn't talked with me in months, I could tell she was on a manic high. Probably cleaning her bathroom grout with a toothbrush or taking apart her piano to clean each individual wire with a cotton ball.

"Zoe, hi. I'm on my way in to the office." I adjusted my headset and watched my latte bump around in the cup holder when I distractedly hit a pothole.

"Well, turn around, my dear. You're not coming in today."

I blinked. Zoe had never given me a day off out of nowhere.

"Would you do me a favor, dear?"

"Yes?" I drew out the word, not knowing if Zoe was sounding just a little bit off because she'd missed her medication or if she couldn't talk freely. Like someone was in the office with her and we had a privacy issue.

"Would you stop off at Starbucks and get me a frappucino?"

I tilted my head, confused as hell. Zoe didn't drink Starbucks. Zoe didn't drink coffee.

"Sure. . . ." I drew it out again. I felt like both *Starbucks* and *frappucino* were code words, but I didn't have the master code word sheet. "Anything else?"

"Ummmm . . ."

Yes. She couldn't talk freely. Now, to figure out which Starbucks I was supposed to go to. There was one on every street between my apartment and the office. And hey, what kind of secret meeting place is Starbucks, anyway? I thought everything was supposed to be superhidden. We were supposed to be sneaking through back doors in private meeting spots.

"Zoe, can you put Renata on the line?" I asked, wishing for traffic to hurry up. Something very strange was going on.

"Spectacular, darling," Zoe said and clicked the phone into holding music.

After a second, Renata picked up. "Mylie, you'd better get here quick."

"What's going on? Zoe sounds weird."

"She's on full tilt," Renata whispered. "We need you."

I hung up and whipped my car around a corner, taking the longer but faster way to the office.

"Zoe! Renata!" I called out as I was keying the door open. No one was in the reception area, so I moved back through the workrooms, scanning each as I ran. The spa. They'd be in the spa.

When I walked in, Zoe was curled in a ball on her recliner, and Renata was holding her, rocking her. Zoe was whimpering, wide-eyed frightened. Her hair had come out of her chignon, pieces sticking out all over the place. Renata looked terrified. We had always shielded her from Zoe's biggest meltdowns.

"Zoe, I'm here." I kneeled in front of her. She clasped my hand. "It's okay, Zoe. I'm here."

She was sleeping. I'd covered her with a yellow cashmere throw blanket, spritzed her with lavender, and turned on some ocean sounds music while we waited for her medicine to kick in. This was a bad one. It hurt to see someone you loved suffering like that, her lips tightened, her eyes wide with terror, her shirt moving where her quickened pulse was making it dance.

"Good Lord, Mylie . . ." Renata ran her hands through her own hair. "What was *that?*"

"She had a panic attack," I explained. "It happens sometimes." We stepped away slowly, satisfied with the rise and fall of Zoe's stomach, her calm breathing, and the more peaceful expression on her face.

"This has happened before?" Renata's eyebrows drew down. "You know about this?"

"Yes, and it's all taken care of now." I was short with her, not wanting to say too much, or else we'd get into the inevitable discussion about whether or not Zoe should be in such a high-stress job, dealing with constant ups and downs when her own body chemistry was so up and down itself. We couldn't bring it out into the open. Zoe wanted Renata never to know, to judge her. She didn't want to be seen as anything other than the superhero she needed to be to do her job well. We weren't doing too well with secrets these days, were we? "Come on, Ren. We have work to do."

We worked in silence, Renata reviewing order forms and invitation templates, me unpacking swatches of new Egyptian fabrics and alençon lace from the distributors. It was a quiet afternoon, as Mondays usually were. Most of our colleagues took Mondays off after working weddings the weekend before, but not us. Quiet days like this meant more could get done.

Chapter 13

Renata was right. I couldn't keep Bryan on a leash, hoping to throw him off of Celia and Kick's scent. So I decided to tell Celia.

I was escorted through a restaurant, asked to dress in black pants and a white shirt to look like the staff. Through the kitchen, with live lobsters screaming as they were dropped into vats of boiling water, sweaty kitchen assistants carrying armloads of lettuce to a chopping counter, chefs screaming at waiters, the glint of steel as sharp knives were waved about, I followed my guide and kept my mouth shut. I was sweating from more than just the heat of the kitchen.

We turned a corner, and the guide, a tall man with brown hair who didn't say much to me other than "It's slippery there" and "Watch your step" opened a rather beat-up looking door to reveal what looked like a red tunnel. The stairs leading below were covered in a plush, clean red carpeting, the walls painted in a glossy red. Even the handrail was shiny, red, and metallic. If it wasn't so pretty, it would look like the first-class stairway to hell. Sconces lined the walls as I descended, not a trace of dust on them.

Downstairs, the secret VIP lounge was busier than it sounded from the top of the stairs. A soundproof door kept the jazz music to silence, the laughter to nothing. Several dozen tables designed like martini glasses (complete with a big, fake olive under the glass tabletop) sat in wide distance from one another throughout the room, and waiters in red shirts brought trays of antipasto and raw clams to the patrons. I moved through the room, scanning for Celia.

"Celia's in the back room." The bartender leaned over the bar, a narrow ledge of metallic red, of course. "They called you down."

I'd been announced. And the secret downstairs VIP dining room had a back room. And probably another secret chamber beneath it. "Which way?" I asked, pointing in both directions like the Scarecrow from *The Wizard of Oz*. The bartender nodded left. "Thanks."

I was probably supposed to tip him a thousand dollars, but I just walked onward.

At yet another door, of course, I was frisked, subtly, in more like a hug with a lot of groping action. I wondered if the guy worked for Celia or if I had just run into some drunk lurking by a locked door. My cell phone was taken away, my purse, too. They might as well have stripped me down, put me in a wetsuit, and sent me in. Finally, after a swipe of my thumb on a glowing blue computer pad, I was allowed to enter.

"Mylie!" Celia sat alone in a corner booth. This room was jewel blue, with silver stars on the ceiling and a checkered floor in light and dark blues. Tiny pinlights illuminated the tops of the tables, and there was no one else in sight. Complete privacy.

She approached and hugged me. I hoped with a deep swallow that it wouldn't be for the last time. "Celia," I said, and she immediately picked up on the nervousness in my voice.

"What's wrong?"

"I have something to tell you," I started, sliding into the

booth after her. She held up two fingers to the waiter, who immediately brought us two martinis with extra olives.

Celia's eyes narrowed. Her arms crossed over her chest as if protecting herself from a physical blow. "What's wrong?"

I took a breath and blew it out. Loudly. "A paparazzo knows that I'm working for you."

Celia closed her eyes.

"I met him in Hawaii at the resort, and I had no idea that he does what he does for a living. He bought me a few drinks, took me to dinner, and . . ."

"You *told* him?" Celia's entire face was different. Pinched. Bitter.

"*No, no.*" I placed my hand on hers, and she didn't pull it away. Good sign. "I thought he was interested in me, and . . . I hadn't had a date in a long time . . . and all the guys on Match.com were . . ."

What was happening to Celia's face? Was that a . . . a smile?

"What?" I snapped, annoyed with her. She wasn't supposed to enjoy this!

"So he charmed you at the resort," she summed up.

"Yes." I looked down into my lap.

"But you didn't tell him anything."

"No."

"So how does he know?" She smiled. *Why is this woman smiling?*

"Because . . ." *Ugh, I can't even say it.* "Because he said that rather than do the cheesy vacation pickup thing where he takes me for a walk on the beach and tries to kiss me, we should just—"

"Exchange business cards." Celia slapped the table, and I jumped. My heart was pounding. I was terrified, and she was smiling. "Good old Bryan!"

What?! She knows him?

"Oh, sweetie, we know his game," Celia said, patting my hand in comfort. "He did the same thing to Angelique." That would be her British, ponytailed assistant. "Only she slept with him first."

"I so did *not* sleep with him!" I defended myself.

"We know," she said and gave me a wink.

"I just—" *Wait. Did she just say "we know"?* "If this is some kind of Willie Wonka trick where the bad guy is a test of my loyalty, then you and Kick are just a pair of twisted whackos!" I cried out. Zoe would so not approve of my tone. Or the Willie Wonka reference.

Celia burst out laughing. "No, Bryan does not work for us. We just know all of them." She took a sip of her martini, pursed her lips against the sour olive taste, and folded her hands in front of her again. "They're always at our windows, always there. We know them by name. Bryan's one of the smartest of the bunch. And the sleaziest."

"Tell me about it." I looked down again, ashamed at my own stupidity. But I had a friend in Celia. She would not let me wallow.

"Okay, so Bryan has your card. Does he know that you're working our wedding?"

"Well, it seems so. He knows I have something big in the works, but I can't be one hundred percent that he knows it's you."

Celia nodded, sipping again at the martini. I hadn't touched mine. "He probably does. He only goes for the big ones."

"I can handle this, Celia," I promised. "He doesn't know that I know."

"We know." *Wait, there it is again.*

"Celia?" I paused. "You already knew about this, didn't you?"

She gave a guilty smile.

"But how . . . ?"

The guilty smile lingered. She knew her timing, being the great actress that she was. Her expressions conveyed volumes, and that was why she got the big bucks. "That night in the restaurant . . ." She nodded, then had to resort to mimicking me to get the dead look out of my eyes. "Hazlenut buttercream, key lime buttercream, carrot cake, espresso filling," she imitated me. "Pure genius."

Did she have me bugged?

"I loved the part where you told him your family was going to *love* him." Celia smacked the table again, her enormous engagement ring making a *crack* sound against the blue metal tabletop. "You really tortured the guy."

"How in the world . . ." I wanted to wake up from this dream I must be having. This was a good time to dig into the martini.

"We had you tailed," Celia confessed, biting her lip a little bit. "I'm very sorry about the invasion of privacy, Mylie, but this is how it's going to have to be."

I exhaled, so glad to be violated like that. "Oh, Celia, I am so relieved." I nearly slumped down into my chair. "You have no idea how scared I was that you were going to fire us."

"Fire you?" Celia wrinkled her nose. Just like she did on the red carpet when someone marveled over her backless and almost bottomless dresses. "Mylie, we like you more and more each day. Sure, the guy's a snake, and he charmed you real good. But we know that you've kept your mouth shut and protected us. Bryan will not be a problem. We have it covered."

"And if he contacts me again . . . ?"

Oh, God, Mylie, shut up!

Celia lifted her chin. "Please don't tell me you want to go out with him again, because I'd really have to fire you for being a moron, not for being unprofessional."

"I just thought I could keep him close, throw him off the

trail." I sounded a little too eager, wanting to redeem myself, and Celia rubbed her chin. "Bad idea?"

"Bad idea." Celia nodded. "I appreciate your motives, even the vengeful ones, and I'd probably do the same thing if pushed too far once too often . . ."

Wait, how much do they know about me here?

"But please leave it to my men. We know Bryan, we know how he works, and we'll take it from here, okay?" Celia had spoken. I would not have Bryan on a leash. "If he contacts you, ignore him. Agreed?"

"Agreed." I swallowed large on my martini. "So we're fine?"

"We're fine." Celia smiled. "Just no more picking up guys for the next three and a half months, okay?"

To make her happy, I'd swear off men for the next three and a half *years*. Which was a milestone I could probably reach on my own anyway.

"Does Zoe know about this?" Celia asked, wanting full disclosure.

"No," I confessed. "I wanted to come directly to you. Zoe would have wanted to take the fall for me."

"She's a good woman." Celia nodded. "There's something a little bit . . . intense about her. . . ."

Uh oh.

"She's just very driven," I said quickly. "She loves her job. She's a perfectionist. She gives two hundred percent to everything she does."

Celia rubbed her chin again. "That I know . . . but there's something else about her. Like she's not there sometimes."

I swallowed. Was I going to get more than two minutes of peace through this whole thing? One crisis over, on to the next one. "You know how creative geniuses are." I smiled. "They're always painting a picture in their heads, a bit of inspiration comes flying out of nowhere—"

"No . . ." Celia tilted her head the other way. She was

going to figure this out. "It's a sadness. Something goes very dull in her eyes sometimes."

She was absolutely right. Zoe did have a sadness. And I would, too, if I'd been through what she'd been through. But we didn't talk about that.

"I'm right, aren't I?" Celia looked me straight in the eyes. "Zoe has a sadness."

I couldn't lie, or pretend, or insult her intelligence. "Yes, she does," I said. "But it's never going to interfere with your plans. Everyone has a sadness. I have a sadness, Kick has a sadness, which made him build that chapel, and you, Celia. You have a sadness. No one gets through life without one if they're living it right and taking chances."

She straightened up, more stunned by the insight than insulted by the tone.

"And without sounding too Dr. Phil," I continued. "It's everyone's sadness that's underneath whether they're nice, or whether they're a jerk."

"I thought it was everyone's character, actually." She winked.

"Sadness is a part of the soup that is the character, along with morals and love and fear and passion," I said, knowing that I had just boiled down hundreds of years of psychotherapy study into a proverbial vegetable soup.

"So we're all in the soup." Celia lifted her glass to clink with mine.

I lifted mine as well. Crisis averted. "We're all in the soup."

We drank down the remains of our martinis, dug out the olives with our fingers, and nodded in contemplative silence. "No one ever talks with me like this," she said quietly. "People don't realize that I appreciate deep conversation."

I nodded, then both of us shook our heads no to another drink offer from the waiter.

"We have to spend more time together, Mylie," Celia said,

liking the part of her that came out when she was with me. "I like talking with you."

Some moments hit me strangely. *Celia Tyranova likes talking with me. The woman who's on every magazine cover likes talking with me.*

"So how would you like to see how *I* live out there in the real world?" She beamed.

Um, no thanks.

"Really." She practically bounced in her chair. "When it's not terrifying, it's actually kind of fun."

I must have looked completely horrified.

"Are you afraid?" she teased, poking me in the arm. "Come on, don't be a wimp. I have bodyguards."

"Yes, to protect *you*," I said, the fear in my voice all too evident. Soup's on.

"We won't let anything happen to you," she promised. "No one's after you, anyway," came out of her mouth, and she immediately reined herself in. "I'm sorry, I didn't mean . . ."

"No offense, you're absolutely right." I laughed. "Zoe wouldn't pay the ransom. But she *would* have sadness about it."

Celia burst out laughing, grabbed my hand, and pulled me across the blue room and out into the VIP red room. Some waves, some happily surprised faces from various B-, C- and D-listers. Someone thought I was Alyssa Milano, then said I was too chunky and big on top to be her. I wasn't sure how to react to that one.

"Wait, Celia," I said, accepting my purse and cell phone from the security guard at the red door entrance. We were going up.

"Just stick close and watch." Celia smiled, and I got the feeling she relished the adventure of it, diving out into the everyday daylight just like diving out of a plane. It was just as dangerous, and apparently just as exhilarating.

She practically ran up the stairs, throwing open the door and disappearing. As I was moving much more slowly behind her, not sure I wanted to fling myself to the wolves today, she popped her head back into view and waved me forward.

The kitchen staff couldn't care less that she was passing through their workspace. Given the location of the secret doorway, they'd probably seen more celebrities than anyone on earth. It turned out that the guy who washed the broccoli would be way more valuable to Bryan than I was.

"Come on, Mylie!" Celia walked back to me and grabbed my hand, pulled me right up next to her. "Let's go greet the public." She looked positively giddy about it. "We're walking up Fifth."

Behind us, five of Celia's bodyguards appeared out of nowhere. Where did she stash them? In the freezer? But there they were, all over six-five, all over three hundred pounds, dwarfing us. They had biceps the size of my waist straining against the fabric of their dark suit jackets, dark glasses on, and earpieces that they not-so-subtly held in place with their meaty fingertips. They alone would draw a ton of attention to Celia.

As we moved through the restaurant, everything clicked into slow motion. *This must be how the Secret Service feels*, and I instinctively searched the other patrons' eyes and bodies for any signs of danger. Having seen way too many movies, I got a momentary flash of myself yelling "Gun!" and then dramatically leaping into the air to cover Celia. In reality, if a gun had appeared, I knew that I would freeze in place and probably wet myself.

Patrons smiled and waved. People hit each other in the arms and pointed at Celia moving through the room. Other people, seasoned New Yorkers who didn't give a toss about celebrities, completely ignored her.

Of course, there were those who sprayed their wine through their noses.

And those who furiously dug through their purses for paper and a pen, knocking their chairs to go skidding backward as they ran up to Celia for an autograph. She obliged, mastering some kind of batlike sense of blind movement that allowed her to write as she walked, stepping over those toppled chairs, her hair bouncing on her shoulders. She turned to hug her fans, and she was smiling. She loved this.

We moved quickly. She had to stay a moving target, otherwise she'd jam the place up and anger the management. "Are you anybody?" Someone pulled at my white shirt and turned me around, and I was quickly rescued by one of the bodyguards who lifted me off my feet to face me in the right direction again. All before I could say I was Alyssa Milano.

It hit me then that this was really quite reckless of Celia. What was with all the security and the secret meetings, the thumb scans and the cell phone seizure, if she was going to parade me through a restaurant and out onto Fifth Avenue? Wouldn't I be recognized? Actually, no. She was right when she said they weren't looking for me. In her presence, I—and everything else in the room—was invisible.

"This is the easy part." Celia turned to me as we both pushed open the heavy glass door, her waving goodbye to the crowd over my head. "The fans are not dangerous. Especially when you take them by surprise like this. They're so busy trying to see if it's you that you're pretty much gone before they can do anything."

Still, she slipped a pair of dark glasses over her eyes as we stepped out onto the sidewalk with the Bruise Crew right behind us. And I was right. It was the security people noticed first, then Celia. Some didn't even recognize Celia. She was just another pretty redhead on the streets of New York. Probably a wannabe model, most thought. When they weren't expecting greatness to walk by, they were blind to it.

"When the hawks descend, you step away," Celia warned,

and I could tell by the raise of her shoulders, how her arms swung a little more stiffly now, that she was bracing for the darker part of her little stroll down Fifth Avenue. "Oh, look at those shoes!" She pointed at a glass window. "The pink ones! Barry!"

From behind us, someone grunted. One of the Bruise Crew. "Tell Angelique."

And he made a cell phone call. To tell Angelique to order the shoes in a seven. I was amazed. The guy was so well trained that he didn't ask "Tell Angelique what?" He had been paying attention. He looked when she said "the pink ones." He was honoring his pledge to get Celia whatever she wanted. He was completely tuned into her, even from five feet back. We were quite the crowded group.

A giant hand landed on my shoulder, and I was pulled back, my hair whipping against my face in a kind of whiplash from not expecting a sudden change of direction.

Someone has seen something!

The Bruise Crew instantly moved into a circle around Celia, and pulled in tightly. Out of nowhere came a band of thugs with cameras, about forty of them, some with baseball caps on backward, some with moustaches, all of them pushing and shouting Celia's name and "Where's Kick? Is he off with another woman?"

Celia told me later that they said things like that to get you angry, so that they could capture your scowl and sell it for more money to tabloids underneath a headline that screamed "Celia Devasted Over Kick's Betrayal." The hawks swirled around us like so much garbage caught in a wind tunnel, jockeying for position, knocking each other around, the flashes going off, shutters clicking a million miles an hour. Some of them moved behind us, taking pictures from behind. Celia told me that those were the ones looking for her panty lines showing, so that they could sell the pictures to the fashion mags with a headline screaming "Celia Vows Never To Wear a Thong Again!" Or if her bra strap was showing, there would be an article about the top ten ways to hide your bra straps, with Celia as the great, big glaring Don't at the center of the article.

Others took pictures of her shoes, all the time yelling things like "Celia, did you gain weight?!" just to make her frown or look concerned. God forbid she take a reactionary glance down at her own stomach or thighs, or that would be the next picture on the next tabloid, right over "Celia's Pregnant! And It's Not Kick's!"

A squeal of tires sounded, and a limo stopped right in the intersection. The Bruise Crew all but shoved Celia into the car, and the straggler of the security guards who had been walking next to me just kind of pointed to the door as my instruction to get in. Then the car door slammed shut, and the limo pulled away. We had left the Bruise Crew behind. I spun around in my seat to see what happened to them. But the car turned a corner.

Celia exhaled and raked her hand through her hair. "Whew! Now *that* was fun!"

I must have looked like I was going to cry.

"What?" she asked, now drumming her hands on my arm. "Did that upset you?"

My mouth hanging open, I couldn't even speak.

"What? They scared you, didn't they?" Celia shook her head. "That wasn't even a bad one."

"Why? Why?" I couldn't get the rest of the sentence out. "Why would you *do* that?"

She smiled. "It's my job, sweetie."

She had to stay in front of the cameras, even if it meant showing up in a tabloid. The exposure kept her on top of her game, even if it was always a danger to her personally. If she stayed hidden, she wouldn't be so in demand.

"Every one of those people I hugged just now," Celia explained. "They're going to remember that forever."

Don't be naïve, Mylie. This is how it works. She just secured a few dozen lifelong fans who would tell their fifty closest friends, who would become lifelong fans by proximity to a great story.

"I'm very careful not to accept a hug from any kind of attractive man," Celia explained, popping open the ice bin and grabbing a water for herself and one for me. "Or else I'm having an affair with him. No babies or little kids ever, or the whole Celia-has-baby-fever brigade will start up again. I pick the people I'm seen with carefully."

It was an ugly reality. A necessity for Celia, but an ugly reality. "I'd be terrified all the time," I confessed, struggling with the top of the water bottle until the plastic seam ripped and it gave way.

"Oh, I was when I first started out," Celia said, nodding, eyes wide. "I was the paparazzi's dream! I'd start crying if they just looked at me the wrong way, and then *snap, snap, snap*. Luckily, I wasn't as—" She stopped herself. *I wasn't as big a star then* just didn't sound the same when spoken out loud as it did in your head. "When I was in the tabloids, I'd get calls from my momma and daddy." *That's right, she's from the South.* "And they'd be so hurt. It just about killed me." She looked to her left, out the window for quite a while.

"And now . . . ?" I tried to break the emotionally loaded silence, apparently by pressing her on a difficult memory.

"Now it doesn't bother me. I've been hurt into numbness by it." She shrugged, and when she turned, I could see the tears where they welled up in her eyes and willed themselves not to fall over her cheeks.

Thankfully, I had enough sense not to ask her if she'd ever sued the tabloids, if she ever wondered if that cozy-cozy photo of Kick and a blonde in Brazil was the real deal, if she loved being on the Best-Dressed List. My gushing fan talk wouldn't do for now. It just wasn't the time.

But it was time for this one: "Is it worth it, though, to be so targeted like this in order to do what you do?"

She didn't even hesitate. "Absolutely."

Chapter 14

"Mylie, it's Bryan."

I'd recognized the Caller ID and picked it up anyway. Mistake #1.

"Hi, Bryan," I said casually, munching on an apple. I didn't have to have professional etiquette with this guy. "I had a *terrific* time the other night." Mistake #2.

Renata rolled her eyes and, angrily, moved her centerpiece to another station. She wasn't going to have any part of my dangerous decisions.

"Yeah, me, too," Bryan said, a smile in his voice. "You looked *delicious*."

Now it was my turn to roll my eyes.

"What are you doing Friday night?" he tried, and I inspected my nails. Not my fingernails, but rather the tiny brads I'd soon be hammering into two hundred mini birdhouse wedding favors.

"I have plans," I said, trying my best to sound sincere.

"Saturday then." It wasn't a question.

"Going out of town."

He might have asked for Sunday, but was aware of how he sounded. "Ah, you're a busy girl."

You have no idea.

"Mylie," he said, and what came out of his mouth next

sent a chill right through me. Renata even said I turned sheet white. "You're safe with me. I would never do anything to hurt anybody."

It was even scarier than being in that rugby scrum of paparazzi with Celia.

"Goodbye, Bryan," I whispered and hung up. I was not going to make Mistake #3. Renata closed her eyes as if in silent prayer.

"Good girl," she said, and without knowing why, I burst into tears.

"One meltdown a week is enough for all of us." Zoe appeared out of nowhere, looking much better, her ability to laugh at herself returned. She was pink-cheeked, polished, her lipstick on fine. I, by contrast, was a mess. I wondered if, like Celia, I would ever get hurt into numbness by this kind of thing.

"Mylie, the guy's not worth it," Renata soothed, shaking her head, and Zoe was instantly by my side, holding out the Kleenex box.

"I know." I sniffled, digging the soft white tissue into my face. "It's not about that guy. It's that I'm tired of getting the lines. I'm tired of having games played on me. That nothing that seems real is actually real. And you can save all that at-least-you-found-out-now crap. The guy targeted me. He played a game on me. That's what *hurts*."

Zoe stepped back. I imagined her thinking *Where is my strong Mylie?*

I'm allowed to melt down, too, lady. Everyone has their breaking point, as you know, and it's often the smallest thing that tips you over. Everyone is the same.

"I know, Mylie, it's awful," Renata said, and her promise was loaded. "Believe me. He will get what's coming to him."

Chapter 15

"*Mylie, you need to fly out to the coast. You're needed in the chapel.*"

That was the extent of Zoe's voice mail, and I knew what it meant. Kick wanted to meet with me. The chapel in their Sonoma estate was his.

By 7:00 P.M., I was there. Escorted by Angelique and left at the rounded-top doors of the chapel, I took a calming breath before I pulled open the door and walked into Kick's sanctuary. It was darker than before, of course, lit only by pillar and taper candles whose flames danced in the unfelt air currents of the room. Faint sounds of monk chants played on a sound system, as distant sounding as if I were standing on a hill in Nepal and the shrines were miles away, the chants echoing through the mountains. He kept it calm and serene in this chapel.

A few steps in, and I was closer to the candle grouping on the altar. My eyes had adjusted to the dim lighting as well, so I could make out the dark silhouette of Kick's back and shoulders. His head was down in prayer. I would not interrupt. So I looked up at the gold designs on the ceiling, looking so different in candlelight than they did in the daylight of my original tour. The gold captured every flicker of the candles, reflected back to me.

"I'll be with you in a minute," he said in a hushed, reverent tone, and I kept myself from answering back with a "Take all the time you need." I didn't want to break the silence with my voice. It was beautiful in there. A true escape from the world, from noise, from any movement at all. It was like no bad thing had ever been allowed to enter and thus left no trace of itself. Amazing that a room could hold the same deep peace as a forest or a mountaintop, a beach in the morning, my favorite park on a hill, or the Hudson River's edge at sunrise, which was my own place to reflect. I still can't get used to the difference in the skyline.

"You're not a praying woman?" Kick stood then, only the side of his face illuminated by the candles, the rest of his face in darkness.

I felt no need to tell the client what I thought he wanted to hear, wouldn't fake being devout for the sake of a business connection. "My faith doesn't fit into any one category, so I do my praying outside," I shared.

"Ah." He nodded, being the absolute first person to respect my belief system. Everyone else wanted a definition. Which box did I fit into? He didn't ask. Not because he didn't care, but because he was the same way. Some things were not for others to ask or know. "So you're probably surprised that I spend so much time in here."

I just didn't answer. It would take too many words to trace the flow chart of my observances about him: from arrogant jerk to morals-conscious celebrity to spiritual being.

"If I didn't, I'd lose myself," he offered.

I nodded, understanding fully the way his world could do that.

"My soul is for sale every day to get ahead," he continued. "And coming here just brings me back to the one thing they can't touch. I make better decisions when I come here first."

"I can understand that," I said, slipping into the cushioned pew seat next to him, both of us looking not at each other but at the pillar candles on the altar. "I do the same thing with running by the river . . . I never make a big decision without being near the water first."

We were quiet then. Not an awkward silence, definitely not the awkward silence of being attracted to someone you're not supposed to be attracted to (even though I was in a candle-filled room with *People*'s Sexiest Man Alive). But a comfortable silence, both of us just absorbing the remaining moments in that chapel. He hadn't called me here to pray with him. We had work to do.

"Celia wants you to stay here tonight," Kick said as we climbed the stairs and I followed him around a bend into their TV room. He clicked on Sports Center on a huge-screen TV and—not taking his eyes off the screen—backed up the perfect number of steps to sit back into his beige leather reclining chair. "Seeing as how you're a jerk-magnet at resorts."

Oh, God, she told him!

For that, he'd take his eyes off of Sports Center. "Nice going, by the way."

Do NOT apologize. Kick won't admire that.

"Yes, I'm quite proud of my ability to be surrounded by hundreds of men and get picked up by the biggest loser there." I smiled, taking my place uninvited on the recliner next to him. "It's a gift."

"Nah, he had you pegged the minute you got out of the limo." Kick reached to a silver end table next to his chair, popped open a hidden front door, and pulled from a mini refrigerator two cold Coronas and fresh-cut lime wedges. He handed a beer and a wedge to me. "We should have put you and Zoe in separate cars. You're helping us refine our game."

"Glad to be of service." I nodded as Kick popped off my beer cap with an opener that also came out of the hidden mini fridge. We clinked bottles and took a swallow.

"Is the guy bothering you?"

Ah, that's why I'm here. Kick's assessing the damage I brought on with the whole Bryan thing.

"He called. I blew him off."

"Good girl," he said, which was exactly what Renata had said. "He got to Angelique, too, you know."

"I know. Celia told me."

"You and Celia are getting along great," he said, eyes on the television, beer held at the ready by his chest.

"Yes, she's terrific." I smiled, taking a sip of my own.

"She thinks of you as a friend, you know." He nodded, eyes still on the scores. "It's not a business-only thing for her, so if it is for you—"

He's protecting her. Making sure I'm not feigning friendship until I get my check.

"It's not a business-only thing," I said and decided to get real with him. "I have to be honest with you. I didn't expect the two of you to be so nice. No offense."

"None taken." He probably heard that—or felt that—all the time.

"And I doubt you invite many workers to come hang out in your chapel and drink Coronas with you in your den," I played. "So I can tell you both see me as a real person, too."

That took his eyes off the scores. "We're hoping so," he confessed.

"I assure you, Kick. You'll have no problems from me."

He nodded. "Good. Now that that's settled, let's talk business."

And I thought we'd be watching the Minnesota game on TiVo.

"What can I do for you?" I shifted in my chair to face him, very unprofessionally swigging from my Corona bottle. Another scene Zoe would not approve of.

"I'd like to plan a series of surprises for Celia on the wedding day." He clicked off the TV and swiveled his chair to face me, too.

"A *series* of surprises?" I blinked. Most of our couples went for the one big surprise: an enormous diamond pendant, fireworks, a celebrity flown in to sing their song. "What do you have in mind?"

He smiled. This was going to be big.

Three hours and many beers later, Kick and I were sprawled out on those recliners, my leg hung over the side of the chair's arm, Kick pushed back so that he was practically lying down, and eight empty beer bottles and a pizza box on the floor all around us. With work behind us, and Kick's surprise plans for Celia written on my yellow legal pad and zipped up into my carrier for security, we were talking football.

"Yeah, I grew up in a football family," I told him. "We have last row under the scoreboard at Giants Stadium. You can't see a thing once they're inside the twenty."

"Nosebleed seats." Kick laughed.

"Yeah, the hot dog guy doesn't come up that far very often." I laughed. "So we stock up."

Kick laughed a buzzed giggle. "Oh, man, I wish I could sit in a stadium like that again."

"Why can't you?" I blinked. "Stars sit in stadiums all the time."

"Yeah, but it's not the same. People interrupt, and security has to keep an eye out; then they put you on the Diamond Vision, and everyone knows where you're sitting. People send their kids over." He sighed. "It's just easier to be in the VIP box."

I threw my pizza crust at him. "Oh, you poor baby! 'I *have* to sit in the VIP box.' Waaaah," I mocked him, and the pizza crust came sailing back to hit me in the lip.

Which was the perfect time for Zoe and Celia to walk in.

"Mylie, you're fired."

Chapter 16

"If you fire Mylie, we fire you."

It was Kick. Standing up for me.

Zoe was fierce, angrier than I'd ever seen her. She and Celia stood there in the doorway, assessing the scene with our pizza box and beer bottles, both Kick and I looking falsely cozy with each other. It wasn't as if I was in his lap, wiping pizza sauce from his mouth. We were having a pizza crust fight. While we were drunk and I was mocking him. What was so unprofessional about that? Nah, I was screwed.

"Mylie, get your things right now!" Zoe assumed the Mom Stance, with her hands on her hips, her lips pressed tightly together. Celia stood blinking beside her, wondering if I wasn't really her friend.

"I'm serious, Zoe." Kick stood up from his chair and crossed his arms over his chest. "Celia and I *like* Mylie. She's a friend, and if you hurt a friend of mine, I will hurt you."

Wow, that was a little harsh. I chalked up his street cred to the Coronas.

"Kick?" Celia asked. "It's fine?"

"Of course it's fine," Kick answered, not the least bit defensive. "Mylie's a real person. She's not kissing our butts or being fake." He looked right at Zoe on that one, and I slumped down farther. His defending me was coming at Zoe's expense.

Yes, she could act a little fake sometimes, but I didn't want that thrown in her face right now.

Celia placed her hand on Zoe's arm. "We have no problem here, Zoe."

"No!" Zoe roared. "This is not how I trained her!"

"*Excuse me?*" I stood up from my chair. "How you *trained* me?" Her lipstick was fine, so this was not some sort of episode. And in a heartbeat, I knew I would never feel the same about Zoe again. I had taken care of her. I had been practically her nurse for the past years, running to her when she needed help, keeping her secrets, shielding her from anyone knowing about her problems. I had no life outside of my job, and apparently part of my job was being *trained?*

Kick must have seen the fury in my eyes, because he stepped between us, blocking her from my view. The last thing they needed was a homicide at their house. They didn't need that kind of publicity.

"Zoe, I will not ask you to apologize to Mylie for that," he said.

Hey, thanks, Kick.

"Because you should know enough to do that on your own."

Zoe looked like she'd been slapped. Which she basically had.

"Mylie and I worked for three hours on the wedding plans, and I'm very happy with her work," Kick said. "She's more attentive to our wedding than you are, Zoe. So if she goes, we go. And if you ever talk to her like that again, you go, and we keep Mylie on to plan our wedding."

Good Lord, Kick, stop talking!

It only made her angrier. Kick didn't know the nerve he was hitting with Zoe.

"Let's just call it a night." Celia stepped in. "It's late, we're all tired, and we don't want to say anything we don't mean."

But the damage was done. My mentor had revealed her true nature. She thought I was a trained puppy.

"Never mind," I said. "Celia, Kick, it was very nice to get to know you, but I'm removing myself from your wedding. And, Zoe"—I stepped closer to her and said the words she never wanted to hear—"take care of yourself." With a slight emphasis on the *yourself*.

"Mylie, no," Kick said.

"Mylie"—Celia grabbed my arm—"don't do this."

"It's done," I said and grabbed my bag, unzipped it. "Here." I handed my legal pad to Zoe. "Just so you know what Kick and I were working on all night."

All I saw as I left was Zoe flipping through page after page after page of plans, one yellow page after another. I had done well. I had been *trained* well. I earned a pizza and a few beers. And the chance to be human and laugh with a friend.

As I closed the door, I heard Celia crying.

Chapter 17

Renata picked me up at the airport. I'd taken the red-eye and just wanted to clear my stuff out of Zoe's office before she got back from the coast.

"Are you sure about this?" Renata helped me fill cardboard rose boxes with my things, my coffee mugs, my suits which I always kept on hand in case clients stopped by. I left my cell phone, my keys, and my laptop on the counter. All were given to me for work by Zoe.

"Abso-friggin-lutely," I growled, my jaw clenched so tightly it hurt.

"She shouldn't have said that," Renata tried, knowing that I was walking away from a dream job and a bundle of cash. And being a good enough friend to comfort me, even though she was going to step into my place and get my commissions. Minus, I'm sure, the Kick and Celia wedding. They'd never keep Zoe on now.

"Maybe she wasn't well," Renata tried.

"No, she was well," I barked, hurt to the core that she'd pull rank like that after all I'd done for her.

"Listen, Mylie . . . think long range. I know you're hurt, and this is a bad time for you to be hurt again, but think long range."

She was trying to help, but I needed to get out of there. I

needed to be away from Zoe, from wedding world, just out of that office.

"Go to Dolphin Dance, then," Renata offered, and when I turned around, she was holding out the keys. To her vacation home at the beach. She and Pete owned a Victorian by the ocean, and they were talking about turning it into a bed and breakfast someday. It needed some work, and their friends had an open invitation to stop by on weekends to relax and paint if they felt like it. I'd always been taking care of Zoe or working, so I hardly ever got there. I hadn't been there in . . . what? . . . a year?

Take the keys, Mylie.

"I'll be down on Saturday." Renata hugged me. "Go relax and then get ready for diaper patrol when we get there." She poked me on the nose, just as Celia had done not too long ago, and I took my surprisingly small box of personal belongings and got out of there, stunned by how little was actually mine.

When I pulled up into the crushed-seashell driveway at Dolphin Dance, having opened my windows on the way to breathe in the ocean air, the rest of the world fell away. Zoe was on her own. I was done with that. Who cared who Bryan stalked now? I was done with that. Working weddings? I was done with that. Celia and Kick? That was the only thing that made me tear up, then bawl.

Which made me a suspicious character to the little girl who was sitting on the porch at Dolphin Dance. I heard her first: "Daddy . . . some lady is crying in the driveway." I looked up to see a little girl with blond, ringlet hair in a pink T-shirt and white shorts, hugging a doll to her chest. As protection from the crazy lady who just pulled up in the rented Sebring. The SUV I normally drove was Zoe's. I was carless now, too.

The little girl was alone on the deck. It being a Thursday, Renata and Pete's friends weren't usually there. I'd expected to have the place to myself. To wander like a ghost, wondering what happened to the last few years of my life. I craved alone time. I needed quiet. I didn't want to talk to anyone.

"You okay?" came a man's voice at my car window. The little girl's father had come to chase the tearful visitor away.

"I quit my job," was all I could say. "Renata said I could come here."

My door opened, and a man's hand appeared before my teary eyes. "Yes, Ren called and said you were on your way. And that I should have some Häagen-Dazs bars ready for you."

I looked up, my eyes stung by the sun over his shoulder. I'm sure I looked fabulous after on-and-off weeping on the parkway for three hours.

"I'm Russell, and this is my daughter Emma," the man said, helping me out of the car. "Your bags in the trunk?"

I nodded.

"I'll get 'em," he said, holding his hand out for my keys. I pushed the button to pop the trunk instead. "Just a sec."

The little girl stared at me, then smiled when I looked her way. "Do you want to hold my doll?" she asked, holding it by the arm over the white railing.

"Em, stand back, I just painted that," the man warned. "I know you like to test me." He smiled at his daughter, and she stepped back, smiling as well.

"I'm Mylie," I introduced myself, for once without a formal, businesslike handshake and eye contact. "I quit my job," I heard myself say again, and Russell laughed.

"Yeah, I know. You said that. Kinda in shock, huh?"

I nodded.

"Well, you're at Dolphin Dance now, so the world out there does not exist," he promised. "We have lunch just about ready, and there's plenty for you to join us if you like, and at six o'clock, my Emma takes the stage."

Now that I was standing, the sun was out of my eyes, and

the man became visible to me. Sandy blond hair, blue eyes, football-player build, and white paint all over him. He had a smear on his cheek, and his hands were striped. The white paint dotted his knuckles.

"Takes the stage?" I managed, looking over to see a very proud Emma showing off some of her dance moves. I was getting a preview of the show. Russell looked up at her like the proud dad he was.

"Do you want my doll?" Emma asked again. Without waiting for an answer, the little girl clomped down the front stairs in her blue flip-flops and shoved the stuffed doll into my hands. "Here!" And then she ran around the house to the backyard.

"She's a handful," Russell said.

"She's adorable." I was coming back to life, taking a deep breath of the ocean air and looking around. "I haven't been here in so long." I marveled at the house, shielding the sun away with my hand against my forehead. They'd done a lot of work. The entire house was painted a sage green, the porch was finished, and a porch swing with a green cushion moved just a little bit in the breeze. Planter boxes showed off plenty of lush greenery and white flowers. The windows were new, arched Andersons with white etching.

"So you're the slacker friend who never showed up to help us," Russell joked with a wink, and I couldn't take offense. "Yeah, a bunch of us have been coming down here all season. We're like a regular Habitat for Humanity, only Ren and Pete aren't in need."

I laughed. "No, they're definitely not."

"You're not going to believe the inside," he promised, taking my bags and leading the way.

The last time I'd seen the inside of Dolphin Dance, it was practically gutted. Sheetrock only on some walls, old, musty carpet covering the big question: what do the floors look like underneath? Wiring sticking out of the walls, capped by little blue security thimbles, no kitchen appliances, mildew on the walls from all that ocean air. It was a mess. I remembered being afraid to walk up the creaky stairs for fear I would fall through to the dark, creepy basement.

No.

It was far different now.

The answer to the big question was that beautiful hardwood floors were waiting to be revealed underneath those musty old carpets. French doors had been put in. The walls were a warm beige color, almost honey. Ceiling fans turned slowly in lazy circles. Comfy, inviting couches touched together in a U shape, and a coffee table held home décor magazines.

"Nice, huh?" Russell led the way, turning to look at my impressed face as I moved through the living room and into the kitchen. "Ren picked out all the furniture."

Of course.

"And Emma picked out the wall color."

Great job, Emma.

"She's very proud." He winked. "Although we did veto her idea of orange for the kitchen. She wanted it the color of orange juice."

I was reminded of how I wanted cinnamon-colored walls for my dream home. It was close in concept to a six-year-old's great vision.

"Oh, wow," I marveled once we reached the kitchen. New appliances, everything gleaming, a twelve-seater table, a chopping block island, copper pots and pans hanging above it. An herb garden potted above the kitchen sink. Framed photos of the people who worked on the house, with Russell holding Emma on his shoulders. "You all did an amazing job!"

"Thanks," he said. "We had an amazing amount of fun, too. Pete would bring in steamed crabs and cases of beer, and we'd all set up in the backyard for a feast."

I should have been there.

"When do you think they'll open it as a bed and break-fast?" I asked.

"This fall, probably." Russell shrugged. "Ren's been so busy with work that things have been slower around here."

"Well, she's got some big weddings going on right now, but it always slows down in the fall," I reasoned, continuing my tour of the place, inspecting the cookbooks in the kitchen cupboard, the collection of white plates and footed coffee cups. Renata was terrific at this. She'd outdone the Williams Sonoma catalog.

"Emma's mother loved this place," Russell said, and the drop in his voice stopped me. I turned from the coffee cups to look at him, and he was looking out the window. Normally, I was great at navigating loaded comments like that, experienced as I was with brides who had something they were upset about but didn't want to say out loud. But I couldn't bring myself to push this guy. He stopped talking for a reason.

"And Emma is how old?" *Good save.*

"She's six." *I was right on target.* "Turning seven next month."

"And she wants to be a dancer?"

"Dancer half the time, interior decorator the other half." Russell shrugged. "And an astronomer on the weekends."

"An astronomer?" I wrinkled my nose. It wasn't the usual thing for a six-year-old to want to be.

"She loves the night sky," he explained. "I took her out to Mesa when her mother left. . . ."

Ah, got it.

"And the sky out in the desert is just unbelievable. Have you been?"

I shook my head no.

"It's unreal, all those stars . . . the Milky Way . . . shooting stars everywhere you look." Russell shook his head. "I've been everywhere, and I've never seen a sky like that. I wanted my little girl to see it, too."

"What did she think?"

Russell laughed and rubbed the scruff of unshaven growth on his chin. "She said it was like the angels poked more holes in the sky so that they could see us better."

My hands felt warm with that one. "That's adorable." I smiled. "She's really something."

"Yeah . . ." Russell was lost in a memory, looking off to the side. But he snapped out of it quickly. "You've got to see the upstairs. Go on ahead while Emma and I get lunch ready."

"Are you sure? I can help out," I offered, feeling like a guest in his home.

"No, you're too in shock from quitting your job." He winked.

I laughed. Somehow, when I passed through the doorway at Dolphin Dance, I had truly forgotten about the outside world. Ren's bed and breakfast was going to be a huge success.

"So what did you think?" Russell said when I returned from my quick upstairs stroll through the eight bedrooms. I had been taking everything in only halfway, as I was listening to Russell whistle downstairs. Emma, I had seen through the window, had been playing in the yard with a big blue ball, kicking it one way and chasing it down, then going back in the other direction, cheering for herself.

"It's beautiful beyond words." I gave my thumbs-up report. "You all did a fabulous job. I love the ceiling beams upstairs." And I ached for the fun I missed out on, the painting parties, picking out light switches, those crab bakes in the backyard. Now, the house was nearly done. I had missed it all. I had been invited a dozen times . . . but my loyalty to Zoe kept me away.

"Yeah, I think we're all kinda sad that it's almost done," he said, placing a big salad bowl in the center of the table.

Glistening red tomatoes sat atop a spinach salad. Garlic bread waited in a basket, cut into one-inch slices, a plate of mozzarella drizzled with olive oil sat beside that, and strips of flank steak perfectly pink in the center waited next to that. The table was set with those white dishes, and pink lemonade with ice cubes sat in front of our dishes. "I'm a chef." He shrugged, noticing me noticing his work.

"Ah." I nodded. "Looks great."

"Let me just go get Emma."

And of course I had to check him out as he walked away.

Chapter 18

*D*on't check your voice mail.
Don't check your voice mail.
Don't check your voice mail.

I walked away from the land line phone in Renata's office, which was a dream of a room with mahogany desks and framed nautical prints.

"Mylie! We're outside!" Emma called, and I had to follow the sweet little voice. The sliding glass door was open, and I stepped out onto the deck, admiring the arrangement of furniture, the open-air fireplace with cushioned seats in front of it. The deck had been designed as an outdoor living room, perfect for parties.

Russell and Emma lay together in a green-striped hammock, the little girl snuggled against her daddy's chest, and Russell had one arm around her. She smiled as I approached.

"Are you ready for your show tonight, Emma?" I asked, walking up to them and sitting cross-legged on the Adirondack chair nearest them. It had just been Armor Alled, so I slid backward on the slippery surface to rest against the chair back. I hoped they hadn't noticed my lack of grace.

"Oh, yes." She beamed. "Piece of cake."

"I'm sure you're going to be great." I winked.

"I'll get it." Russell rolled out of the hammock, and it was only then that I heard the phone ringing inside. He sprinted off, that football build still having strong speed, and I watched him go.

"Don't even think about it," adorable Emma said to me, and I blinked at the little girl's keen observation.

"Don't even think about what?" I tried.

She centered herself on the swinging hammock and crossed her hands behind her head, with a dead-on glare that even I couldn't muster in a business meeting. "Liking my daddy."

Okay, then . . .

"It's for you, Mylie." Russell stood on the deck, the cordless in his hand. Wanting to get away from the now-frightening little girl, I scurried off the Adirondack and jogged over to him to take the call.

"Mylie?" It was Renata.

"Ren, hi."

"You got there okay?"

"Yes, everything's fine. How are things there?" I couldn't stop myself from asking.

"Zoe's . . . fine," Renata said. "Surprisingly fine."

"Whatever." I feigned indifference. I had actually been pretty worried about her. If a *P* that looked like a *B* on a wedding invitation sent her into a depression for four days, what would my quitting do to her?

"Don't worry about Zoe," Ren said. "Celia's called six times for you."

I swallowed, never wanting to hurt her. Or Kick. They had opened up and trusted me.

"Can I give her the number where you are?" Ren tried. "I think you should talk to her."

I thought for a moment, pacing on the deck.

"Mylie," Ren pushed.

"I can't come back to work for Zoe." I sighed.

"Well, that's what Celia wants. And you need to swallow

your pride, put away the hurt feelings, and just do what you need to do for the long range."

She was right.

"You're not Zoe's caretaker. You don't even have to be her friend. In fact, it's probably better if you're not."

Again, right.

"Here's what I'm going to do," Renata said, ever the problem-solver. "I'm telling Celia you're at the shore for the weekend, but you'll call her on Monday. I'm telling Zoe that you'll be back on Monday, and that she owes you an apology, a raise, and a kidney donation if you ever need one."

I smiled.

"Now you and Russell just enjoy yourselves." Was that a smile in her voice. "We'll see you on Sunday."

"Wait, Sunday? You said you'd be down for the week-end!" *Don't leave me alone with the little girl who gave me the "Don't even think about it" about her father.*

"We'll be there Sunday. You need a little bit of time . . ."

Interesting how this all worked out according to plan.

"How are you and Russell getting along?"

Yes, according to plan. Renata was really something.

"Well, Emma just told me 'Don't even think about it,'" and before I could go on, Renata was laughing loudly. "What?"

"You really are a raw nerve, aren't you?" Renata giggled. "Now you're offended by a six-year-old? Mylie, sweetie, just enjoy the man's company. And if you happen to get lucky . . ."

"Goodbye, Ren." I hung up.

Okay, so my life would be back together on Monday morning. I'd be stepping back into my old world, just a little bit wiser, and the Celia/Kick commission was still mine. I'd get my dream apartment with the cinnamon-colored acces-sories, most likely a raise from Zoe, and I wouldn't be on Xanax patrol anymore as Zoe's nurse. The SUV, the laptop, everything would be mine again. And I'd be back in Celia

and Kick's life in just a few days, which I was far more relieved about than getting my cell phone back. Renata had
solved everything. Including force-feeding me some perspec-
tive about the six-year-old, who was just looking out for her
daddy.

"Everything okay?" Russell called from the hammock,
and I jogged my way back to his side. "You look happy," he
said, shielding his eyes from the sun and squinting up at me.

"Good news." I beamed. "Ren has fixed my life. I have
everything I wanted and more."

Russell smiled. "Good, then you can afford Emma's very
expensive tickets for tonight's performance."

My eyes shifted toward the cherub. "Tickets?" I asked.

"The ticket for Daddy is one dollar." Emma held up one
tiny finger with red sparkly nail polish almost all bitten off.

"That much, huh?" Russell remarked, pushing her bangs
off her face.

"And for you, Mylie"—she thought for a second, counting
on her fingers, looking up at the cloudless sky as she did her
math—"a million, bazillion, gabillion dollars."

Russell's eyebrows drew down. I could tell he was puzzled
by his little angel's insidious streak. I, on the other hand, didn't
miss a beat. "That's *all*? No problem. I have that much in the
trunk of my car." I winked at Russell, who was clearly crossing from embarrassment to relief at my fine footwork.

"You *do*?" Emma squealed.

"Do you have a wheelbarrow so we can get all that money
into the house?" I joked, and Emma was undoubtedly imagining a very long visit to the American Girl store in the city.

"Daddy, get the wheelbarrow!" she yelled, thrashing around
on the hammock, all arms and legs flying everywhere. *Get
this kid off of sugar right now.* Russell visibly turned to protect himself, laughing the whole while.

"Ah, you got tricked, pumpkin." Russell effortlessly collected her wrists in his one hand. "Mylie's kidding about the money in her trunk. And you should be a little bit nicer to Daddy's friend, okay?"

"She's *not* your friend." Emma pouted, then yanked her wrists out of her father's clutch. She folded her arms tightly over her chest and glared at me, her lip curled down in defiance.

"I'm sorry, Mylie." Russell's eyes turned to me. Very clearly, he had seen this side of Emma before. "She's just . . ."

"It's okay," I assured him with a touch on his arm.

"*Don't touch my daddy!*" Emma shrieked, and there was no hiding it. Russell looked mortified, apologizing to me with his expression while Emma wailed without actual tears.

Get this kid some therapy.

"Emma, stop!" he ordered. "You apologize right now!"

"No!"

Where's the "She's not my mommy!"

"She's not my mommy!"

There it is.

"Emma," Russell pleaded. "Go inside."

"No!" She beat against him with her fists and screamed no over and over.

I'm sleeping with my bedroom door locked tonight.

Russell rolled up off the hammock and scooped Emma up. Instantly, the little girl stiffened her body out flat with her hands in fists at her sides, head thrown back, wailing, "She's not my mommy! Make her go away! I don't like her!"

What a sweetheart.

I considered hopping in my car and getting a head start back to the office where it was considerably safer for me to be, but Russell came jogging out of the house a few seconds later red-faced with apology. "Mylie, I am *so* sorry, and I'm so embarrassed. She's *never* done anything that rude before."

Your daughter is possessed.

"Seriously, Mylie. I'm going to have a talk with her, and

she'll apologize." He was talking way too quickly. "I'm very, very sorry about this. It's not—"

I held up my hand to quiet him, an understanding smile on my face. *She's just trying to protect her daddy.* "Go talk with her, Russell. I'm going for a walk by the ocean." With a smile, I turned away and walked around to the side of the house where it was just a cross of the street to get to the dunes, the hot sand, and the water. And I could feel it as I went . . . He was watching me walk away.

Chapter 19

This has been quite a day.

In the past twenty-four hours, I had a pizza crust fight with Kick Lyons, quit my job, took the red-eye home, cleaned out my desk at work, came to Dolphin Dance, and walked into the best "After" picture ever, met Russell and found myself hated by his troubled little daughter, got my job back, got my life back, and now I was here by the ocean. Baby crabs scuttled through the last lick of the surf, disappearing into the sand. Broken seashells scattered the beach like rose petals at a wedding. Seagulls called out overhead, and the sun was flickering beautiful blues and purples in each arch of movement on the water's surface.

Not caring about my jeans, I sat down in the damp sand and looked far out into the distance. Boats were just dots out there.

This was what I needed. For time to slow down.

Everything had gotten too surreal there for a little bit. What in the world was I doing drinking beers with Kick Lyons? How did I get to be insta-friends with Celia Tyranova that she would cry upon my leaving?

Their world was a fast one. Fast and dramatic.

My world was like this. Quiet and peaceful. I'd forgotten

that. I was lost in the fast-paced jungle of glue guns and con-centric circles of crystals stuck into roses, ice sculptures with enraptured doves, seven-tier cakes covered with edible gold leaf, and replicas of Carolyn Bessette Kennedy's wedding dress. Exactly twenty-four hours ago, I was driving to Kick and Celia's house. Now I was sitting wet-butted in the sand on the opposite coast.

And time had slowed down.

I loved it here. This was the beach where I had summered with my family. *Wait, summer is not a verb. You've been hanging out with the Hamptons crowd too long.* My parents won me an orange bicycle on the boardwalk. I'd come here for the first time without them after high school graduation, which was the summer I met Renata. Renata had met her husband Pete on this beach, and they bought their dream home, the run-down Victorian that was now Dolphin Dance. Now she had a baby, and she'd soon be leaving Zoe's to open her bed and breakfast. If I didn't love her so much, I'd envy her. But never hate her.

It seemed my whole life was connected to this beach some-how. The most important things, at least.

What have I been doing with my life? Working seven days a week until 3:00 A.M., taking care of Zoe, watching *Gilmore Girls.* I used to love tennis. I used to love going to football games at the stadium. I used to love to dance. Without notic-ing it, I'd become boring. One note. I'd sealed off all the chambers of my life, like owning a big, gorgeous home like Dolphin Dance and never leaving my bedroom.

Now would have been a good time to truly walk away from Zoe's, to open up the doors and windows to all the rooms of my proverbial house, to own the whole thing. I've been afraid for too long.

I told Kick that I never made an important decision with-out being by the water first. Well, here I was. And my decision was this: work would get thirty percent of me. I wanted the other seventy percent to get all the things back that I loved. And figure out what else I loved at the same time.

"Mylie, it's Celia. Call me, okay?"

"Hi sweetie, it's Mom. Just wanted to check in, see how you're doing, wherever you are." My mother didn't even know where I was. I hadn't talked to her in over a week.

"Mylie, babe, it's Bryan—" I deleted that one.

"Renata tells me you're coming back on Monday." A big, long pause and a sigh from Zoe. *"I'm very sorry for what I said and how I treated you. The work you did with the groom was good work. I apologize, and I'll hug you when I see you soon. Enjoy the shore."*

"Good messages?" Russell appeared behind me, standing with his hands in his pockets, his eyes wide with not knowing what to say to me.

"Yes." I blinked back a tear. "I've been living it all wrong for so long and I didn't even know it."

Russell nodded and looked down, a silent message that he was perhaps in the same boat, or just respectful of my revelation. "But you know it now," he said quietly.

"I do," I breathed, placing the phone back in its cradle. "I do know it now."

"Good," he said. "I've put Emma to bed. She hates me right now."

No dance recital tonight. "She doesn't hate you, Russell."

"Feels like it."

I nodded.

"I have no idea what set her off," he confided, opening the fridge and pulling out a bottle of wine, lifting it toward me in a silent offer. I nodded again, knowing that it was time to listen, not talk. "It's not like you were—"

"No," I interrupted.

"It's not like she picked up on—"

Say it.

He exhaled and turned away from his thought, slid open the gadget drawer, and rummaged through for the corkscrew. Renata had filled her kitchen with the best quality gear, so the model that came out of the drawer was gleaming, top-notch. Russell opened the bottle with a quiet pop. "It's nice outside," he said. "Want to join me on the swing out front?"

I was hoping for the hammock. I'd always wanted to do that, to lie next to a man on a hammock. I made a mental note to list things like that, the little things in life that were the brushstrokes of contentment, and pursue them. And then I stopped myself. No, that was work mode, making lists, setting goals, crossing them off the dry erase board wall and moving on to the next one without ever fully appreciating the thing I'd just done. I wouldn't make a list. I'd just let things happen. Fly without a plan. In a few months' time, I'd see what wound up on the list of things that came to me without effort.

Russell held the bottle of wine and two wineglasses in one hand and led me through the house to hold the front door open for me. I stepped through. The evening air was getting cooler, a welcome relief from the drowning humid air we'd had this summer, the wet heat, the drenching sweats. Now fall was starting to introduce itself to us.

He poured the wine and set the bottle on the deck, both of us sitting down on the porch glider swing, which corrected itself in a forward movement as we lifted our feet in respect to it. I could faintly smell the paint from the work Russell had done earlier on the porch, as well as the blissful scent from the fudge store a few buildings down. Peanut butter fudge and autumn were in the air.

"Mmmm, great bottle." I admired the wine after my first tentative sip. "Australian?"

"New Zealand." He nodded, smiling. "I prefer it over the Argentinians."

He knows his wine.

"So what else needs to be done on the house?" I asked a little too quickly, sticking to safe topics as it was not quite the moment to ask what in the world was wrong with his daughter.

"Oh, don't worry . . . I'm putting you to work tomorrow." He winked and patted me on the knee. "No free rides here. Ren would never forgive me."

"And how do you know Ren and Peter?" I asked, smitten with both the wine and the weather. I tilted my face back and closed my eyes, just welcoming the scented breeze on my hot cheeks.

"You don't know the story?" He seemed puzzled. "I thought Ren told you. . . ."

Uh oh. He thought I had backstory.

"Well," I stumbled, tried to cover for her. "We've been so busy at the shop. . . ."

"A likely story." He grinned. "Okay, well . . . Peter and I went to high school together. He and I came down to the shore after graduation, and there was this girl on the beach. . . ."

He was there when Peter met Renata? I was there when Peter met Renata.

"Pete didn't have the nerve to go up to her, so we left the beach."

No, he definitely approached her. I was there.

"We went back every day, looking for her, and some days we saw her and some days we didn't."

They were watching us. I was with Ren.

"Until finally, I just sat my man down and told him that if he didn't go talk to the girl the next time we saw her . . . he'd regret it the rest of his life."

"And he did," I helped him with the story. "He had blue bathing trunks on, and he was really badly sunburned on his chest."

Russell raised an eyebrow. I doubted he remembered those details, but he was getting the gist of it. "You were there?"

I laughed. "You didn't notice her hot friend for yourself?"
Easy there.

"No, my focus was on getting my boy to approach the girl of his dreams. I wasn't even looking out for myself."

I remembered that day so clearly. Ren and I had seen Peter wandering around, very obviously trying to stay in the vicinity, working up the courage to come over. We called him The Pacer. I never noticed a guy friend with him.

"And he asked me to Cyrano him." Russell shrugged.

"*What? You* fed him the lines?" I nearly spat out my wine, and that was a very good bottle. Not good for spitting. "You did the whole Cyrano de Bergerac thing with him?"

"Not like hiding in the bushes while he called up to her window, but I gave him some lines, yeah." Russell blushed. "Don't tell me you remember . . ."

"Of *course* I remember!" I kicked my feet excitedly. "We women remember these things! It was the best approach ever! I can't believe the words were yours. And I quote, '*Excuse me, but I've noticed you every day this week, and I haven't had the courage to come over. But I knew that if I left, that would be it.*' It was the most honest and revealing pickup line ever. Great work."

"I like to keep it simple and direct." He nervously brushed through his hair with his hands, that sandy blond hair coming right back into position in the short, neat haircut he had. "I can't believe you remembered the words. That was a while ago."

"I can't believe you were there."

"Can't believe you were there."

"Didn't you stay and watch him? I mean, you would have seen us together, right?" I tried, wanting details on top of details.

"I was . . . with someone at the time. Married her."
Oh. Okay.

"And our demon spawn is probably cutting the heads off

her dolls upstairs right now," Russell joked, looking up as if he could see through the porch ceiling and into Emma's room right now. "I guess she did inherit some of her mother's charm." He laughed, then caught himself. "Sorry. Not very gentlemanly of me to trash her."

"That wasn't trashing, and you can blame the wine." I nudged him.

"Yeah, all two sips." He laughed.

I cupped my wineglass in both hands. "Divorce is in process?" I ventured.

"Finalized last week," he said. "She doesn't want custody or visitation with Emma at all." He shook his head. "I can sure pick 'em, huh?"

No visitation? What kind of mother would even be capable of such a thing?

"Emma didn't fit into her lifestyle." He pushed off with his foot to swing us a little bit, which we had forgotten to do. I imagined Emma's mother as one of the lionesses from the resort in Hawaii, all decked out and overtanned, wearing stilettos, looking for a good time, more interested in being watched than in watching a child.

"I'm sorry," I whispered. "I can't even imagine that."

"Neither can I, which makes it pretty easy to deal with things being over." He half laughed. "I'm just upset for Emma. She has a pretty rosy image of her mother. I hope I never have to tell her the truth."

"Ah, so Emma wants you two back together. . . ."

Russell nodded. "Not going to happen."

"Good," I said, surprising myself with my honesty but not backing off of it. "I'm glad."

Russell smiled. "So what about you?"

"What about me?"

"What's your relationship saga?"

"Saga?"

"No one gets to this age without one." He smiled.

"They do if they've . . ." *Don't say it. Don't ruin this with the I'm-a-workaholic-who-dates-unavailable-men-on-purpose speech.*

"What?" He wasn't letting me off the hook. He grinned playfully and nudged me in the leg. "You've been hurt?"

"Not hurt, exactly," I tried, for the first time in my life lost for words. Well, lost for acceptable words. I felt the walls closing in and willed them to stay open. *Don't shut him out, Mylie. Take the risk.*

"More like operating on the wrong level?"

He nodded. He knew exactly what I meant.

"And then I see couples like Ren and Peter and Kick and Celia—" *Oh, no.*

"Who?" He choked a little on his wine. "Oh, please don't tell me you're one of those girls who holds up celebrity relationships as some kind of guidepost."

"No," I covered immediately. If I was going back to work on Monday, I was still bound by the confidentiality agreement. How to be honest without being too honest. "It's just that . . . I saw a moment between them. In real life. He defended her. He was protecting her. And the way he looked at her . . ."

Russell was searching me. He knew there was more to my story.

"But like I was saying"—changing the focus like a train changing tracks, with just a little bump you hardly notice— "with Renata and Peter, it's like they—"

"Were always together."

"They just fit."

"And they've built this unbelievable life."

"To Peter and Renata . . ." I held up my wineglass to clink his.

"For their being smart enough to be friends with the two of us." He smiled.

"For their great taste in friends, yes." I giggled.

"And for their bringing us together," he confessed, and we both took a sip on that one. "You do know that Ren's been trying to introduce us for a while, right?"

I blushed and looked into the swirling burgundy in my glass. "She's mentioned that she had someone she wanted me to meet."

"She told me all about you," he said. "She speaks very highly of you."

"Yeah, she'd better!" I joked, unwisely deflecting the serious tone.

"Mylie?"

I looked away from my glass and right at him. "You're operating on a different level right now . . . with me. The right level."

The tenderness in his voice, the encouragement, the understanding. The wine might have been of great quality, but it was nothing compared to the quality of that moment. How he had the courage to speak such truth. And the way he looked at me, protectively.

"I know," I whispered.

Chapter 20

"Miss Mylie . . ." Emma stood next to me at the kitchen table. Out of the corner of my eye, I'd seen her shuffle into the room in her pajamas, move along the wall, circle a little bit. No shiny objects, like a knife, in her hands.

"Yes, Emma?" I looked up from the morning paper and smiled.

"I'm sorry I wasn't nice to you." She blinked, her brown eyes round and remorseful. "Daddy said I was a bad girl and that he's appointed with me."

She meant *disappointed*.

"Apology accepted." I nodded.

"*Really?*" She seemed surprised. " 'Cause I was really a brat. . . ."

I laughed. "Emma, I can tell that you're a sweet little girl, and you were just having a bad day."

She rubbed her nose, and her hand came away moist. "I was just having a bad day. . . ." She seemed to absorb it. Her little eyes looked upward, and she was thinking hard. No doubt I'd just given her a weapon in her arsenal to disarm her father upon future outbursts. *But, Daddy, I was just having a bad day* after she shaved the dog or threw her dinner plate across the room.

"Would you like me to make you some eggs, Emma?" I'd awakened early and padded quietly down to the kitchen to start the French vanilla coffee and assess the refrigerator for eggs and blueberry pancake makings.

"No thanks." She made a yuck face.

"Blueberry pancakes then?" That did it. She was such a dramatic little girl, always dancing and twirling, seemingly fascinated by the movement of her own arms, ballet hand gestures. Her smile grew big as she leaned toward allowing herself to befriend me over blueberry pancakes. "Wanna help?"

She nodded fast and clapped her hands. "We can surprise my daddy!"

"Emma, that's a great idea. What do you think we should drink?"

"Orange juice!" she screamed, then danced around singing, "orange juice, orange juice, orange juice." The kid had a thing for Vitamin C.

As expected, the chef had no Tropicana in the refrigerator, just a bowl full of oranges, and I spotted the handpress juicer to the left of the fridge. This was going to be fun.

"What's all this noise down here?" Russell walked into the kitchen, freshly showered and shaved. I had been yelling "Pull!" like I was skeet shooting, only it was my signal for Emma to grab on to the silver juicer handle and pull with all her might. A few times she actually slipped off the kitchen chair and dangled from the thing until I lifted her back up, both of us laughing hysterically. Tears ran down my cheeks. Everywhere on the counter lay spent orange halves, probably not entirely squeezed through, but Emma always wanted a fresh half to juice.

"Try it, Daddy! It's fun!" Emma held out a fresh, dripping orange half to him, then threw it to him when he held up his hands in receiver position. Ah, the football background. He had played at some point.

I'd never gotten the eggs and pancakes started, as my assistance was needed at the juicer, so the minute Russell took over duty with the silver handle, I opened the refrigerator and pulled out the bowl of enormous, fresh blueberries and the carton of organic brown eggs.

"Are we cooking together?" Russell smiled, pulling playfully on Emma's ponytail as he looked at me.

"Yes," I said. "Be prepared to be impressed with my skills."

"I'm already impressed with your skills." He winked.

You haven't seen anything yet, mister.

"Hello!" cried a strange voice in the house. We had company. Six of Renata and Pete's friends had taken Friday off of work and come down to work on Dolphin Dance. I'm sure the disappointment on my face was very noticeable, but it matched Russell's expression perfectly. In they walked, bearing gifts for the home: potted Gerbera daisies, a basket of lime soaps, bottles of wine, and a box that made noise. Scratching noises. Someone had brought a case of fresh crabs to be steamed. I was going to experience that crab bake in the yard!

"They're blue claw," one of the men said. I didn't recognize any of the people, but I was hugged just the same by the three men and three women, all dressed in cutoff jeans shorts or overall shorts, the women with their hair in ponytails or tucked into baseball caps, the men in ratty T-shirts and shorts. All dressed to work on the house.

"This is Mylie," Russell announced as the hugs commenced, the kitchen growing loud with the wonderful sounds of friends catching up with one another. I noticed he didn't follow my name with any qualifier like "She's Renata's friend" or "She works with Renata."

"Ah, you're the wedding woman," one of them said.

Because they already know who I am.

"Ren told us you'd be here," a short, pixieish woman with

blond hair and a pregnant stomach hugged me tight. "That's funny, you don't look like you need any cheering up."

"Take care of that already, Russ?" one of the men chided, and I liked them all immediately. They dropped their bags, left their gifts on the table, and we all worked together on the blueberry pancakes and eggs as Emma sang, "orange juice, orange juice, orange juice," dancing across the kitchen floor.

As he stirred, as he tilted the griddle from side to side to spread the melted butter, I watched his hands. And his friends watched me watching his hands. The only thing that could have been more obvious was if I was drooling, and I lifted my own hand to my lip to see if I was.

"You've got it bad," the blond pixie said to me with a hip to hip nudge, and she popped a blueberry into her mouth. "Come with me for a minute." She did the directional tilt with her head and bounced out of the room.

I hated to leave the sight of him, to miss one second of his hands at work, but I followed her. She waited for me in the foyer, grinning.

"I'm Katie," she said, holding out her hand to shake mine. "I'm Russell's sister."

Shaking her hand, I blushed. I had no idea she was his sister, of course.

"Glenn is my husband." I didn't remember which one Glenn was. Hopefully not the unshaven, hungover one with the baseball cap who was checking out my butt. "I've heard so much about you from Ren, and we've all been waiting *so long* for you and Russell to get together."

"Well, we're not *together* together," I stammered. "We've only just met yesterday."

"Let me put it this way." Katie smiled. "He's been waiting a long time to meet you."

I couldn't keep the smile from my face. It was nice to be awaited.

"I can see how much you like him." Katie hugged me in. It

was a little too early for the sisterly thing with me, but her enthusiasm was contagious. "He and Emma have had a rough year, so all I'm going to say is that I'm glad we finally have you two in the same room together after all this time."

I had to ask. "Um, Katie? How long has Ren been talking me up to him?"

"Four years."

I expected *three weeks* or *a month*, but four years? Was that how long Ren had been saying, "I have someone I want you to meet?" She *did* say something to that effect at the start of the Bryan thing, and—come to think of it—after every bad Match.com date I ever had. And I had always blown it off. Just like I'd always blown off every invitation to come down to Dolphin Dance.

Four years. So that means when Emma was two . . . and he was married.

"You're doing the math. I can tell." Katie took my hands in hers and looked me right in the eyes, not blinking. She wanted me to listen well. "We never liked his wife."

I hesitated. Was it right to ask what happened? Shouldn't the details come from him?

"Her being gone is the best thing that ever happened to him, and to Emma," Katie said quietly. She gave my hands a little squeeze and let go.

"Emma seems pretty much against what we're . . . what's . . ." *Whatever this thing, this attraction, is.*

"It's been hard for her," Katie confided, leaning to the side to see if anyone in the kitchen noticed our little secret meeting just a very subtle twenty feet away. "She was kept from most of it, of course, so all she knows of her mother is very . . . created by her."

I understood. Bravo to Russell for not being the type to trash-talk Emma's mother to their daughter. He seemed like a decent guy. I could hear him laughing and talking about the Notre Dame game in the kitchen with the men. I could smell the pancakes cooking, hear the clinks of utensils and the rack of ice cubes being released from their trays. Ren's home was filled with so much right now.

"Ren said she's coming on Sunday?" I checked in with her, confused about the gaggle of visitors when Ren had implied Russell and I would have the place to ourselves for a few more days.

"Nope." Katie smiled. "They couldn't keep us away from here, so they're coming down, too. They'll be here for dinner."

Good. We have a lot to talk about.

"I'm so happy you're here, Mylie." Katie hugged me again and led me back to the kitchen. Russell smiled at my return as he expertly flipped a pancake on the griddle. He was the only one I saw in the room. The rest of them, as loud as they were, just faded away.

Chapter 21

Ren and Pete showed up just as dinner was served. We'd just laid out the red plastic tablecloth on the long picnic tables set end-to-end in the yard, and the four dozen crabs steamed bright red and generously dusted with Old Bay seasoning had just been ceremoniously dumped across the table. We were in the process of handing out cold beers when the happy couple and baby James in his Snuggli came tiptoeing dramatically around to the backyard.

It was a celebration, as if they hadn't seen each other in years, while it had only been since last weekend. Baby James slept through the hugs and the backslapping by the men, the cheerful compliments on Ren's new, shorter, Mommy-Must haircut. Russell moved from the fray to stand by my side, while Emma practically pushed the others aside to get to the new baby.

"Just in time for dinner!" someone shouted.

"Actually"—Pete lifted Emma up to give her an eye view of James—"we got here twenty minutes ago, but we thought we'd wait 'til you guys got dinner ready."

A jeer sounded, and someone handed Pete a beer bottle.

Ren searched for me with her eyes and beamed the smile of a mother looking for her long-lost daughter after . . . apparently . . . four years. She saw me standing side by side with

Russell and brought her hands to her heart. I wasn't sure if it was wise dating decorum to have everyone so invested in us, so over-the-top rooting for us, but it seemed to bring a smile to Russell's face, so I didn't give her the silent "Cut it out." What could it hurt to have a team of cheerleaders behind you? At least it wasn't a roomful of saboteurs, with all of them acting like Emma. Now *that's* a tough gig.

"*There* you are!" Ren couldn't exactly run to me, or else baby James would bounce against her, but she did the best she could. "Mylie! Russell!" Hug. Hug.

"Hey, Ren." Russell smiled, then touched the top of James's head. His curls were coming in auburn. "He's getting big."

"Yeah, he's a load." Ren lifted the baby by his bottom, and he barely even stirred. "Sleeps like a champ, though. I hear I'm very lucky."

"Hey, the crabs are getting cold!" someone shouted, and it was a hurried walk to our places at the table. Ren wasn't too obvious about stepping back so that Russell could sit next to me. All eyes were on us. Once we were safely next to each other, everything going according to plan in their eyes, the rest of them launched into the food, clinked their frosted mugs, and chattered about everything from their ski lodges to the price of gas, their kids' summer camp schedules, Katie's due date, and the fabulous paintwork we all did on the backyard fences that afternoon. Ren and Pete, fabulous Tom Sawyers that they were, admired our work and applauded our only a *little* bit selfish dedication to their dream home. We all had open passes to stay for free whenever we'd like. And that included me, too, even though I put in a grand total of six hours on the place. But no one seemed to mind my last-minute entry into their little club.

"How's it going?" Ren leaned in to me as I cracked open my first crab, splitting it at the hollow to reveal the tender white meat strips separated by chambers of cartilage. We had no dainty seafood forks here. It was all about picking with your hands, slurping on the legs, pounding the tougher shells with a wooden mallet, and laughing while crab juice squirted on your neighbor.

"With what?" I teased her.

"With Russell," she whispered.

"I'm two feet away, Ren!" he surprised us, and the table cracked up.

"Just eat and you two girls can run away giggling and gossiping later." Pete rolled his eyes. "Russ, man, you're in trouble now."

"It's a nice place to be." Russell cracked open the stubborn shell of a blue claw leg and handed it to me. No one had ever done anything so sweet and so chivalrous in all my life.

And down at the end of the table, eating her specially prepared coconut shrimp because she didn't like crab, Emma glared steely hatred at me.

"Look at the kid!" I whispered to Ren, and the moment Ren turned to look, Emma was gleefully smiling, wiggling in her chair, and making her coconut shrimp dance across the plate. *Little demon.*

"You know, you don't get full when you're eating steamed crab; you get *tired* of the effort," Ren said, placing the still-sleeping sweet baby James in his playpen and tucking a blanket around him. The evening air was cool, and we had the windows open. In the backyard, the crew had started up a game of volleyball with the pregnant Katie sitting on the sidelines cheering for her husband Glenn, who it turned out *was* the hungover guy in the baseball cap checking out my butt.

With her baby in for the night, Ren turned and dove onto my bed, hungry for details. "So . . ."

"Oh, Ren, he's phenomenal," I breathed, finally able to let it out. I'd been keeping my smiling to half wattage all day, and my face was killing me.

"I *knew* it!" Ren kicked her feet on the mattress. "Oh, God, Mylie, you don't know how happy I am right now! We've wanted you to meet Russell *forever!*"

"Yeah, like four years?" I winced. "How did *that* happen?"

"You were in your work bubble and dating losers on-line, and he was married to that bitch Melissa." She shook her head. "Evil woman."

I sat up and hugged my knees in. "I need backstory."

"Oh, no." Ren slapped my arm. "You've been waiting a day for your details; I've been waiting four years. I get my dirt first. How was last night?"

I rolled my eyes. "No, I didn't sleep with him, so you can forget—"

"Oh, *please!* Like Russell would sleep with someone on the first date," Ren snorted.

Um, hello? Like I would?

"Did he kiss you?" Ren's eyes bulged, her hands slapped up over her mouth. She really wanted the answer to be yes.

"No."

"No?"

"No . . . he's a gentleman."

"He's a *man*, Mylie."

I smiled. "It was better than if he did." Here I was again, although I hated to bring any remote reminder of Bryan into this delicious situation, being very, very excited that a man didn't try to kiss me. *What is wrong with me?* "We just sat out on the porch swing for hours, had some wine, talked . . ."

Ren faked a big yawn.

"It was great." I smiled. "The stars were out, we could hear the ocean . . ." In my mind, I traveled back there. "He went in and got a blanket for me . . ."

"That's *so* him."

"And then when it hit that quiet moment . . ."

"Where you *would* have kissed." Ren nodded.

"When it hit that quiet moment, we just said good night and went upstairs to our rooms." I beamed. "And I barely slept, knowing he was just two rooms away."

Ren clapped her hands and stole a glance out the window at the volleyball game. We had to get back down there as soon as possible or else risk looking like high school level idiots. "Seems you're off to a good start, then." Ren nodded.

Words failed me. I didn't expect to have a good start this week.

"Oh, everything's zipped up at work," she assured. "Monday's going to be a big day for you."

"Oh." I squinted. "Don't even talk about it. Work can wait."

As I got up, I didn't realize that Ren hadn't stood up next to me. I turned around, and she had a blank, unblinking expression on her face. "I have *never* heard you say that before."

True.

"I *like* this version of you." Ren hugged herself with joy. "Someday I'll have to tell you about all the times you missed out on meeting Russell . . . so that you can kick yourself over and over and over. . . ." She giggled.

"Oh, there's just one thing." I held up a finger before opening the bedroom door, half expecting to see Katie there with a glass to her ear, listening in. "Emma positively *hates* me."

Ren laughed. "Yeah, she has a little bit of her mother in her. Cute girl, but definitely inherited the bitch gene."

Great.

"You'll win her over, Mylie." Ren checked on James, it being only a few weeks since she stopped holding a compact mirror under his nose to check if he was breathing. "I'm going to stay up here with the baby. You go down and play with the other kids." She winked. "And hey, Mylie . . ."

"Yeah?"

"I've never seen you look like this, either. You're all lit up. Your eyes."

I stopped with my hand on the doorknob. Suddenly, I was in the soup. "But Ren . . ." My eyes itched with tears, way back there, that wanted to come out. "I don't know him and he doesn't know me. What if you're wrong?"

She wrinkled her nose. "What if I'm right?"

Chapter 22

"You have *got* to be kidding!" Glenn took off his baseball cap and scratched his head. His side was waiting to serve. "What is she doing?"

"I'm biting off my nails." I shrugged. "I want to play. And it's better than breaking them."

Jaws hung open all over the place. "Russ, man, marry her now."

"Now that's low-maintenance!"

And of course, the two other women, not Katie, frowned at me. I was making them look bad. Unintentionally.

"What?" I shrugged. "They'll grow back." I spit out the last little curl of pinkie nail and took my place next to Russell, barefoot and ready for the serve. The other two women looked at their nails, decided against it, and assumed their playing positions.

I'm good.
I'd forgotten.

"Okay, you know way too much about Sinjin Smith and Karch Kiralyi." Russell put his hand on my shoulder as we all walked from the volleyball court to the outdoor sitting area with the couches and chairs. Ren had brought out some snacks and drinks. And by snacks and drinks, I mean goat cheese canapes, mini meatballs on toothpicks, bacon-wrapped scallops, and blended margaritas with color-salted rims.

"I used to watch the pro volleyball circuit," I explained. "They play in Belmar every summer, right, Ren?" At one point, one young summer, Ren had hatched a plan to pursue, flirt with, and sleep with Sinjin Smith. But now that she was holding baby James, and her husband, Pete, looked at her with pure adoration, it didn't seem appropriate to share that particular summertime blast from the past. And she didn't land Sinjin, by the way. Which was probably a good thing now that we know how Pete stalked her most summers.

"Right." She giggled, and Pete smiled knowingly. Perhaps she had told him about her efforts to snag the richest pro volleyball player in the country. Good thing she settled for Pete.

"Hey, Mylie." Russell sat down next to me, and like a very bad sitcom, everyone else immediately and loudly started talking to each other. "Want to go for a walk on the beach in a little bit?"

What's a little bit? Five minutes? An hour? After everyone else goes to sleep? When? Tell me! "Sure." I nodded, and the back of my neck felt warm.

"Good." He smiled, and then he was right back in the mix with his friends, talking about us all going on the boat tomorrow morning. *There's a boat? How much did Renata get for finishing the Montgomery wedding without us?*

I had no idea what the women were talking about. I was zoned out, with a stupid, blissful little smile on my face, knowing enough to nod and appear as if I was listening to one of the women who didn't bite off her nails during the volleyball game complaining about the rude treatment she got during her bikini wax.

What's a little bit?

*   *   *

It turned out "a little bit" was right after Russell put Emma to sleep. We'd been expecting her dance recital again this evening, but the baby diva decided to spell out "I hate Mylie" in M&Ms on the kitchen counter. Only she spelled it *MyLee*. I hadn't seen it. Katie had cleaned up the cry for help before I walked in with an armload of dishes and margarita glasses. I could hear the kid screaming upstairs, "It's not fair! It's not fair!"

"Everything okay?" I'd innocently asked Katie, who munched on the offending M&Ms. Get rid of the evidence.

"Yeah." She paused, waiting for a good lie to take shape. "Emma's just having a meltdown. Too much sugar."

If there was one thing that kid couldn't be associated with, it was sweetness.

"She's just acting out." Katie nodded, then grabbed another handful of the M&Ms.

I flashed forward into the future, a surly Emma with half a shaved head and a piercing above her eyebrow, standing in court next to a lawyer who said, "Sorry about the twelve murders, Your Honor, but my client was just acting out."

Russell appeared at the doorway, out of breath, tired from the struggle upstairs, but he did a great job of faking the everything's-fine smile and holding out his hand for mine.

"We're a little ahead of the sunset." He seemed to be thinking aloud as we walked over the dunes, the deep, thick sand sucking at our ankles and making it a little bit hard to walk. I almost toppled over, and he instinctively reached for my elbow to steady me. Another piece of chivalry I'd never experienced before. In the past, and only on rare occasions, if a man reached for my elbow, it was because my bra strap had stopped there while we were undressing.

"Thanks," I said, trying not to resemble a horse or grunt my way through the upclimb. They never showed this in coffee commercials. Couples walking on the beach were always right at the ocean's edge, the wind blowing their hair (but not into their faces), the woman's skirt fluttering lightly, and their feet barely leaving tracks.

"Almost over," he encouraged me, and in a heartbeat or two, we were leaning backward a little into our descent down the other side of the dunes. It was smooth walking from there, just a short distance to that gentle ocean's edge. Beach grass poked up through the sand, hollow reeds, and a tiny cloud of sand gnats hovered over something appetizing in the distance. Seagulls dive-bombed a family throwing bread crusts in the air, and handfuls of vacationers remained in their chairs or on their blankets, their bright blue and red coolers all but baked by a day's worth of sun. Behind us, the ice-cream man's truck rolled slowly along the street, playing a cheery version of "Pop, Goes the Weasel."

"What a great day," I heard myself say, with a deeply satisfied exhale, and Russell laughed.

"Yeah, we all live for coming down here." He nodded. "Ren and Pete are very smart. They knew we'd get hooked on the place."

"I wish I'd come down here a long time ago," I confessed, and I knew what he'd say before he even said it.

"Me, too."

Okay, let's not dance around this anymore.

"So . . ." I gave him a little wink and positioned myself so that our arms would brush together as we were walking. I'm quite good at the ultrasubtle contact. "I understand Ren's been talking me up to you for quite a while. Four years, she says."

A pink blush moved into his ears and then over his cheeks. He smiled and shrugged. "I've been waiting," was all he said.

It can't be this easy. It can't be that one day your life falls apart and you pull into a driveway and there's the Right Guy

*who's been waiting for you for four years, and it all clicks to-
gether. It just can't be this easy.*

It didn't even occur to me to ask what Ren had said to him
that kept him intrigued and interested for so long, but it
didn't matter. All that mattered was that I trusted Ren. She
wouldn't persevere for that long without a deep belief in . . .
something.

"You're lost in thought." He smiled, and did a little subtle
arm brush against me of his own. "Where are you right
now?"

"This is just . . . very strange," I said, then dove in head-
first, not wanting to be my own downfall by not speaking up
when the moment was right. "I wasn't expecting . . ."

He laughed, almost a giggle of nervousness. "Yeah, you
were a mess when you pulled into the driveway."

"Thanks a lot!" *Yes, I'm sure I made some first impression.*

"But you were still beautiful."

There's that warm feeling in my neck again.

"I wanted to kiss you last night," he confessed and
stopped walking, moving to face me but still a respectful distance away. "I really did."

"Me, too." It came out as a whisper, carried off by the
ocean breeze. Our conversation was being carried out to sea,
so that only we had access to it before it would float out to
those boats in the distance.

"Didn't have the courage, though." He smiled. "I didn't
sleep all night."

I grinned. "Me neither."

"And you're not the come-a-knocking-on-the-door type."
He nodded, and I hoped that meant he knew I wasn't the
type to knock on his door at 3:00 A.M. for a bed dive.
"Which I like."

Not being an aggressive, desperate whore pays off. I remembered the lionesses by the resort pool. Subtlety, ladies. Subtlety.

"And if you make me wait one more minute to kiss you, this whole thing is over," he said, and was already moving in as he spoke, his hands raising to hold my face, the soft touch of his lips in a gentle, respectful introductory kiss. The kind you savor, absorb those sparks, separate for only a quarter-inch, and make that lightning-fast decision to lean in again for another one, and another. His hands moved along my jawbone and into my hair, my arms now around him and my hands on the muscles of his back, moving up to the back of his neck.

I have no idea how much time passed. But we missed the sunset. The sky glowed a dark purple and dark pink when we finally stepped apart a little bit, out of breath, dizzy with hormones and bliss. "Wow," he said. "Worth the wait."

I laughed. A few times. Lost for words and amused at myself for being so taken away.

He took my hand, and I had to say it. Funny how all the thoughts could come rushing out after the electric charge of that first kiss. "I have to tell you . . . I've been looking at your hands all day."

"My *hands?*" He held out his free one and inspected it for paint.

"Oh, yeah." I laughed. "They're gorgeous."

"No one's ever called my hands 'gorgeous' before, but I'll take it." He smiled. "Thanks."

"You're welcome," I said, and we walked along the water's edge. Finally, I was part of one of those couples you saw walking along the beach, hand in hand, their smiles way too big it seemed, throwing off extra light as one or both turned to look at the other in an I-can't-believe-I'm-so-lucky kind of way. I'd seen it in young couples, young families, and older couples who you knew had been together for fifty, sixty years. Their hands just fit together, and they walked in stride without that obvious pacing, the little foot stumble when one or the other got out of synch. We'd get that together, Russell and I. We'd get our paces to match a little better. Right now, we alternated between smooth matching steps and the syncopation of my smaller steps bouncing me alongside of him.

"They're back!" someone called from inside the house. Apparently, they had assigned a lookout. I almost expected to walk into the living room and find it filled with candles, a bottle of champagne and two glasses, the fireplace going, and blankets set out before it, but our supportive friends settled instead for everyone being lounged out on the couches, watching television and eating pizza off of paper plates. They were quite drunk, as well.

Chapter 23

I so wanted to go to his room.

If we were alone in the house, maybe I would have. Actually, I *know* I would have. But Ren and Pete were on one side of his room, and Emma—dear, precious Emma—was on the other side. And I doubted this team of weekend house-painting warriors soundproofed the walls.

He had kissed me good night by my doorway, another face-holding kiss (God, I loved that!), and looked back at me as he opened the door to his room and disappeared inside. Not a come-a-knocking look, but more a look of "patience, patience."

I slipped into a pair of boxers and a sweatshirt and climbed beneath my sheets, turning over to look at the empty pillow next to my head.

At 4:00 A.M., it was not empty.

"Get out of here, Ren!" I groaned and rolled over.

"I'm up feeding the baby," she whined. "Talk to me."

"I signed a thick confidentiality agreement with Russell," I played, turning back over again to face her. "Thumbprints, retina scans . . . He's serious about his privacy."

"Whatever." Ren rolled her eyes. "How was the kiss?" She was dying to know. She'd worked on my behalf, behind the scenes of my life, for four years, and this entire day was made possible by her. She deserved some scoop.

"Ren . . . I get butterflies just thinking about it," I said and pulled the sheets over my face.

"You should go to him," Ren suggested, still sporting some of her youthful pursuit spirit.

"It's 4:00 A.M.!"

"So?"

We're at a beach house. And we're not that old. Ren and I used to . . .

An idea hit me. Something that Ren and I did once during our notorious summers down the shore. It was Russell's last night here, after all. He wouldn't be staying Sunday since Emma's mother had visitation that day. She had been granted one Sunday a month, and given the court system's usual lean-toward-the-mother attitude in custody cases, that said a whole lot about her character.

"Later, Ren," and I flew out of my own bed, out the door, and down to the kitchen.

A half hour later, at 4:30 A.M., I stood in front of his door, my knuckles poised to knock lightly.

I took a breath.

And I did it.

No answer.

I knocked lightly again, and I could hear his footsteps coming to the door. *Thank God they didn't fix the floor-boards too well.* The light from the hallway slanted into his room, and he squinted against it. He had been looking down, expecting to be talking at Emma's level. His hair was messy, and he had pillowcase marks on his face. "Mylie," he said, blinking the sleep out of his eyes, looking dazed, probably thinking he was dreaming.

"Come with me." I took his hand and with my other hand made the "quiet" signal in front of my lips.

"We're going into the bathroom?" he said from behind me, significantly more awake now.

"We're going *through* the bathroom." I turned to him and smiled as I approached the wide-open window, curtains blowing in the nighttime breeze. "Follow me."

And I climbed out the window.

He joined me on the roof, slightly slanted but standable, and we walked around to the front of the house, away from Emma's bedroom window. I'd set out a blanket, candles in hurricane lamps, the leftover strawberry shortcake from after dinner, and two forks.

"What's this?" he marveled. "A picnic on the roof?"

"Check out the stars." I pointed up to an incredible sky filled with stars, Emma's angel-poked holes to heaven. "It's no Mesa, but it was so beautiful I had to move our picnic out here."

He took his place on the blanket and lay back, signaling for me to join him, to lie against him. The shortcake could wait.

"Mylie," I heard his voice in my ear. I had drifted off. We'd never gotten to the shortcake, and since I didn't see it anywhere nearby, I assumed in my groggy state that we had kicked it off the roof. "Mylie . . ."

"Hmmm . . ." I rolled over to bury my face in his chest. "No . . . don't wake me up."

"We have to go inside. They'll be waking up soon."

By *they*, he meant Emma. The kid would burn the house down if she found us sleeping out on the roof together, naked under the second blanket he'd run inside to get.

"Wake up," he half sang into my ear, kissing it for good measure. "Do I have to tempt you with another offer?"

I still kept my face in his chest, hooked my leg around his. "What offer?" I giggled.

"We missed the sunset last night." He squeezed me. "Because *you* distracted me."

I laughed into the warmth of him.

"But there's a sunrise waiting to happen." He kissed the top of my head. "I'm leaving today, and it's my *wish* to see the sunrise with you."

"It's your wish, huh?" My voice was muffled in his chest, and the minute I answered, gallons of water fell on us. Gallons. Cold water. We looked up, and on the higher roof, not the second-floor level roof we lay on, our housemates laughed, pointed, and shook the three big coolers they'd filled with water, dancing at their own cleverness. Ren was up there, too, and I knew it was her idea. We'd done the same thing to a friend of ours during one of our summers down the shore.

Russell quickly made sure I was wrapped in a blanket and gathered the bottom blanket around him, very gentlemanly accepting the role as the one who would be seen naked by all. We stood, took a bow, and then ran around the corner to climb into the bathroom window before Emma came to see what happened. As we ran, we could see it. We had kicked the shortcake off the roof. It lay splattered on Ren and Pete's car, completely covering their windshield.

Chapter 24

So there I was, waving at the end of the driveway. Russell pulled his truck away with Emma diabolically waving at me through the back window.

Keep smiling, kid. You haven't gotten rid of me.

"You okay?" Ren put her arm around my waist, baby James sleeping against her chest in the Snuggli.

"Okay doesn't sum it up," I said, and I was teary-eyed, so sad to see him go, wanting more days, wanting more time with my face against his chest, wanting more of those hands, more of his voice.

"So I take it you'll be back next Friday." Ren laughed, and at that moment Pete came out of the house and discovered his windshield covered with smashed strawberry shortcake.

"What the—" he barked.

"Emma did it," Ren called over her shoulder to him, then pinched me on the waist and leaned in toward me, speaking quietly. "The little bitch wrote 'I hate Mylie' on my kitchen table with maple syrup."

"Wow." I shook my head. But I wasn't thinking of Emma's ability to say "I hate you" with edibles. I was thinking of her father's ability to say other things with his hands and his lips.

Chapter 25

"Honeymoon's over," Ren said as we keyed open the door to Zoe's studio. "Back to reality." It was 5:00 A.M., and I had missed four days of work. That meant I probably had about six hundred e-mails to return. As expected, a mountain of mail and packages awaited me on my desk, and the workroom dry erase board was covered from floor to ceiling in tiny little printed tasks. *Welcome home.*

I smiled.

"Good to be back?" Ren looked at me hopefully. "I hated being here without you."

"It's great to be back." I grinned, almost happier with an overflow of work than with my usual conveyor belt of To-Dos. "I really do love it here."

"Zoe will be in at nine," Renata reported, flicking a Post-it off of her computer screen. "That should be fun."

I exhaled, not looking forward to it, not wanting to get back into the which-way-was-she-spiraling mode. Would she make a big deal out of apologizing? Or would she completely ignore what had happened, preferring not to acknowledge it at all?

"I can't believe you and Russell had sex on my roof." Ren interrupted my worrying and brought me back to a much better place. "Pete and I haven't even done it on our roof yet."

I just smiled.

"Nice job with the shortcake." Ren laughed.

"Shortcake? Who's having shortcake? We have no orders for shortcake." Zoe tornadoed into the room, picking up file folders here, dropping them there, papers fluttering to the floor in her wake. And like that, she was out of the room.

"There's your apology." Ren giggled. "Now let's be business-like."

"Good idea."

"I can't believe you and Russell had sex on my roof."

This would get her. "Twice, Ren."

I'd never forget the look on her face.

"Mylie!" It was Celia on the phone. We had our scrambled cell phones delivered to us, so we could talk freely to her. I kept mine in a pink case.

"Celia!" I cheered, dancing in my office chair, boxes of stephanotis on the floor all around my feet. They filled the room with a sweet scent, like being in a rain forest. "I've missed you!"

"We missed you, too," she said. "I'm *so* happy you're still on board for the wedding. Kick practically threw that horrible boss of yours out of the house."

I flinched. Zoe wasn't good with confrontation. I imagined her frozen to the ground at Celia and Kick's place, not knowing what to do or say to unwind time and make that whole scene not have happened.

"Seriously, Mylie, if you ever decide to split from that boss of yours, I'll make sure every A-lister has you on her speed dial," Celia promised, and I could hear a small dog barking close to the phone.

"Thanks, I'll keep that in mind." I mouthed *Oh, my God!* to Renata and waved her away when she wanted me to mouth the rest of the message. "Now, let's get talking about the big day. . . ."

"Oh, that can wait," Celia huffed, and I immediately froze. I had a sixth sense, a radar that told me when a bride and groom were on that dangerous slope of indifference toward the wedding. Something was up. "How was your vacation?" she asked.

"Oh, Celia, it was great." I leaned back in my chair, swiveling it back and forth as I kicked off of my desk with my bare feet. "So romantic . . ."

"Romantic?" she squealed. "Oh, Mylie, I can hear it in your voice!"

In the background, I could hear Kick saying, "Which tabloid does he work for?"

"Shut up, Kick."

"Hi, Mylie," he called into the phone.

I loved these people.

"Tell him I said hi."

It was like chatting with college roommates rather than a power couple who made a combined fifty million per picture. "Mylie says hi. Now, Mylie . . . I'm going to be out your way this weekend, and we have a lot to do."

This weekend? I'm going to Dolphin Dance.

It was exactly eight minutes since I walked in the door, eight minutes until I was in that familiar, crushing spot where my work life smothered my personal life. How could I tell Russell, "Sorry, can't make it, gotta work. But thanks for the sex on the roof."

"Which day are you coming in?" I tried, hoping the disappointment didn't sound in my voice.

"Saturday," she replied.

Good, that gave me Friday and most of Saturday to get down to the shore house. I wished I could bring her there, wished she and Kick could have steamed crabs with us in the yard and drink margaritas out back, walk on the beach at sunset with us. But that confidentiality agreement . . . No one could know that we even knew each other. I couldn't invite her, even though I knew that would be a surefire way to get Emma writing "I LOVE Mylie" in M&Ms, Skittles, chocolate syrup, and bathroom caulk on every surface she could find.

"Anything in particular you want to work on this weekend?" I asked Celia, and she giggled, but not at the question. Were she and Kick in bed or something. With the dogs? "Celia?"

"Sorry, we're watching *Access Hollywood*. We TiVo it. My birthday was two days ago, and they did the whole who's older, me or Jennifer Aniston? I've got her by two weeks."

"Happy Birthday!" I beamed, then motioned for Ren to get me a pen. In bold letters, I wrote, "Celia's birthday, two days ago, send flowers and Mounds bars." Ren nodded and headed out to the other office to make the call.

"Thank you." She giggled again. What was going on over there?

"Anything in particular you want to work on?" I tried again.

"The invitations and the menu, we think," Celia reported, shrieking for a second, then admonishing Kick to stop. Yeah, they were definitely fooling around. "One thing, though, we don't want to go with the usuals, the established big-name chefs and cake people. So find us someone unknown, okay? I'm sure you have a collection of those. Oh, and I changed my gown from the Reem Acra to my friend Rowena."

"Rowena?" Oh, man, I hated working with what we called "climbers." So many of our celebrity brides handed their wedding plans over to their friends (or parasites pretending to be friends) just to get them the publicity, the spread in *InStyle Weddings*, and these up-and-comers could sometimes be . . . difficult. This Rowena was going to be a *thrill* to work with.

"Yeah, she's a friend of mine. We're doing *feathers*, little ones like Keira Knightley wore in *Love, Actually*. Crystal trim along the bare midriff, mermaid train with a crystal heart at the edge." *Sounds tacky as hell.*

"And the menu?" I tried, used to the everchanging world of weddings. Very few plans stayed the same from day to day. Not with this kind of money to bat around. They'd walk away from a ten-thousand-dollar deposit if it just didn't "feel right" after a night of hard partying. Not that Celia and Kick were like that. This was the first plan they were changing.

"We want an unknown chef, someone great, no press yet." Celia swallowed something, and I hoped it was a morning mimosa.

I thought of Russell. He was a great chef. But he was a personal chef, not a cook-for-nine-hundred kind of ultraelite party chef. Wolfgang Puck may crack the whip over his forty thousand employees for the Oscars, but Russell wasn't like that. And I didn't know if he would want the press. It would help him, I pondered, and had no idea what rougher currents I was dipping my toe into.

It would make life easier on me if I could share the secret with him.

"Angelique will fax over a list of the chefs we have in mind."

Ah, there goes that. They'll all be friends of Celia's.

"We'll be doing tastings at 2:00 A.M. at my friend Sarah's loft," Celia instructed, and I scribbled it down. "I'll call with her address closer to then. Be ready to eat . . . and drink."

"Sounds like a plan," I agreed, then decided to check straight-on with her. "Do you have plans to have a lot of your friends in on the action?"

Celia paused. She may have sensed a tone she didn't like.

"I mean, it would save a lot of time and energy if we knew you already had wish lists, and of course, we're very happy at how personalized your wedding will be with all of your closest friends devoting their talents."

She liked that one. "Yes, we have a lineup for you. It's what we've been doing the past few days. We don't trust your boss and her contacts. Can't take the chance of everyone being flip with us."

I understood. Tighten your circle. Bring in your friends. Give them the break they've been waiting for. Celia had told me how Nicole Kidman had told her and Naomi Watts that it just took that one thing, that one moment, to change everything. And Celia was the type to help her childhood friends, not cash in on the prestige of being affiliated with the new, hottest name. She preferred to share the joy with her sister (who made jewelry), her oldest friends (the favors), some musical performers (who would surely get discovered if Clive Davis attended the wedding), but not for the cake. Sylvia Weinstock would be hand-making that baby for her. I grinned at the mention of her. Sylvia had once wanted to set me up with her grandson. I turned down that one, too.

"Whatever you want, Celia, I'll make it happen."

"I know you will, Mylie." There was a rustle, a drop of the phone. "Just a sec, Mylie, Kick wants to talk with you for a minute."

"Mylie?"

"Yes, Kick."

"You still have the papers we worked on?"

"Yes, Kick, they're here in my briefcase. Everything's set."

"Good, 'cause I'd like to talk about those some more."

"Sure thing."

"Oh, and just so you know, we moved the wedding date."

What?!

"Yeah, moved it up to two months from now," Kick said plainly, as if it was no big deal to pull off a ten-million-dollar wedding in two months using untried and untested personal friends of the bride and groom, while I would be sneaking off for half weekends with the man of my dreams. And couldn't tell him where I was going. Yes, this was going to be fun.

"Why?" I tried not to be angry or condescending, or assume a little baby Kick was on the way.

"Oh, Sasha Worthington got engaged, and she announced our weekend, just up the street from us in Sonoma." Celia had taken the phone back.

I blinked. Sasha Worthington was one of those bimbo heiresses who could basically pee on Mother Teresa's grave and people would think she was adorable because of the Manolos she was wearing. "So that would throw off the press, right?" I tried. "If they're all over Sasha, they won't be focused on you."

So naïve, Mylie. Celia laughed, practically choking on her mimosa, or so I imagined it. "No, it's a timing thing. I don't want our wedding even mentioned in the same reports as that diamond-studded trailer trash. We're putting some breathing time in between ours and theirs."

"Any word from their camp on the plans?" I asked, and Celia really could have fired me right there. That was the kind of stuff that our team should have known. But I'd been busy painting a fence, cracking open crabs, and having sex on my friend's roof. A lot could happen in four days.

"It's going to be big," she warned. "Really big."

I'm sure. They'd probably be giving out stripper poles as wedding favors. They were the new breed of old money, completely removed from decency and all about the cameras. Sasha's great-grandmother, who built the company, must be downing martini after martini in heaven, wondering what happened to her bloodline. Now Sasha was going to mix that bloodline with a rock band guitarist who was unknown before stumbling down a few red carpets with Sasha.

Everyone in town knew to steer clear of the stink of Sasha's wedding.

On my legal pad, I wrote a note to Renata: *Sasha Worthington wedding.*

Ren made a disgusted face.

Find out everything you can. Same weekend as C&K, in Sonoma.

"So do you have a new wedding date picked out?" I asked Celia, glad that we hadn't made the invitations yet. Ren's face fell. Moved-up dates were a nightmare logistically. Someone else would get only ninety-eight percent effort from us. It was necessity. So were *looong* hours.

"Yes, but we're going to talk about it when we see you." Celia's breathing had changed, and I knew our time together on the phone was limited. What was in the air these days?

"Okay, I'll line up Sylvia for you for Saturday night, and we'll get everything else rolling as you see fit." I snapped into dynamo mode. "If you'd like to send me your list of other wedding experts"—careful not to say *your friends*—"we'll line that up, too. Two months . . . no problem."

That's why we get the big bucks.

"Thanks, Mylie, we knew we could count on you," she said and hung up just as I heard a very distinctive moan from Kick. Didn't do a thing for me.

I placed the phone back in its holder, turned to Ren, and said, "Two months from now."

"Oh, my God!"

"Sasha Worthington grabbed the same weekend, and the same street."

"Oh, my God!"

Ren had her head in her hands. "And I can't help you?"

"You've got to work all the others, Ren." I cringed. "I'll work on Zoe to get you fairly compensated, don't worry."

"Can you do this and still get . . . weekends off?" Ren physically flinched.

"Try and stop me," was all I said, and I was quickly on the phone. Sylvia had a call coming, and I had six hundred e-mails to answer. Minus the eighty from Zoe just asking if I was on-line.

The rest of the day was a blur. Appointments were set. Orders were changed. Celia e-mailed me the sketch of her wedding gown, and I had to say it was beautiful, ethereal. Her friend Rowena was definitely going to make a mark. I lined up two dozen tiara and headpiece images and sent them back to Celia. Kick, to my knowledge, was sticking with his Armani tux, unless his friend Skippy from high school had become a fashion plate and wanted the media coverage.

I researched and found the wedding favors that Celia and Kick had expressed interest in, those oversized fortune cookies that Kevin James had at his wedding, only we were white chocolate dipping them and covering them with white chocolate chips. They'd be part of a swag bag, along with a perfume to be created by Celia's friend Donielle (we'd already arranged that), watches for all, new digital cameras, and earrings designed by Celia's friend Werner. With a quick few strokes on the computer, I had those swag bags done. Twenty minutes after arriving at the office.

Done.

Next. The honeymoon. Celia and Kick wanted the Maldives. A private villa on the water, massage and spa treatments, private beach, yacht approach and escape, personal butler and chef (no, they couldn't have Russell), and new wardrobes awaiting them so that they didn't have to pack. Two weeks in paradise. Done.

"Hey, pace yourself," Ren warned, watching me get frantic and yell at an Indian dealer about the fabric for the napkins. Celia left the choice up to me. Burgundy brocade, monogrammed, mini gold tassles. Done.

The cake table. Silk dupioni studded with pearls, matching swag, mirrored base. Done.

The guest book. Handmade by artisans in Thailand, hand-pressed paper with a woven cover, hand calligraphy of their names, and Kick's favorite scriptures written into the artistic design to match the designs on his chapel ceiling. Done.

"Hey, you can't plan this wedding in one day." Ren showed up with an iced latte from Dunkin' Donuts. I hadn't even realized she'd left.

All fifteen bridesmaids confirmed for their fittings.

All fifteen groomsmen confirmed for their fittings.

The flowergirls' parents had been called to make sure none of the cherubs had screen tests that day.

The officiant had been confirmed, but I received an e-mail from Kick that his father would be ordained for the day to perform the ceremony—which touched me—so the officiant needed to be let go. Firings always happen with a phone call, so she was out.

Wines and champagnes would be tasted and tried at our meeting next weekend.

Fifty images of floral bouquets sent to Celia, with my choices of top ten ranked for her.

Twenty images of boutonnieres sent to Kick, who was a linear thinker and would more likely avoid the topic than have to choose between fifty of anything.

Celia wanted it to rain orchids inside the tent. Well, it was going to be an orchid monsoon, with each one lit inside by a tiny, tiny cube light.

No ice sculpture. Too pedestrian.

Speaking of ice sculptures . . . "Celia sent this." Ren strolled by my desk with an ice carver in her hand and a parka on. Most likely, it was her turn to spend hours in the freezer chipping off a dove's facial expression or a phallus from a Roman statue. We kept cases of Reese's peanut butter cups in there for long stays. I looked at the fax, and it said, "I have some surprises that I want to plan for Kick. We'll talk Saturday."

The surprises. Kick had a dozen planned for Celia, and who knew what Celia had in mind. I *loved* this part of things, the impact the surprises made on everyone, especially when they were sentimental and time intensive. I knew what Kick had in mind, and I liked him more for it. Now, though, with two months remaining, it was almost time to start them on the weekly countdown surprise schedule he had wanted. Next week would be the first one. I made a note to call him . . . and the jeweler.

While I was at it, we would bring the jeweler in—sworn to secrecy on the piece for Celia—so that we could design their wedding rings.

"Mylie, phone." Renata held it out, and by the look on her face, I knew it wasn't good. My eyebrows knit down, I accepted the phone.

"Hello?"

"Mylie, it's Bryan."

I breathed and gripped the armrest.

"Did you have a nice weekend?" he asked, demonically. "See any stars?"

The double entendre there was chilling. Did he mean stars as in celebrities? Or stars as in angels-poking-holes-in-the-sky stars?

"What do you want, Bryan?" I answered him icily.

"An exclusive on Celia Tyranova and Kick Lyons's wedding."

I swallowed. "I don't know what you're talking about." And I hung up.

He called back a second later. "I think you do know what I'm talking about."

"If you call here again, I'll have the police all over you for harassment," I promised and hung up again. It didn't ring with a callback.

"Mylie?" Ren was white-faced.

"Bryan."

"Oh, no." Ren slumped in her chair. "You have to let Celia's team handle it."

Which was exactly what I did. They'd keep him away from the wedding. But could they keep him away from me?

Shaking it off, I set into calling the beading artists for Celia's purse and her bridesmaids' purses, plus the women's gloves. I called Stuart Weitzman to step up the shoe order, and I nearly gave the rental company for all those tables, chairs, couches, and serving tables a collective heart attack when I said the wedding was in two months, but I didn't know which day yet. I was cursed at in Spanish, and they jacked up the price. I said, "Fine," and responded—in Spanish—with my reply to what was just said to me. They'd never get our business again.

"How are my busy little bees?" Zoe breezed into the room, fresh from lunch with a new client, setting a big packet down on the desk. We had a new one to work on.

"Fine, Zoe, how are you?" I answered, clicking Save on the spreadsheet I had open. Zoe had a way of leaning over me and pressing buttons, sometimes wiping out what I was working on. I now had an auto-save instinct when she walked into the room.

"I hear we have some competition with our big wedding." She hummed. "Sasha Worthington is all over the place, blabbing about her wedding, selling the rights to everyone."

"We heard." Ren nodded. "Tacky girl."

"She wants everything *pink*, I hear." Zoe giggled, "Even the doves."

"The doves?" I smiled. "Pink doves?"

Zoe beamed. She loved trashing the competition. "Apparently, Miss Sasha wants six dozen doves dyed pink and sprinkled with shimmer powder so that they catch the sun when they fly."

"Isn't that unsafe?"

"Like she cares."

"And she wants a pink horse to pull her carriage?" I joked, and from the look on Zoe's face, I wasn't sure if I had just hit it on target.

"White horse with pink hair pulling a pink carriage," Zoe delivered.

Ren and I groaned.

"Pink gown with pink crystals," Zoe had heard from her spy. "The men will be in black, thank God, but the ties will be pink."

"Hello, 1985 prom." Ren laughed.

"And the food needs to be pink." Zoe giggled.

"So undercooked pork is on the menu?" I imagined. "What else is pink? Vodka sauce, lobster bisque . . ."

"Oh, you're thinking way too traditionally, Mylie." Zoe shook her head in mock pity. "She wants a pink brioche shell around filet mignon."

Ren and I dropped our faces into our hands. A pink presentation for filet mignon, a pink bread dough wrap around that wonderful beef.

"Where are you getting these details?" Ren stopped her.

"Off her Web site." Zoe shrugged. "Sasha is an attention hound. She's doing a blog about her wedding plans, taking suggestions from her fans, and she's running a contest." Zoe shuddered. "One lucky fan will win the chance to be Sasha's maid of honor."

"No!" Ren and I both exhaled that one.

"Oh, yes," Zoe went on. "And it gets worse. . . ."

"How could it be worse than that?"

"People *love* it." Zoe shook her head. "I'll never understand this world."

"What do you mean by 'people love it'?" I asked, dumb-founded that people weren't shaking their heads in scorn at the whole raffling off your maid of honor position.

"People *love, love* it." Zoe shrugged. "Her Web site is a hit, people are participating, the talk shows are covering it, all the major magazines are covering it. And Sasha's started baiting Kick and Celia."

Hold the phone. "What did you say? She's baiting Kick and Celia?"

Zoe nodded, not pleased at how Sasha Worthington, by being as tacky, tasteless and media-frenzied as she was, had just turned our entire industry on its ear. A few months from now, I knew, I'd be helping other celebrity clients with setting up their blogs and raffling off positions in their bridal parties. Whatever the big-name stars wanted, whatever made a splash in the media, we had to arrange for the next crop of brides. But this . . . baiting Kick and Celia . . . what was this about?

"Sasha set her wedding date for the same weekend as Kick and Celia's on purpose . . . ," Zoe explained.

"But how did she know the date?" Ren asked, naively.

"You won't be seeing Angelique again." Zoe nodded to me, and there we had it. There was our leak. Bryan must have bedded good ol' Angelique again.

"So Sasha set her wedding date to compete with Celia's, right down to the same town. When that didn't create the de-sired effect—because Celia and Kick didn't run to the media with it, which is what Sasha's trying to drag them down to—Sasha started up her Web site and has been making snide comments, taking real shots at Celia and Kick, basically call-ing them 'snooty' and 'too good for the rest of us' by wanting to keep their wedding private."

"That's so juvenile." I was digusted. Celia and Kick didn't need this kind of gamesmanship. They just wanted to get married.

"So anyway," Zoe was not done, "Sasha has set the bar, and the tabloids are running with it. We're now in the middle of an imaginary wedding competition, Sasha versus Celia. The press is speculating, doing their usual disgusting, creative work."

"Sasha's wedding is going to be all pink. She's dyeing doves. I don't think we have anything to worry about." I smiled. "Let me get Celia on the line and make sure she knows everything's okay. Sasha's going to crash and burn with this game of hers."

"I don't know . . ." Zoe pulled on her earring. "It's working for her right now."

"She's disgusting." I hit a few buttons and had Sasha's Wedding Web site on my screen. "Good Lord, look at this."

Zoe and Renata leaned over both of my shoulders, taking it all in. A giant photo of Sasha, topless and holding her hands over her bare breasts, with her punk fiancé behind her, was the opening screen, what they call a "splash screen."

"Very classy," Ren drawled. "It's the next cover of *Modern Bride*, I'm sure."

"Hardly," Zoe sniffed, then motioned with her hand for me to click the Enter Site button, and I almost didn't want to. It could get much worse from there.

And it did. Sasha and punk fiancé in bed, covered only by a champagne-colored satin sheet, holding flutes of champagne. The words "Welcome to our wedding" danced across the screen to the sounds of "The Wedding March."

A note from Sasha: *"You're invited to the wedding event of the season, and we want you to be a part of it. You've been such loyal fans for so long, we wanted to give you what you want. Because we all know that Donnie's been giving me what I want every night . . . and twice in the morning."* Smiley face icon.

"At least she can spell," Ren snorted.

The diary entry went on: *"On August 10th, we'll make it*

official. I will be Mrs. Donnie O'Connell . . . oh, who am I kidding? He *will be* MR. SASHA'S HUSBAND.*"* Smiley face icon. Exclamation point.

"Make it stop." Ren shielded her eyes.

"Oh, look." I laughed. "Look at these! Dress Sasha. We have to see this."

I clicked on the little pink bubble wording, and up popped a lingerie-clad model of Sasha, looking like a Barbie version of her. We clicked on a series of numbers, and the little figure suddenly sported different wedding gowns. Vera Wangs, Monique L'Huilliers, Reem Acras.

When the Reem Acra came up, we all caught our breath. Because above that gown, in a pink bubble, with an animated version of a Cupid shooting an arrow into the dress were the words, *"Celia Tyranova turned down this dress."*

"Oh, God," I moaned. Angelique had really screwed Celia by leaking these details. She had signed that confidentiality agreement, too. I'm sure the Bruise Crew was right now harvesting her corneas with toothpicks.

The Dress the Groom button gave us two options. Naked and Armani tux. Her visitors had voted ninety-seven percent for Naked.

For the location, Sasha announced it would be in Sonoma, *"right down the street from Celia and Kick's house, so stop on by for a nightcap."* Celia must have been thinking of putting her estate up for sale. There went the neighborhood.

For the menu, there we had our pink menu. Pink brioche-crusted filet mignon, of course, pink penne with pink vodka sauce (Grey Goose, darlings), vodka-soaked watermelon cubes, port wine cheeses, pink rice sushi, and something she called "blushing duck."

Next, her fans could pick her wedding song. And her hairstyle. What she should wear underneath her gown (ninety-eight percent said La Perla).

A photo gallery page of near-naked photos of them also showed closeup photos of her engagement ring, surprisingly not pink. *"That's been done,"* Sasha's little note scorned.

"Donnie and I are so happy you've visited our wedding site," I read aloud. "Because we're just like you! We don't think we're above you! We're not hiding our wedding from you, like some people we know. We're just a happy, happy bride and groom in love, and we want the world to know it. We want *you* to know it, and we want *you* to find the same kind of love."

"She's a moron." Ren shook her head. "People have to be laughing at this."

"Well, they're not," Zoe warned. "I've had six calls today from the top bridal magazines, asking if celebrity brides are going to be sharing their wedding plans like this in the future. They think it's marketing genius, and they'd want to host the sites and promote them if we were willing to share our celebrity client list."

"Yes, we were born yesterday." I laughed. "Nice try."

"What's that button?" Ren pointed to a Shop icon, which took us to Sasha's wedding store. She was now designing honeymoon lingerie and selling it from her site. What an enterprising young lady!

"What a hollow, little person." I couldn't stand it anymore, so I closed down the screen. "It only makes Celia and Kick look classy in comparison."

Zoe's face soured. "Actually, Celia and Kick are taking a hit in the media. The press wants details on their wedding. Sasha's making them look bad."

"This is making Celia and Kick look bad?" I could hardly believe it.

"Sasha hit a nerve with the whole we're-not-hiding-anything-from-you thing." Zoe shook her head. "The people, and the media, are buying into that. And Celia's taking some heat."

"Celia's used to heat," I defended her. "She's not going to want to get in this fight with Sasha. She doesn't need the publicity."

"Actually"—Zoe looked down, afraid to meet my eyes—"Kick wants it."

"What?!" I couldn't believe it. "Kick has been protecting Celia from this kind of thing!"

"Well, his career's not doing so well right now." Zoe shrugged. "He got wind of this, and since Angelique spilled some of their secrets, he wants me to drop a few things to the press."

"Like?" I raised an eyebrow. This didn't sound like Kick. Not at all.

"Like the surprises he has planned for Celia."

I sat there, looking at her. I didn't believe her. Kick was a great actor. His career was fine. I saw the emotion in him when he and I outlined the surprises he had planned for Celia. He would never sell out like this. No, this was Zoe's plan. Zoe wanted the publicity for herself.

Who was the soulless whore here? And at my moment of thinking that, a pop-up screen came on, with Sasha Worthington in a little white bikini, pretending to toss the bouquet. *Well, there's your answer.*

"No, we're not dropping anything to the media," I stood up and announced, and Zoe took a step backward. Yes, she was the boss. But I was Kick and Celia's friend. And Celia said she would hook me up with all of her A-list friends if I ran my own wedding planning company. So I had no reason to be loyal to Zoe, no reason to play underling. I had not been *trained* to sell my soul. "Zoe, I'm telling you that I can use the media, too."

Zoe blinked at me.

"You drop any of Celia and Kick's secrets to the media, and I will go right to the press about you," I promised.

"Now, let's partner up nicely on this wedding, do a great job for Celia and Kick, and then I'm leaving. I thought I could come back and work for you, but I can't."

Ren suppressed a smile.

"You fire me, they'll fire you. Celia already offered me the job of doing her wedding, which you know about." I was All-Business Mylie. No one messed with my friends and got away with it.

"But Kick wants—"

"I'm not buying it, Zoe." I shook my head. "Now go inside and pay attention to your other clients. I've got this one. You're still getting your commission on this wedding, but it's all on me from now on. Consider it my gift to you."

Zoe just stood there and blinked. She really was painted into a corner. She fired me, she lost everything. I quit, she lost everything. Better to just do as she was told right now.

"Ugh, I feel like I need to take a shower." I slumped back into my chair when Zoe left the room.

"You were great," Ren whispered, leaning to see if Zoe was truly out of range. "She had that coming."

Ren's assurance didn't make me feel any better. I hated strong-arming Zoe, but she'd left me no choice. She just walked in here like nothing happened and did an awful job of trying to pull a scheme right under my nose, blaming it on Kick.

"I have to call Celia," I said and reached for my little pink case containing the scrambled-line cell phone.

"Good job, Mylie, I mean it," Ren said and returned to her overflowing task list. She was carrying the load for us, working four weddings right now, managing the rest of Zoe's staff in the other workrooms, and she always brought in bagels in the morning.

"Celia, please," I spoke into the phone, having reached a new assistant. A male one.

"Mylie!" She laughed into the phone. I didn't expect her to be in a good mood, but she was far stronger than I gave her credit for.

"Hey, Celia." I was given the relief of being able to smile while talking with her. "Just checking in to make sure everything's in line."

"Yes, the stuff you sent was *great!* You do amazing work. So fast!"

"Thank you. Once we nail down your date, the rest of it will just fall into place," I promised. "Piece of cake."

"But would that be *pink* cake?" She laughed. She'd seen Sasha's site. "Can you *believe* that tramp? God, she must be making your stomach turn right now."

"Yeah, we're all pretty nauseous over here." I smiled. "If you ask me to create a blog for you, I'm going to fly out there and slap you."

Ren's head jerked up. *This* was how I talked to the biggest celebrity client we've ever had?

"No worries about that." Celia giggled. "My publicist has a plan. Letterman's doing a Top 10 list tonight that we faxed over. Very 'Sasha's Trashy Wedding Plans.' It's going to be great."

Okay, so it was a little juvenile, but Celia's sense of humor was intact, and if Letterman could help us, I was all for it. This was way better than having to console a tearful bride over the phone. "I'll have to tape it." I smiled.

"Oh, it's great. Kick and I wrote it this morning, actually." Then she told someone 'good serve,' and I knew she was out at her tennis courts. "Let Sasha whore out her wedding plans. The world knows she's just desperate for publicity. It may get her ink right now, but in the long run . . ."

She didn't have to finish the sentence.

"Oh, and you know Angelique is no longer with us, right?"

"Yes, I know. I'm sorry to hear about that."

"I'm not," she said, and I heard clapping in the background. Someone had scored. "Now what was this you were saying last time about having had a *romantic* time this weekend?"

I blushed. *Oh, those hands.* "Oh, Celia, it was *amazing!* He's . . . he's . . ."

"So he's got you speechless, huh?" She giggled. "Good for you."

That's right. Good for me.

"I want to hear all about it when we get together on Saturday, okay?" Someone said something to her on her end of the line. "Kick wants to talk to you, all right? I'll say bye now."

"Bye, Celia," I said, but she was already gone.

"Mylie," Kick's voice now. "I have a question for you about the bar menu."

The bar menu? What is he talking about?

"The twelve choices for the bar," he said, and with the mention of "twelve," I knew he meant the twelve things he had planned as surprises for Celia.

"Okay, got it. I know you can't talk freely."

"Right."

"I've got Harry Winston working on the copy of her mother's wedding ring," and as I spoke, Ren's head shot up again, listening. "The suite is booked at the Kapalua for next Thursday, and I found Evelyn Greenberg."

Ren mouthed, "Evelyn Greenberg?" I shook her off.

"You *did?*" Kick coughed, then said something to Celia about my finding a rare bottle of cognac for him and his friends. "How did you do that? I tried, my people tried . . ."

"She was on Match.com." I shrugged. My subscription was good for something. I had found Celia's childhood best friend whom she hadn't seen in years. It had been a good morning.

"Wow, Mylie, you're really something. . . ."

"And hey, Kick, I have to ask you something," I started, searching for the words. "Did you have a request to drop some details to the press about the wedding?"

"What?! No," he answered, offended. Just like I would be.

"That's what I thought."

"Who said—"

No need having them hate Zoe any more than they did. "Media request," I lied. "We get them all the time. 'Kick Lyons said it was okay,' that kind of thing."

"Never," he answered, and I believed him. "Celia and I are funneling everything through you. No one else. Just you."

So he knew what I was talking about.

"Gotcha. No problem. I'm on it."

"I've got to run, Mylie, but we'll talk to you later," he said hurriedly. "And thanks."

Click. He was gone.

My instincts were right. I was cutting Zoe out of the information flow. Better yet, I'd feed her false information. How quickly I'd switched from wanting to protect Zoe, from seeing her as a wounded little bird I wanted to nurse back to health, to pretty much being disgusted by her. She had been the leak in all of the celebrity weddings we had planned. I wondered if Angelique was fired for no reason at all, if it was Zoe.

I was on my own with this ten-million-dollar wedding. And that was the way I wanted it.

Chapter 26

I had missed the beginning of Letterman. But he was on #5 of the Top 10 Reasons Sasha Worthington's wedding would be the wedding of the decade:

"*Number 5 . . . it will be the last time Donnie has a job to do . . . showing up on time.*

"*Number 4 . . . the wedding favors? Body piercings.*

"*Number 3 . . . the videographer does double duty: tape the wedding and then the sex tape they'll sell afterward.*

"*Number 2 . . . naked Macarena.*

"*And the number one reason why Sasha Worthington's wedding will be the wedding of the decade . . . the bride will NOT be wearing white.*"

The crowd cheered, and I smiled for Celia and Kick's late-night revenge. I popped a Lean Cuisine into the microwave and checked my messages.

"*Mylie, it's Zoe . . . I can't get into the file for Celia's wedding. Call the computer guy and get that fixed.*"

I'd changed the password.

"*Mylie, it's Zoe. I can't reach Renata, so give her a call and tell her to call me.*"

Bite me.

"*Mylie, it's Ren. Zoe's called me like fifty times. Go tranquilize her.*"

"Mylie . . . it's Russell."

He sounded disappointed to reach my voice mail.

"Sorry to call so late, but I just wanted to hear your voice. Been thinking about you all day, especially when one of my clients requested a strawberry shortcake."

I smiled, wondering when exactly we'd kicked it off the roof. When he was on top or when I was?

"Okay, well, I'll hope to reach you tomorrow night, unless you want to call me during the day. It'll just be me with my gorgeous hands, working in the kitchen. And I go out for deliveries at three. If you take a coffee break or something, just give me a call. Later."

Oh, I'm so glad he didn't say "Ciao."

I felt guilty eating a Lean Cuisine when Russell was a professional chef and didn't eat anything prepared. I felt like I should have been stripping sausage of its casings, chopping fresh green and red peppers from the farmer's market, smashing a garlic clove with the side of a butcher knife. Instead, I was peeling the melty plastic cover off a cardboard box of angel hair pasta and tiny little shrimp. If I ever got to the point of Russell coming to my place—Who was I kidding? That was a *when* question—I'd have to gut my freezer and fridge, my cupboards and my snack table, completely getting rid of anything prepared, the mac and cheese boxes, the Dinty Moores. I'd have to go to the gourmet supermarket with a mind-set of "What would Rachael Ray have in her kitchen?" For some reason, I felt a very strong desire to have artichokes on hand, and chèvre.

This was a man who went to the Culinary Academy and now made meals for the fabulously wealthy and fabulously busy in New York City. They ordered, he cooked, he delivered and prepared. He could definitely have his own cooking TV show, I thought. *The Hot Guy in the Kitchen.* I smiled at that one.

We had a lot in common, workwise. We both were artists of a sort. And we both had to be extremely discreet about our celebrity clients. Who knew what he'd seen in their homes, in their kitchens? He didn't tell me the celebrity angle of his job, of course. Ren had filled me in on that. He just said he was a personal chef. Like he was cooking for college kids in their dorm rooms, nothing more than that. Trust was a big element in our jobs . . . and in our lives.

Ren had also filled me in on what happened with Melissa. No one had ever liked her. She started out sweet and adorable, but Katie could sense something was off. It was just a scent about her, Katie had said. Ren had seen something dark in her eyes during a game of Cranium, of all things. Sure, she could slap on a smile and bring a tray of brownies to family gatherings, complimenting Russell's parents and earning gold stars all over the place. But Katie saw it first . . . the mean streak.

And Katie also saw her out for dinner with another man.

Russell didn't believe her at first, smoked as he was by her lovely exterior and how charming she could be. There was a reason why *charming* and *snake* showed up in the same sentence so often.

Melissa had joined the community pool, having chosen not to work after Emma was born. And she was said to have been like one of the lionesses at that Hawaiian resort, interested in any man who looked at her. She would leave baby Emma in her stroller, in the noonday sun, unattended and without sunscreen, while she strutted around the pool, posed, and said of a sixteen-year-old boy, "Now that's *hot*." Her friends slowly deserted her, and soon she was sitting at the pool on overcast days with her hair and makeup done, earrings on, giving the come-hither look to the lifeguards and the maintenance men. She was an empty shell, needing constant attention from all men, to feel like she had some value.

The man Katie saw her out with . . . was the landscaper from the pool. And he was married, too. Empty shells seemed to find one another.

Russell filed for divorce, and she didn't want custody of Emma. She said she had other priorities. Like banging landscapers and sixteen-year-old boys from the pool. Her family apologized, said she always was in an arrested development, that they'd hoped Russell would "straighten her out," that she threw away the best thing that ever happened to her. Small comfort. Russell had been devastated at first, gaining weight, more humiliated than missing her. He said he was glad she cheated, because that was the only thing that would have made him break his wedding vows. He'd always thought they could work through it, but she was being fake even in couples' counseling. Even their shrink seemed horrified by her callousness, how she referred to Emma as "It."

She was secretive, amused by her deceptions, even went so far as to plant fake evidence of an affair once just because she wanted to see Russell get mad. She thought it was funny.

Their counselor took Russell aside and shook his hand, congratulating him on being free of such an evil wife. That sparked his healing. He could see her clearly then.

"He needs to be with someone like you, Mylie," Ren had said during the weekend at Dolphin Dance. "And you need to be with someone like him."

Chapter 27

"Hey, it's Mylie."

"Mylie!" I could hear something sizzling. He was at work. "I'm glad you called."

I feel like a teenager, and not one of those insecure, gangly ones.

"Is this a good time?"

"Yes, yes, it's fine," he said. "I just have ten things going at once, so it's a slow day."

I can relate.

"So how are things in wedding world?" he asked. "You're not doing that Sasha Worthington's wedding, are you?"

"Nooo," I drew it out.

"Good, because if you were, I was never going to sleep with you again."

I laughed. *God, he's funny.* "You saw Letterman last night, I take it?"

"Yeah, Emma had a stomachache, so I was up late."

Poor baby.

"Is she feeling better?" I asked, because I do have a heart.

"Yeah, she's fine now," he said, sounding distracted. Probably flipping something in a pan with those gorgeous hands. "Thanks for asking. I know she's not your favorite kid."

Ouch. Clean this up fast, or the kid gets what she wants.
"It's okay," I assured. "Really. This can't be easy on her."

"Yeah, but *still* . . . I'm doing the best I can with her."

"I know you are. You're doing a great job. Ren tells me you're an impressive father."

"Still figuring out the whole discipline thing. It's rather new," he confessed, opening right up to me. "I just don't want her to turn out like her mother, so I have to be tough now. She doesn't like it very much."

"It'll be worth it."

"Still . . . when your little girl says 'I hate you . . .' " The sound of sizzling came again. "Let's get off this topic," he said, more lightly.

"Yes, let's."

"Are you free for dinner tomorrow night?" he said quickly, like he'd been rehearsing it. "I'd ask you for tonight, but I'm catering a dinner."

"Yes, tomorrow's perfect," I breathed, thrilled that I wouldn't have to wait until Friday to see him at the shore house.

"Good, I'm cooking for you. What do you want on the menu?"

I want everything to be pink. "Surprise me."

"Ah, my favorite answer." He laughed. "I like your adventurous spirit. I've got a bunch going on in the kitchen right now, so I'll call you tonight with the details."

"I'll be home at ten," I offered.

"I'll be home at eleven. Too late to call?"

Ah, I love the superpolite beginnings. "No, that's fine."

"Good. Talk to you later."

"Okay, bye."

"Bye."

And I hung up the phone, screamed, and danced around the office. Renata said she should be taping all of this. "You've never been more of a giggling idiot," she said, shaking her head while I sang, *"He's* cooking for *me, he's* cooking for *me!"*

"The best part is, he's probably dancing around his kitchen right now, too. You two idiots were made for each other," she said. "What have we done?"

"Something very, very good." I leaned over and kissed her on the head.

Chapter 28

I've learned to expect the unexpected in my job, that things you could never imagine happened quite regularly. Every time the phone rang, it could be anything.

But I never expected Kick Lyons to knock on my door in the middle of the night.

Luckily, I wasn't asleep. Russell and I had talked until 2:00 A.M., so I was up making some tea. Sleep wouldn't come tonight, I was too excited. So I thought I'd brew up some lemon tea and dig into work. In the quiet hours without my phone ringing, I'd get a ton done and open up my weekend for my trip to Dolphin Dance. The knock at my door made me jump and knock my hand against the hot tea kettle.

"Who is it?" I called through the door, standing a safe distance from it in case the police were about to break down the wrong residential door with a battering ram again. But I doubted they knocked first.

"Your favorite client," came Kick's unmistakable voice.

I hurriedly unlocked the four safety latches and opened the door to see Kick all dressed up like he'd been at a club. Since he smelled like vodka, that was likely the case.

"Is Trump Tower all booked up?" I joked, leaning out to look down the hall. He was alone. No Bruise Crew, no body-guards, no assistant. Just him. "You need a place to crash?"

He laughed and came in when I swept my hand to gesture him inside. Never mind that I was in stained sweatpants and a Derek Jeter jersey, my hair in a ponytail, my face scrubbed of all trace of makeup, shiny from moisturizing cream. I didn't need to look good for Kick Lyons. He loved me for my mind.

"Sorry for not calling," he said and assessed my place. It was a mess. Magazines and files on the dining room table, bottles of nail polish on random surfaces, Post-its every-where. "Spur of the moment decision. Better for no one to know. Everyone thinks I'm at the club still."

"Ah," was all I said. "Lemon tea?" I offered and immediately felt about eighty years old for offering tea.

"No thanks, Grandma." He agreed, shaking his head. "You need to get a life, girl."

"Right now, your wedding *is* my life," I warned. "I've hip-checked Zoe right out of the picture, so it's all on me."

"Good. That's the way we want it." He sat down on the couch, first removing some empty packaging wrappers from Victoria's Secret, raising an eyebrow at me. They were the small squares of plastic. From the bras and panties. Luckily, I had put my new collection of lingerie away already. Kick would never let me live down the red lacies and the salmon-colored boy shorts with matching demi-bra and white em-broidering. And the garters.

"Okay, boss. What can I do for you?" I grabbed a nearby yellow legal pad and a pen, sat cross-legged on the couch next to him, and readied my hand.

What we didn't know at the time was that Bryan had fol-lowed him. And like a true shape-shifter, he had flattened himself against my neighbor's door to take a sneaky picture of Kick being welcomed into my home. The next day, the tabloid headlines had me in my ponytail and Jeter shirt, wel-coming a smartly dressed Kick into my home in the middle of the night. "Kick Falls For the Wedding Planner—Celia Crushed."

* * *

"Celia, it's not true!" I paced with the phone in my hand. "I swear it's not true."

Renata just shook her head. She thought I should have called Russell first.

"Yes, Kick did come over. To talk about a surprise he's planning for you," I explained, saving the whole truth that it was actually twelve surprises. I listened to her, Renata listening to me listening to her. "I swear to you. Look at how I was dressed! Is that how someone dresses to seduce someone?" I listened. "*Role-playing?* Oh, come on, Celia. You know I have to meet secretly with both you and Kick to get this wedding together." I listened. She was calming down. "I swear to you, Celia. Yes, it was the middle of the night, but Kick had nothing but good intentions. He was doing something nice for you."

Hey, I thought you were hurt into numbness by these tabloid stories. Why the hysterics?

"Celia, you have my word. Kick was there planning something really nice for you. I promise."

A half hour later, she was calmed.

I exhaled, brushed the wisps of hair out of my face, and dialed Russell's number.

"You should have called him first," Renata warned. "Remember his past . . ."

I got his voice mail. A drop of sweat ran down my back, and I shivered. "Russell, it's Mylie. I'm having a little bit of tabloid hell here and wanted to make sure you didn't get the wrong idea of anything." *Was I talking too fast? Was I sounding guilty?* "I'm sure you haven't even seen the paper yet, and you probably have no idea what I'm talking about, but I wanted you to know that nothing's going on, okay?"

Ren rolled her eyes. "You sound insane," she sang behind me. "I'm going to have to clean this up, I just know it."

I ignored her and spoke into the phone. "So aside from

that, I'm looking forward to seeing you tonight. Can't wait for our dinner. Okay? Talk to you later."

God, that was the worst tap dance ever. I almost convinced myself that I had a guilty conscience.

"Excellent work, Mylie." Zoe stormed through the room with the newspaper in her hand. In the picture, I had too big a smile on my face, my arm swept to welcome Kick into my apartment. Good thing I didn't hug him. That would be bad. "Do you know how many calls I have to make now? Everyone knows we're doing Kick and Celia's wedding. Thanks."

It wasn't my fault. Kick shouldn't have shown up like that. And it was Bryan's fault for . . . for . . . for doing his job.

I laid my head down on the desk. Zoe slammed her office door, and I could hear her explaining to the team of lawyers over the phone that it was not our misstep. She defended me. I was at home at 2:00 A.M., and Kick came to my door. It was sloppy work on *his* part.

The rest of the day was a blur. Every second I waited for Russell to call was agony. Renata even tried calling him, but there was no answer. I tried to remember. Did he say he had some all-encompassing job to do today and wouldn't be reachable by phone? Three hours . . . four hours . . . He wasn't calling back.

"Mylie, you have to go to him," Renata suggested. "This is a raw nerve for him, even the idea that you'd have another guy to your place after just talking with him."

"It's not 'another guy,' it's Kick Lyons. He knows I work celebrity weddings," I reasoned.

"No, you'd really better go to him now," Ren warned. "I've known Russell for a long time. This isn't good."

I grabbed my bag and stood to leave, and Zoe blocked my path. "You're not going anywhere. The lawyers are on their way over, and you *will* be here."

"Get out of my way, Zoe." I had tears in my eyes. How did this happen? All I did was open my door.

"Sit down, Mylie."

"Zoe, I will knock you over, I swear," I said through tears. "This is my *life* we're talking about."

"And it's *my* life I'm talking about," Zoe said in a fury. "You're not going to destroy what I've worked all my life to accomplish just because you want to get—"

I moved closer to her. "Don't even finish that thought, Zoe."

"Mylie, go," Renata said with all urgency, putting her own job in jeopardy. She had no pull on Zoe, nothing to hold over her. She put friendship above her job every time. If Zoe fired her, she could get an earlier start on Dolphin Dance.

"I'm going," I said, sidestepping Zoe. "Stall the lawyers. I'll be back in an hour."

I didn't even look back, but I heard Zoe's bewildered voice behind me: "Where is she going?"

I knocked on his door. Waited. Pounded. Paced. Waited some more. Knocked some more. It seemed like an hour had gone by, but it was only ten minutes. I sank down onto the carpeted hallway floor and wiped the tears out of my eyes. I would sleep here for a week if I had to, just to get to see him. I couldn't get this close to happy, finally, and have it torn away by Bryan.

The elevator doors slid open with a ding, and the best I could say for myself was that at least I wasn't curled into a fetal position.

"Mylie?" It was Russell . . . and a woman.

I stood up quickly, wiping my eyes, taking a wipe at my nose in case.

"Mylie, what are you doing here?" he asked, his arms filled with grocery bags, his eyes filled with concern.

"I was . . . I was . . ." I couldn't take my eyes off the brunette holding a few grocery bags of her own. Jealousy. I was already on overload. A nice dose of jealousy in my unbalanced state was going to tip me over the edge, and I'd go running back to hide in my work world forever.

"This is Carla. She's interning with me," he explained, seeing—and probably being frightened by—the look in my eyes.

"Carla . . ." I breathed. "Hi."

"Are you okay?"

"I'm having a *really* bad morning," I confessed, holding both of my hands out in total surrender.

"Do you want to cancel dinner?" He stepped back, a little defensive. He didn't know anything yet. He didn't get my crazy voice mail.

"No, *no*, I can't wait for dinner." I half smiled through the sobs that wanted to come out but didn't. "We're still on."

"What's going on? You look kind of . . . weird." He raised an eyebrow and fumbled for his keys. I took a bag from him so that he could open his door. He, Carla, and I walked inside to his gleaming studio that was mostly kitchen, all silver and streamlined.

I exhaled. This wasn't the entrance I wanted to make into his place, all teary-eyed and frantic over nothing. Now I had just carried the problem into the room. "The tabloids printed something untrue, and I didn't want you to get the wrong idea."

Carla smiled and turned away, unloading groceries right into the refrigerator. She was tan and wore a midriff-baring shirt, and when she turned I could see the tattoo at the small of her back. And another tattoo on her shoulder blade, *Carla* entertwined with *Jennifer* in a big heart with roses. Nothing to worry about there.

Russell's arms were now free to hold me. "I know, Renata called me."

Every muscle, every cell, every vertebrae in my body relaxed as I leaned against him. "I was so worried," I confessed and decided to keep it at that. If everything was fine, no need to muck it up with too many words and assumptions and . . . too much *me*.

"Ren was worried, too, and she explained the whole thing," he comforted me, rubbing my back and rocking me back and forth. "I know how the business works," he assured me. "They once snapped me with Catherine Zeta-Jones, and she sued the living hell out of them. We were just shopping for porcino mushrooms, and they always get that one moment that *looks* like something. I know how it is."

"I just didn't want you to think—"

"That you hung up the phone with me and invited Kick Lyons over for a quickie?" He laughed. Carla laughed, too. "No, I didn't think that."

"Good."

"But I have to tell you"—he stepped back and looked me in the eye—"I am upset about one thing, and it could be the end of us."

What?!

"The Derek Jeter shirt." He sighed, and I knew he was kidding by the smile he couldn't keep off his lips. "I'm a Red Sox fan. I don't think I can date a Yankees fan. Sorry."

"Jerk." I smiled, then accepted an all's-well kiss from him.

"Now get out of here." He turned me around and patted me on the butt. "I have a *very* important dinner I'm doing tonight." That would be the one he was making for me. "And we have to focus. And you, my dear, have to get back to the office and face the sharks, apparently. I know you'll be great."

He kissed me at the door before I had the presence of mind to see what was in those grocery bags Carla was unloading. And as the elevator arrived for me, I firmly decided not to worry about looking like a neurotic moron in front of Russell. If he was going to be with me, he'd have to get used to that. It was, as my mother said, what made me endearing.

* * *

"Here she is." Zoe announced my arrival with a smile, as the five suits with angry faces sat in a line before her desk.

And Zoe was phenomenal. She took the heat. She strong-armed the contract-waving barracudas. She found a way to lay it on Kick without actually blaming him. And she assured there would be a lawsuit against the tabloid. Which would give Kick and Celia some of their money back for this ten-million-dollar wedding.

"We have this Bryan's contact information, so we're suing him personally as well," Zoe announced.

Nice!

"I've spoken to Kick and Celia, and they do not want to break their contract with us, gentlemen, so if you'll excuse us, we have a lot of work to do." Zoe was magnificent, calm and cool, what we call Butter Tough—appearing to be soft as butter but really being hard as the plate it sat on. "Your clients have moved up the date of their wedding, which could be construed as a violation of their original contract. But we don't count pennies like that. We're not charging them extra."

The suits exchanged glances. Since they lived by codes and sub-clauses and fine print on contracts, and not in the human world of nuance, their little rat brains probably computed a dozen different potential lawsuits opening up in our favor. So they stood, bowed a little bit to Zoe, and single-filed it out of our office.

"All taken care of." Zoe slapped her hands together like she was getting chalk off of them. "Now, Mylie, go get me some tea."

"Yes, Zoe," I agreed. She was my boss again. The part of me that revered her talent just woke up from its nap, and I hurried to get her a tea, light and sweet.

Chapter 29

"**Y**ou look *much* better."

It wasn't exactly the compliment I was hoping for when I made my arrival at Russell's—I'd have far preferred "You look beautiful" or "You look amazing"—but I brought this one on myself. So all I could do was laugh at myself, shake my head, and accept the glass of wine he so wisely brought to the door for me. "All right, all right." I smiled. "Bring it on."

He just laughed and gathered me in for a hug. "Did your day get better? I assume so, since your face isn't swollen to twice the size right now and you don't have crazy eyes."

"Wow, you really know how to impress a woman," I said, snuggled in.

"You make it so easy." He gave me a little extra-tight squeeze and then stepped back enough to kiss me. Hands on my face. I loved that. I melted so much, relaxed so much that I feared I might have tipped my wineglass. That would have been perfect. Two seconds inside and I spill Cabernet on his rug. Luckily, he didn't fill the glass to two-thirds.

"Where's Emma?" I asked, not wanting the little hellion to come walking in . . . with or without a butcher's knife.

"Katie's got her," he said and took me by the hand, started walking. "Let me give you the tour. . . ."

His kitchen, as seen earlier, made up most of the place. Shining silver counters, a phenomenal silver sub-zero refrigerator, a super-clean stove with not a drop of sauce or grease on it, everything organized, everything reachable. Then into the living room with its brown leather couches, bamboo stalks in vases as counter accents, warm amber lighting, a bookshelf I'd surely analyze later, lots of framed pictures of Emma, clay mugs that Emma probably made in preschool, and a sizeable television set with a neat stack of kids' movies piled in the console.

The hallway was lined with wood-framed photos, mostly of his family, of Emma, and the gang at Dolphin Dance. Katie and Glenn at their wedding, which was the only clean-shaven appearance by Glenn that I'd seen. No celebrity-with-the-chef photos, which impressed me. Russell wasn't the type.

Leading me by the hand, he walked onward.

Emma's room. Buttercup yellow with a floral motif, big daisies painted on the walls, dance costumes hanging on wooden pegs on the walls, fairy wings suspended in the line, ballet slippers and tap shoes lined up on the floor. "She loves to dance, huh?"

"Yes, she loves it." He nodded. "Her teacher says she has talent beyond her years."

I'll say. She has high school level bitchiness perfected. Quite an overachiever.

"Are we ever going to get that dance recital?" I asked, taking his other hand in mine and clasping them together.

"When she behaves herself." He shook his head, and I just laughed it off. No need dampening the mood with any more reminders.

Russell clicked off the light and closed Emma's door. Now we were getting to the good stuff. His bedroom. Burgundy and black, but not in a 1980s way. It was streamlined and sexy, a warm burgundy with a comfy rug underfoot, dark burgundy closet doors, a ceiling fan. "Nice," I approved, only naturally looking with interest at the bed surface, at the smooth stretch of comforter that issued a very intentional invitation. Not now, though. It would wait. I stopped myself from asking "What's on the menu?" as the risk of seeming too suggestive was clearly there and instead gave him a smile and a wink as I sipped from my glass, stepping past him and out of the room.

If you ever got a chance to have a personal chef cook for you, take it. The warmup was better than the table set for two, once you took to the kitchen and insisted on helping out. I wasn't the wait-to-be-served type, so I had direct access to those gorgeous hands of his, dripping with mango juice as he tiny-cubed the fruit to sprinkle over the crabmeat-stuffed salmon. Just the sight of him from the back, even, as he pulled a mesclun salad from the refrigerator, his shirt pulling over his back, made me shift my footing a little bit. I had butterflies, those deep-in-your-stomach ones that were like the opening act to an orgasm but came from just your thoughts. All from watching this guy pull a salad out of the fridge.

We talked effortlessly as I washed the berries for dessert (hadn't Carla done *anything* ahead of time?), and he finished the presentation with a few sprigs of mint, instructing me to set the berries aside so that they'd be at room temperature for better taste delivery later.

I noticed a distinct lack of garlic and onions on the menu as well. All the better.

Rosemary potatoes sizzled in the oven, as did a foil-wrapped length of garlic bread, which he'd sprinkled with Romano cheese. ("Parmesan is too everyday," so I'd ranked in the higher echelon of cheeses. A good sign.)

His bistro table with the very cool metal chairs was set with burgundy linens, a single low gardenia and a single votive. He'd put some time into this.

Finally, dinner was served, right after a toast to a great evening (No cliché "To us!") and a confession. . . .

"I have to tell you . . ." he started. "When you dug into those crabs at Ren's house that afternoon, knowing exactly what to do, getting messy, not being afraid to lick your fingers . . . that was great."

He had been watching me slurp my way through a half dozen crabs, pushing the stray bits of green slime away with my finger, and not dipping the crab shell into the bowls of water to remove any trace of muck—and flavor—as the beginners usually did.

"I didn't know I was impressing you." I grinned.

"Oh, yeah, it's a major turnoff when a woman picks at her food, afraid to eat, afraid to break a nail." He shook his head. "I don't like the pretentious type."

As the woman who bit off all of her fingernails to play volleyball, I didn't think I qualified.

"Ren told me that you're down-to-earth, funny, the real Girl Next Door," he said, serving me up a slice of salmon after first asking for my serving preference with a few silent placements of his knife. Impressive. I hated it when men just decided your portion for you. It seemed all of our most respect-inspiring moments were actions, not words. "And I can't believe someone like you really exists."

I can't believe someone like you really exists. Sigh.

"I mean . . ." He stumbled on the words. "Ren described you, but . . ."

She didn't do me justice.

"You just . . . *shine* in person."

You're killing me here, Russell. No one's ever said such

amazing things. "Thank you," I said quietly, that reverent quiet that makes the words mean more.

And he just smiled, looking manly and boyish all at once, shining just as well. So we two shiny people savored our meal, which was *phenomenal*, and took the room-temperature berry bowl with us to bed.

Chapter 30

"You didn't go home last night!" Ren gasped. Wearing the same outfit back to work the next day kind of gave that away.

"Mylie!" she tried, but she'd get no details. I wasn't that kind of girl. I was the Girl Next Door with Discretion. "Is he incredible? I always got the feeling he'd be incredible . . . all attentive and gentle . . . with the whole cuddling and talking thing afterward, right? Mylie, come on!"

I just grinned with my mouth pressed into a tight almost-smile and got to work.

"Mylie! Come *on!* Give me something here . . . ," she begged. "Hey, we got you two together!"

"He's incredible," I relented, but that was all I'd give her.

After a while of feeling her stare holes into my back, she said something wonderful: "You two are so alike. He'd never talk about it either."

My face hurt from the smile I'd been wearing all day.

"Just give me a number," Ren begged. "Just the number."

"Forget it, Ren."

She was losing her mind. "Pete and I haven't . . . in *ages* with the baby being up all hours. Come on, just give me the number so I can be jealous of you and get Pete back in the game."

I laughed. "Oh, that's cold, Ren! I'm sure you can get Pete back in the game without dropping a number to activate the male competition thing."

"Wanna bet?"

I swiveled in my chair to face her. "I'm not giving you a number." It was *eleven* for me, *three* for him. "But I will give you a little advice for getting Pete back in the game."

Ren leaned in.

"*Cook with him.*" I nodded. "Get him in the kitchen. Make something juicy, get a little sloppy, lick something off his hands, make something that smells amazing, drink some wine, watch his hands, let him watch your hands. I'm telling you . . . I could barely get through the sit-down dinner portion of the evening."

Ren considered it, fabulous cook that she was.

"I'll watch James that night," I offered. "You need to feel like this again, Ren."

Ren smiled and brought her finger to her lips, perhaps imagining mango juice there.

"Mylie, it's Kick."

"Hey, Kick. What's shakin'?" Again, Zoe wouldn't appreciate my tone with the client, and since she had brought herself back onto the case, I made sure to be more professional when she was around.

"I need you to pick something up for me."

"Sure, where am I going?"

"Harry Winston."

Gulp.

"The boys will be by to pick you up," and by that he meant the Bruise Crew. "And you'll go pick up an order for 'Charles the Magnificent.'"

Charles the Magnificent? Please tell me that's not his pet name for—

"Mylie?"

"Charles the Magnificent? Are you serious?" I coughed. "Can't you use *Stanley Markovski* or something a little less . . . attention-getting?"

"Nah, they know what it means."

"And then I'm supposed to do what with the package?" The package being the $750,000 diamond and sapphire necklace he bought Celia as her first wedding surprise.

"Hang on to it until Saturday. I'm flying in with Celia, and I'll take the handoff from you at dinner." He had it all figured out. In the meantime, I was going to have a $750,000 treasure in my house . . . as my responsibility. There was no way I was going to leave it at home when I went to Dolphin Dance on Friday. I'd have to take it with me. That made me very, very nervous. Suddenly I had an image of Emma ripping it apart and spelling out "I hate Mylie" in her most valuable work to date.

"Okay?" He sounded impatient. I was supposed to just say "Yes, boss" and make it happen. "And you've got her friend flying in for the wedding. She's going to love that." He seemed to be counting off in his head. "You've got the suite all done, so we're at . . . what?"

"The Mounds bars." He wanted me to fill her trailer at the movie set with a thousand mini Mounds bars.

"Got 'em on order," I promised, nodding as I flipped open my own list.

"I've got Chris Botti confirmed to fly in as a surprise and play 'When I Fall in Love' for you," I continued, and Ren's head jerked up. The order for a thousand Mounds bars had the same effect on her. "And her mother's ring is in, being worked on right now, almost ready."

"Actually, it is ready. Winston's called on that."

Great. So now I'd be picking up a $750,000 diamond and sapphire necklace *and* a $100,000 replica of her mother's wedding ring. This was worse than walking to the bank with their ten-million check. Because these were *jewels*. Jewels were different than a rectangle of paper, even when you knew the number on it. Jewels could get lost. Very big men could pound you into the ground if you lost them.

"And what about the drum line?" He was going down the same list I had.

This one surprised me the most. Celia had a thing for marching bands. She had been on the flag squad in high school, and it was the best time of her life. She wasn't the cheerleader type, so she did the tall silks in her high school's marching band, didn't make captain, loved the competitions, and even considered joining a professional drum and bugle corps before she got discovered at a Krispy Kreme store by Robert Redford. Who had a life like that?

Kick's idea was to bring in a professional drum line. Not the whole band, as that would have been too tricky with the security clearance thing. Just the drum line to play a hot percussion solo at the close of their ceremony. Kick sent me videos of the DCI competitions and told me to take my pick. Of all the tasks assigned to me, this one was the toughest, as the corps were all traveling and competing right now. I'd have to go to a competition, wear a push-up bra, and try to talk a group of drummers into agreeing to background checks and retina scans. The twenty-five thousand dollars I was allotted to pay them might open the door, I thought.

"That's it for now," Kick announced. "I've got to run. Don't forget . . . Charles the Magnificent."

I rolled my eyes and repeated, "Charles the Magnificent," hoping I'd get more comfortable with it before I had to walk into Harry Winston's and potentially humiliate myself.

The Bruise Crew stayed right with me. Not talking. Not breathing all too quietly. Seemed our boys had a group case of deviated septum. There was a lot of mouth breathing going on.

The limo pulled up in front of Harry Winston's, and the

boys climbed out ahead of me. I hopped out, in my wrinkled dress that had spent the night on Russell's bedroom floor, my hair pulled back in a tight chignon with oversized black sunglasses on. I wondered if the paparazzi was already on their way, only to be disappointed when they reached me. I had to admit, I loved the gawkers on the streets, the people who leaned and whispered, trying to figure out who I was. No Alyssa Milano references this time. But I did hear an "Isn't that the girl who hangs out with the girl who hangs out with Paris Hilton?" The dress must be giving off an aura.

Chin up, I strode confidently into Harry Winston, trying so hard to look like I belonged there. Which was exactly how *not* to look like you belong there. The long-necked, balletic woman behind the counter—with a diamond pendant the size of my eye gracing her chest right between her pointy collarbones—gave me a you-must-work-for-someone smirk and asked if she could help me.

"Yes." I decided to mess with her a little bit. The Snooties, as we called them, wouldn't get away with their condescension. "I'm looking for something . . . *ruby*. A bar pin, I think."

She flinched. She'd pegged me all wrong, and her demeanor changed. "Yes, ma'am." She nodded, her bony fingers all jangly as she turned the key in the display case latch.

If I was on my own, I could have gotten away with trying on the bar pin, maybe holding ruby danglers by my ears with an ambivalent, bored attitude while the sales clerk danced for the chance to run my Platinum card. But the Bruise Crew shifted position behind me, one or two of them clearing their throats, not in the mood to watch me play "dress-up ruby princess."

"On second thought, I'd like to just pick up for," I could barely get it out, "Charles the Magnificent."

Snootie stopped in her bent-over position, then straightened in full haughtiness, turned on her heel, and walked away. A moment later, she dropped a bag in my hand, turned on her heel, and walked away from me again without so much as a "Have a nice day." I could hardly blame her. The commission probably wasn't hers, so why waste time with me?

With my little velvet satchel of ultravaluable jewels in my hand, we walked back out of the store and climbed right into the limo. These rocks were mine for the next few *days*. I smiled. I knew exactly what I was going to do the minute I got home.

If only I had a tiara.

If I couldn't roll around naked in the ten million dollars, I was definitely going to dance around my house in lingerie, wearing the necklace and the ring. With the ring on my pinkie so that there would be absolutely no chance of it getting stuck on my ring finger, I turned up some Tina Turner on my CD player and had myself a little half-naked jewelry dance party, singing at the top of my lungs. Halfway through, I shut the curtains and the blinds, just in case Bryan was dangling from a telephone pole outside snapping pictures of me dancing around in Kick's wedding-gift jewelry.

Chapter 31

The parkway was *jammed*. And it was hot outside, wavy heat fumes rising off the paved road, baked-looking people in their cars as we inched forward. On the radio, the deejays had to rub it in by talking about their air-conditioned studio, heckling those of us who took to the roads for our weekend getaways. What else could they do, stuck at work while the rest of us were decompressing with every mile we traveled, however slowly?

Ren said she'd never seen anyone run so fast after quitting time. I grabbed the handle of my suitcase, grabbed the velvet pouch of jewels, and ran for the door. I guess I wore my heart on my sleeve, huh?

"Drive safely," Ren called after me, then went on to tell me what time she and Pete would be arriving at the house. The door was closed behind me before she finished.

Waiting for my car wheel to make the next single revolution, I looked to my passenger seat. I'd all but buckled the little velvet pouch in with a seat belt. I wanted it in my sight at all times and knew the perfect hiding place for it when we got to the house. Inside the vase by my nightstand, so the jewels would sleep right next to my head. I reached over and felt the bag for the tenth time, just to make sure all the hard little bumps were still in there. *Fine.*

*   *   *

His truck wasn't there yet. The seashells of the driveway crunched beneath my wheels, and no other car was in sight. Dolphin Dance was even more beautiful than I remembered, with its gables and curled wooden window accents, the looks-professionally-done plants on the porch, and the rich green sod lawn in front. I noticed with a degree of amusement and a blush of memory that there was no trace of smashed strawberry shortcake on the ground. We'd given the seagulls a treat, it seemed.

The house was quiet inside. Just the hum of the refrigerator. I clicked on the air-conditioning to make it a little more welcoming to the other guests on their way and spun the dial to start the ceiling fans on low. Mimosas, I thought, then set out for the kitchen. Yes, Ren had three bottles of champagne chilling, and a big bowl of oranges waited for Emma. I had no guilt whatsoever juicing them up, delighting in the splash of each pull of the lever. I lined up eight crystal champagne goblets, and for good measure put together a cheese platter with water crackers, rinsed some grapes, sliced a kiwi, and took off the fuzzy skin from each circle.

A tube of Pillsbury bread dough waited in the refrigerator, and although Russell would not approve of the prepackaged variety, I peeled off the label, pressed a spoon to the seam to hear that fabulous *pop* as the dough broke free of its captivity. I rubbed a baking sheet with sweet butter, turned up the oven, and stretched out the cold, yeasty bread dough onto the pan, making five angled knife gashes across the top.

With my mini feast well on the way, I hurried upstairs to unpack, to hang my clothes against the quick wrinkle factor of the ocean air, tuck my socks and lingerie away in the back of the dresser drawer, and drop the velvet pouch of jewels (worth more than I made in several years combined) into the vase next to my bed.

Downstairs, the front door opened.

"Mylie!" It was his voice.

Followed by the little cherub. "*Daaa-ad! Stop* it!"

Where was Joan Crawford when you needed her?

As I headed down the stairs, a blur of white T-shirt passed me with a sneer. Emma was running to her room. To slam the door.

"Looks like no dance recital tonight either," I joked and bounced down the rest of the stairs. I landed right at his feet, and he held me in. "Hi," I breathed, accepting his kiss.

"Hi." He smiled, his nose nuzzling into my hair, inhaling. "Something smells good."

"It's Pantene," I sighed, and he started laughing. "What?"

"I meant the bread." He squeezed me.

I forgot about the bread!

It didn't smell burned, so there was no reason to panic and slide in my socks across the kitchen floor as I scrambled for the oven door. He followed behind me, finger hooked into the back of my shorts, brushing against the top strap of my thong. The bread was perfect. Golden brown.

"Nice welcome buffet there, Mylie." Glenn winked, still too creepy with the flirting eyes while his wife was pregnant and I was sleeping with his brother-in-law.

"Thanks," I said, keeping my eyes down on the cheese platter. Russell placed his hand over mine, either reassuring me or giving Glenn the "Back off, buddy." I'd be happy with either.

The kitchen was a blend of sounds: laughter, clinks of champagne flutes, pops of more champagne corks. (Ren had additional bottles in the basement refrigerator. You knew you were living right when you needed downstairs storage for your extra champagne.) Russell took my hand and led me away from all that . . . to the hammock in the backyard. We set our champagne glasses down on the table, climbed in, and then I handed him his glass before reaching for my own.

"I have to work tomorrow, but I'll be back tomorrow night," I said, accepting his free hand in mine.

"Uh oh, demanding client?"

"No, busy client." I winked. "And I'm not at liberty to discuss it."

He knew what that meant. "Ah, you've got a big fish on the line."

"You could say that." I nodded.

"Are you bringing them here?" he asked, and it struck me immediately. Celia would *love* this place. And how great would it be for Ren and Pete to have a celebrity stay here? They could . . . Wait, no publicity. My mind whirred. How could I arrange this? It would be stupid for me to waltz Celia Tyranova and Kick Lyons into a summer house with eight other people and still keep the wedding plans a secret. Although . . . Bryan's tabloid photo *did* bust our secret wide open on an international scale . . . Hmmm . . .

"Ren," I called out as she strolled across the lawn, champagne glass in one hand, sleeping baby cradled in her other arm. She joined us, pulling up an Adirondack chair with one free finger. "What do you think about my bringing our bride and groom here this weekend?"

She was stunned into nonblinking. "Here?"

"Yes." I nodded, hoping that she'd come up with a way to make it work. I just didn't want to leave the house and drive back up to the city. Ah, priorities. Some hard-core business-woman I was, not wanting to climb out of the hammock with my boyfriend long enough to talk to a client and make a six-figure commission.

Ren looked from side to side, assessing our crowd as they mingled on the lawn. Glenn would definitely be a problem. He'd be all over Celia. Then Ren smiled. Something had occurred to her. "Russell, what's Emma's favorite movie?"

Russell's answer was just what we wanted to hear.

A few minutes later, Ren and I were in her office, pacing and whispering up the possibilities.

"Isn't it a little wrong to bring them into a house full of people who are going to *freak out* over meeting them?"

"Aren't they used to that, though?"

"They wanted privacy for their wedding."

"We promised them that."

"Bringing them here and letting them get bombarded by questions . . ."

"We can tell everyone to just act normal."

"*Right*. Like that's going to happen."

"And then there's Glenn . . ."

A knock sounded at the door. Russell. "You ladies need to whisper lower," he joked. "I have an idea if you'd like to hear it."

That's my guy. He asks first.

"What if I take everyone out on the boat tomorrow, and you guys stay here to meet with your client?"

Ren and I stood silent. His perfect solution took a while to slide down and sink in.

"Celia, it's Mylie." I cradled the phone in my neck as both Ren and Russell listened in. "I have an idea about our meeting tomorrow. How would you like to come to a bed and breakfast right on the beach?"

I nodded, gave a few *uh huh*'s, then held up the thumbs-up sign. Ren kicked her feet in the air, not having met Celia and Kick yet, and Russell smiled with pride at his being Mr. Fix-It.

Then my smile faded. "A helipad? No, I don't know where you can land a helicopter at the beach. But I'll find out."

The plan was for Russell to take our crew out on the boat at 8:00 A.M., and Celia and Kick would show up around

10:00 A.M., helicoptering in from New York City. That gave us two hours to clean the place, set out fresh flowers, make some hors d'oeuvres, chill some wine. We were planning a stealth party right smack in the middle of our weekend with friends. If anyone could do it, Ren and I could.

Until . . .

"Daddy, I don't want to go on the boat." She must have sensed that it was important to me. Little saboteur.

"You love the boat, Emma," Russell coaxed her, looking up at me with a what-do-we-do-now? expression.

"Don't you want to go fishing and help Uncle Glenn reel in a great white shark?"

"No." She turned out her bottom lip, which I'd heard Russell couldn't resist. Somehow it didn't look so cute to me. "I want to stay here and watch television."

"Well, we're going on the boat, Emma, so go get your sneakers on," he said more firmly. "Go on."

And the tantrum started with a squinting of one eye. A twitch, really. Her lips quivered. Her chin throbbed. She was summoning up a good one, with all of her might. Her little hands balled into fists, and I swear her eyes turned black. "I . . . said . . . I . . . don't . . . *want* . . . to . . ."

"Emma!" Russell shouted, and even I stepped back a little bit. "Stop it right now. Go get your sneakers."

"I *hate* you, Daddy!"

"Forget it, Russ, we can go on the boat another time." Good old Glenn. Always saving the day.

Ren panicked, looking at her watch. It was getting late. "I have an idea," Ren chirped, always the calmer and soother. "Why doesn't Emma stay here with us? While we're working, she can watch television."

Ren, are you out of your mind?

"I hear there's a Kick Lyons movie on HBO Family," she said, and that was when it all became clear to me. Emma's tantrum face turned back into cherub face. She was a fan.

"Kick! Kick! Kick!" Emma danced, one of her other personalities apparently taking over the Dark Force she'd just unleashed on us now.

"Ren, are you sure?" Russell asked, but looked at me. I must have looked mortified. All I needed for my you-come-to-us meeting with Kick and Celia was for adorable little Emma to spray paint "I hate Mylie" across the walls of the kitchen.

"It's going to be fine." Ren smiled a little too cheerily. "We'll have Girls' Time Out."

Russell ran his hands through his hair, seeing Doom written all over this one.

Was it so bad of us to try to win Emma over by flaunting our connection with Kick Lyons? Was it worse than my original priority not to leave my very sexy boyfriend for a meeting? We were painting it up nice with an offer to come relax by the seashore in a refurbished bed and breakfast, and weren't we sweet to find a place of pure privacy for Kick and Celia. It was all a not-so-finely crafted scheme with plenty of potential pitfalls.

Russell seemed to be adding them up right now. "Mylie, are you sure? Emma can be—"

A handful. Difficult. Demanding. Evil.

"Emma's going to be fine." Ren put her arm around the little girl. "Or else she sleeps in the attic with the ghosts."

Emma was terrified of the attic. *Isn't Auntie Ren the best?*

"The . . . the attic?" Emma's mouth drew into a little circle. "You'd make me sleep in the attic?"

"If you're bad . . . ," Ren sang.

Emma turned to her father, all sweetness and light, and crossed her finger over her heart. "I'll be good for Auntie Ren and Mylie, Daddy, I promise."

"Okay," Russell said, with just a hint of fear in his voice. "I'll have my cell with me, so if there are any problems, we're turning the boat around," he said to Ren. "Just tie her up with duct tape until I get back." He winked. "Kidding, angel." A kiss on the top of her head.

A few short moments later, Ren, Emma, and I were standing on the porch, waving goodbye to our SUV full of boat-bound friends, and the clock started ticking on our scheme. We didn't even bother trying to swear the kid to secrecy about who was coming over. It would be fine for her to tell, since Kick and Celia would be long gone and no in-person damage could be done. Glenn couldn't grab Celia's butt.

Singing a little song, Emma skipped off to the television room and clicked it on to HBO Family. Ren had done her homework. Kick Lyons's only PG movie, *Knights in Nantucket*, was about to start. As the movie's opening notes sounded, we checked her out. Her eyes were glazed over. She was in deep focus and concentration. Her heart rate had probably slowed. She wouldn't react to anything going on around her, being in a kiddie TV coma, mesmerized by Kick Lyons riding on a horse through a field of grass.

"Okay," Ren said, pushing her closed fist against mine. "Let's rock it."

Ren Swiffered from floor to ceiling, while I took on bathroom duty. Fresh toilet paper on every roll, fresh hand towels spritzed with Febreze, seashell soaps set out in Lenox dishes at every sink.

Floral arrangements brought in from the garage, only slightly wilted but salvageable, and placed in the entryway foyer and on the kitchen table.

Wineglasses on the table, ready for a toast before business.

"What are you doing?" Emma padded into the kitchen in her socks. "Why are you cleaning?"

"We have work friends coming over," Ren answered her. "That's why we're not on the boat with everyone else, sweetie."

"Can I help?"

Oh, God, no, please. Send her to the attic right now.

"You can make sure your room is clean, okay?" Ren suggested, and Emma rolled her eyes.

"That's not fun," Emma whined. "I want to cut something up."

Ren and I looked at each other. We wouldn't even speak it aloud.

"Emma, go watch your movie. I'll bring you some popcorn, okay?" Ren tried, and that did it. The kid had mastered the halfhearted can-I-help? offer and wound up with a tray full of goodies brought right to her lap on the couch.

I, of course, was the delivery girl. "Want anything else, Emma?"

"Yes." She smiled devilishly. "I want you to leave."

"Emma." I sat down next to her. "Why do you dislike me so much?" Hate was a strong word.

"You're not my mommy, and I don't want you to be." She shrugged, bored with me.

"But you know . . ." I smiled, even though I wanted to throttle her. "There are some advantages to being my friend instead," I sang. The kid smelled presents. I had her hooked.

"Like . . ." She looked at me out of the corner of her eye.

"Like I have very good friends," I baited her. "And I think you'll like them."

That dumbfounded her. *Friends?* What did that mean?

"Mylie," Ren called me. "What are you doing?"

Trying to entice the kid to like me.

"We have a lot to do," Ren called out, and I could hear platters coming out of the refrigerator. Someone had gotten into the Alouette spread already, so we had to smooth over the missing section to make it look untouched.

"Mylie." Emma stood in the doorway, shifting from foot to foot.

"Yes?" I just couldn't bring myself to say "Yes, sweetie." It just wouldn't form on my tongue.

"I'm going to go upstairs and clean my room, okay?"

I smiled. "Okay, Emma. Just your room."

She ran away, her arms flailing around, and her little feet made surprisingly loud stomping noises on the stairs. Unwisely, we trusted her.

"What did you *do?!*" I could hear Ren upstairs, and I ran to the scene of the crime. Emma had stripped my bed, taken all my clothes out of my closet and jammed them into the trash basket, and dumped my purse all over the floor.

The angel just stood there and smiled. "I was *helping,*" she said. "Daddy says that when you start a new project, things get messy."

"Go downstairs and watch your movie, Emma," Ren warned, and we had no choice but to shove all of my things into the closet and deal with it later. We had food on the stove, things in the oven, and we had about fifteen minutes before Kick and Celia were scheduled to arrive. Luckily, Hollywood types were always late.

And they were. About twenty minutes late.

"Celia! Kick!" I hugged them both, hoping the Bruise Crew had come along so they could keep Emma in line. No luck. They were probably at a dogfight somewhere.

"Mylie!" Celia hugged me and rocked me back and forth. Kick gave me a quick kiss on the cheek. He handed over a bottle of wine, a gift for the house.

Ren stood to the side, starry-eyed, breathlessly waiting for introductions. "Celia, Kick, this is Renata. She owns the house."

"With my husband Pete. He's on a boat," she stammered, and Celia and Kick shook her hand. She was almost hyperventilating.

"Ah, a fishing man," Kick said, assessing the entryway and nodding. He had a thing for architecture, I knew, since he designed the additions to Celia's estate. We didn't have a chapel here.

"I *love* the place!" Celia clapped her hands. "I've never been to a bed and breakfast. This is *lovely*."

"Thank you." Ren beamed. "Let's take you on a tour." She swept her hand outward and led the way. The two hottest celebrities in the world were walking through her home, looking at her photos on the walls, complimenting her kitchen.

And then we reached the television room. Emma sat slumped on the couch, her head on a pillow. "And this is Emma," I announced. Without looking up, Emma gave a bratty wave. Her eyes were on the movie.

"You're watching my movie." Kick smiled.

"It's not *your* movie," Emma huffed, until she realized she wasn't talking to me. Ren and I stepped back, crossed our arms over our chests, and watched it sink in. Emma looked from Kick to the TV screen and back again. Then at Celia, who she blinkingly didn't recognize. Celia didn't make PG movies, but Emma had a vague realization of who she was. "You're . . ."

"Kick Lyons." He stepped forward to shake her hand, and she got all smiley and shy. I almost expected her to run to Renata and hug her leg with her finger hooked into the side of her mouth, swaying from side to side adorably. But Emma didn't do that scene. She beamed at him, blinking slowly, then again looked at the TV screen. "Yes, it's me. I'm a friend of your Aunt Mylie's."

Big mistake!

"She's *not* my aunt. She's *not* my mother!" Emma yelled, and Celia's eyes widened.

I leaned in to whisper to Celia, "I'm dating her father. She's *not* happy about it."

"Ah." Celia nodded and stepped forward to help. "Well, you're lucky to know Mylie. She's our favorite person in the world."

"That's right, she is," Kick said, sitting down next to

Emma and draping his arm around her. If she was two years older, she'd be on her cell phone calling all of her friends.

"*My*lie is your favorite person?" Emma blinked, looking at me with an unmistakable message saying "What could you possibly see in her?"

"That's right." Celia nodded. "You should take the time to get to know her. She's very fun."

"Would you like to see my dance recital?" Emma jumped up and down in her seat, and Celia and Kick laughed.

"Later on, sweetie," Ren promised. "We have work to do, so you stay here and watch the movie, and we'll be in the backyard talking, okay?"

"Okay," Emma promised, little angel hands folded in her lap. Her eyes having turned back to blue.

As we walked out to the kitchen for wine and snacks, we could hear Emma's heavy footsteps on the stairs. Probably going to get her doll or something.

"She's adorable." Kick looked up at the ceiling, as if he could see right through. "Whose is she?"

"Mylie's boyfriend's daughter," Ren announced proudly, having waited four years to say "Mylie's boyfriend" about Russell.

"Yeah, she's not warming up to Mylie so well." Celia shook her head. "I had the same problem with my step-mother."

"Isn't that the one you buried in the backyard?" Kick joked, and we clinked our wineglasses together. It was time to get to work.

"Ta da!" Emma showed up in the doorway, prancing, leaping, plié-ing, spinning around a little too fast until she banged head-first into the sliding glass door.

"Ooooh, that's going to leave a mark." Kick laughed, and Celia punched him in the arm.

"Emma, sweetie, we're working now," Ren called out from our table in the yard. "Go practice your routine inside and we'll call you when it's showtime."

"Look at her outfit, it's so cute." Celia smiled, and I could tell from that warm grin she had a baby craving going on. Emma's costume was white with silver sparkle edging at the hem and neckline. Her little white tights were twisted around her legs, a little too big for her scrawny body. Her ballet shoes were white as well. She was a little mass of sparkles. And when she moved closer, I could see why.

Around her neck was the diamond necklace. The one from the vase in my bedroom. I saw it first. Kick saw it second. Ren probably thought it was one of those Barbie Sparkle necklaces, but it was in reality a six-figure necklace from Harry Winston, Kick's gift to Celia. Which was now being worn by a six-year-old.

"Mylie," Kick warned, and I sprang toward the little girl, grabbing her by the arm and pulling her inside. Celia was baffled. Why was I being so rough with the little girl?

Safely inside with the glass door closed, I grabbed her by the shoulders. "Emma, this is *mine*. You stole it from my room."

I reached around to the back of her neck, and she struggled against me, pulling so hard I swore she might break the necklace. A string of obscenities came out of my mouth without my knowing it, and I looked to the front door for a moment. With my luck, that would have been the perfect time for Russell to walk in holding a big bass in one hand and seeing me ripping at his daughter's throat, which I pretty much had wanted to do since the minute I met her.

With the necklace safely in my hand, I tore up the stairs to my room. There on my bed sat the velvet pouch. The necklace box lay open, the contents in my hand. And the ring box . . . was gone.

"Emma!" I yelled. "Get up here right now!" The windows were open. Kick and Celia could hear everything. In a heartbeat, Kick was at my bedroom door.

"What the hell, Mylie?" He was angry. Crimson angry. "I asked you to protect the jewelry."

"I had it hidden in a vase," I nearly cried. "*Emma!*"

She was hiding. The ring box, Celia's wedding ring, was gone.

Oh, you are so sleeping in the attic, little girl.

Emma showed up at the door, with her lip curled. "I was just playing," she sniffled.

"Where did you put the small box?" Kick got face-to-face with her.

"What small box?" She played innocent.

"The small box that was in this pouch, Emma," I warned. "Don't mess with me." Somehow I doubted the line "Don't mess with me" was in too many of those "How to get along with your boyfriend's children" books and articles.

"I didn't see a small box," she lied. "Mylie must have lost it."

Kick looked at me, deflated. "This kid really does hate you."

Ren could hear the arguing, the shuffling of furniture, and it was harder and harder to keep Celia occupied. When I leaned my head out the window, I could see Renata expertly trying to distract Celia with images on her laptop, but Celia's eyes were turned up toward my window. For all she knew, Kick and I were having a knock-down, drag-out fight. My room certainly looked as if we had.

Into Emma's room we went, sifting and sorting through her little bags of clothes, her toy bag, her hamper, under her pillows, everywhere. "Emma, that box is not Mylie's. It's mine," Kick said. "I'd like you to give it back."

"Get out of my rooooom!" Emma cried, scared now for the seriousness of the matter.

"Emma, where is the ring box?" I tried, softer. "Kick paid a lot of money for that, and if you don't give it back to him, he's going to call the police."

On me.

Her eyes grew wild, and she started to cry. "I don't know!" came her self-protective answer.

We continued like that for a half hour, tearing the place apart, down in the living room now, checking underneath the sofa cushions. I could hear Ren calming Celia outside, assuring her that Kick and I were working on the computer inside. Because that always involved things crashing to the floor and a six-year-old crying her head off.

This was a nightmare.

The ring was gone.

"Kick and I have to go," Celia announced, looking at her watch. "We're taking the copter back up to the city and catching a show."

Kick looked around, glancing at the bookshelves, still trying to find his ring.

"I'll find it," I promised. "I swear I will."

"You'd better," he said. "I know it's not your fault, Mylie, but I'm pissed off right now. Of all the things for her to take . . ."

"I know." I took both of his hands in mine. My cell phone rang. It was Russell.

What else was going to happen?

"Mylie, we're on our way back." He sighed. "Chip's girlfriend doesn't like boats." Ah, Chip's girlfriend. The self-absorbed twenty-year-old he left his wife and kids for. She'd spent the whole morning complaining that the ocean air was drying out her hair. And talking on her cell phone about a rave this weekend. We hated her. Chip lusted for her. We were stuck with her.

"Yeah, we're done here," I moaned, and he could hear it in my voice.

"What did she do?" he asked, sensing exactly what was wrong.

"The *ring?*" Russell paced. "And how much was it?"
"Over a hundred grand." I winced. "I had it hidden in the vase next to my bed."
"Emma, get over here!" he boomed. She scurried up, innocently, ready to charm her daddy. "Where is the box you took from Mylie's room?"
"I dunno." She swayed back and forth sweetly, her hands held behind her back.
"Emma, this is not funny."
To her, it was.
"Daddy could get in a lot of trouble if you don't find it."
In the other room, the houseguests made a racket, opening wine bottles and beer bottles, none the wiser about whose empty wineglasses were in the sink. They had missed the megacelebrities who left just moments ago. Now the men produced the fish they caught, and the women kept their distance from Chip's girlfriend, who preferred the company of the men anyway. She flirted shamelessly with Glenn and with Pete, bending over to make sure everyone saw the lines of her thong, then tossing her peroxide blond hair. "Renata, want me to help with anything?" she breathed, trying really hard to sound like Marilyn Monroe. It just sounded like she had asthma.
"No thanks," Ren quipped, cutting the bread into slices, very tense. Pete looked at his wife and gave her a hand signal to calm down. She gave him a hand signal of her own, down below counter level where most of the others couldn't see.
"I'll just get some ketchup." Chip's girlfriend nodded, stunning us all that she wanted ketchup to go with her shrimp cocktail. It was red. It was "dippy." What was the problem?
The noise in the kitchen continued, until we heard a squeal.
"Oh, my God, oh, my God, oh, my God!"
Everyone turned, hearts beating fast. Chip's girlfriend

Staci stood in front of the open refrigerator, jumping up and down, her hair flying all over the place, her hands flapping. With all the jumping, her breasts—of course—didn't move an inch. "Chip, honey! Oh, my God!"

What? She really likes our brand of ketchup?

In her hand . . . the ring box. Opened to reveal the dazzling diamond ring that Kick designed for Celia.

"Of *course* I'll marry you!" she yelled out, then dove onto Chip, nearly knocking him over. Chip, just in it for the ride, looked *terrified.*

That's what you get for dating a bimbo, Chipper.

"Um . . . ," Chip said, and Renata grabbed the box out of her hand, tossed it across the kitchen to me, Staci's eyes following it hungrily.

"Thanks for finding it, Staci," Ren said shortly. "I've been looking for my mother's ring box all day. Emma must have been playing with it." And with that, she stabbed the serving forks into the salad over and over, the messiest salad toss I'd ever seen her do.

I ran for my cell phone to call Kick. Russell ran for Emma, hopefully to punish her. And Chip ran from the house to throw up in the rose bushes. Another day in paradise.

"Emma is just never going to get to do her dance recital." I giggled, now safely nestled in Russell's arms, the hammock swaying gently. The houseguests huddled in groups, men and women separate, both circles talking about Chip and his girlfriend, who were upstairs fighting right now about the ring debacle. The girl could screech. Pretty on the outside, ugly on the inside.

"I wish I could blame her age, but that's not it." Russell sighed, and it took me a second to remember that I'd just commented on Emma, not Chip's girlfriend.

"Now she's mad that I made Kick Lyons go away." I shook my head. "I am her worst nightmare."

"I thought for sure . . ." Russell started, then allowed the thought to trail off. We were both thinking the same thing. We both thought that having Emma meet one of her favorite movie stars was going to swing her over into the I-Love-Mylie camp. But no dice.

"Do you have any ideas?" I tried, loving the warmth of his hand in mine, hearing his soft, slow heartbeat against my cheek.

"She's just going to have to get used to it. Don't let her scare you off, okay?"

He's concerned about that.

"Never going to happen," I assured him.

"Good."

"Meet me on the roof tonight at 3:00 A.M.?"

"No, three's not good for me," he joked. "How does 2:00 A.M. work for you?"

"I'll pencil you in."

Chapter 32

"*Hey, Screwup.*" It was Kick on my voice mail. Seemed I had a new nickname. I'd been called worse, and that little fiasco with Emma and the ring certainly could've earned me a much worse one. "*You're coming out here to the estate this week, so try to keep track of the ring box long enough to get it to me, okay?*"

"*Mylie, it's Mom. Just checking in. Everything's fine here. Your father's working on the lawn right now, and your sister is on her way to Cancun with some friends. And her new boyfriend. Speaking of which—*"

I hit the Save button before she launched into a thousand questions about "the nice boy" I had hinted at last week just to get her off my back. I wasn't in the mood for a lecture on how hard it was to date a man who had children. "They're never really yours," she had said in the past, preferring genetic grandchildren over incidental ones.

"*Mylie, it's Ren. Freezer broke at Zoe's. We have puddles, not ice sculptures. So make sure you bring your hip boots when you come in to work tomorrow, okay? I've called to order replacement ice sculptures, and Zorro's charging us double for the rush job.*" Yes, our ice sculptor went by the name Zorro. *"So work your magic with the budget, because it's going to cost us."*

I sighed and pushed my hair back over my ear, pencil in my teeth as was usual for me checking my messages.

"Mylie, it's Zoe. Freezer's broken at the shop. That's all for now. Ta!"

I checked my watch. In ten minutes, I'd be out the door to catch the Sunday night practice of a drum and bugle corps at a nearby college campus. Two hundred sweaty college kids performing to Lionel Ritchie's "All Night Long" and me running across the field in a suit and chignon, waving a twenty-five-thousand-dollar check at the drum line. Should be fun.

I've underestimated the drum and bugle corps. Instead of running across the field in my stocking feet, I sat in the bleachers and watched them. A primal surge ran down my back as the drums beat, the brass blaring, the entire line of musicians moving into a single-file line, stopping for a beat, and then blasting out a high note as they all moved forward in high, dramatic steps. Behind them, enormous wispy curtains in purple and gold dashed back and forth, their human carriers hidden by the tight lineup of brass players. *I have an idea!*

Before I could whip out my cell phone, the boys came forward.

The drum line, chins jutting the rhythm of their solo, their hands *flying*, fast as anything, switching to play each other's drums, tossing their drumsticks to one another. They tilted their heads backward, all the way, to look at the sky, with their hands still playing the drums, still crossing over to play the other guy's drums, *still* tossing their drumsticks to one another. All with their eyes upward. It was impossible not to move to that rhythm.

My cell phone was out in a heartbeat. "Zoe . . . authorize me to pay double. I've got gold here."

* * *

"Did you get them?" Ren asked, wet circles on her knees, a bucket next to her, a giant yellow sponge in her hand. Our job was so glamorous.

"I got 'em." I smiled, and Zoe followed me into the room. "Hey, Zoe, Ren's one hundred percent in on this wedding. She saved the day when I met with Kick and Celia at the beach, really distracted Celia and got a boatload done while I worked with Kick." *Looking for the lost wedding ring with Kick, actually.* I was talking too fast, but getting the job done, clearing my friend for her due part. "So I'm splitting my commission with her."

Zoe nodded. She'd probably already thought of that. "Done."

Ren beamed. Since she was working the rest of our weddings pretty much on her own, now splitting this commission with me, she'd be making more than both of us. Dolphin Dance would be open for business very soon, it seemed.

"Now, here's what I have from the drum and bugle corps . . . the *entire* drum line, twelve of them. They're *hot*. They play with their eyes closed, hands like lightning. It's the most exciting thing ever, and you have to see it and hear it to believe it." I was out of breath. "So what we're going to do is this . . . I got two trumpeters to play the "Trumpet Voluntary" before Celia walks down the aisle. We're going to regal them up with fabric hangs sporting her family crest."

Ren and Zoe nodded.

"I have two dozen tall silk handlers who are going to be standing in a half circle around the back of the altar throughout the ceremony. They have ten-foot-high thick wire flag-poles that bend, so the effect is an arching, waving fabric backdrop, a really ethereal curtain of sorts."

Zoe nodded, impressed.

"We'll sew up white and silver with Swarovski crystals on each fabric panel so they'll catch the sun," I continued. "And then they'll switch to just the lightest lilac-colored flags to match the color of the sunset at the close of the ceremony, also with Swarovskis. So we have interactive backdrop." I could see Ren adding up the amount of sewing she'd be doing. Each Swarovski had to be hand-placed and sewn. Well, she had to know something big was coming after my announcement that she'd get half my commission.

"When the ceremony is over, all the flags move to the sides, like a curtain opening in front of Kick and Celia."

"Nice!" Zoe clapped her hands. "Then the doves?"

"No, not yet." I smiled. "Then the drum line. All twelve of them will march forward, and I've asked them to play the solo I heard them play at their practice. It's just incredible, so primal you wouldn't believe."

"I think you've used the word *primal* about ten times today," Ren joked.

"Seriously, Ren, it's like something takes you over," I breathed. "It's going to be *amazing*. Celia's going to love it."

"And the damage was . . ." Zoe raised an eyebrow.

"That's the best part. . . ." I stood taller. "I got it *all* for the twenty-five thousand. The trumpeters, the flagbearers, the entire drum line, and their staff to set up the equipment."

"And the confidentiality thing?" Zoe blinked.

"I didn't tell them who the clients were." I danced in place. "They think it's some corporate bigwig throwing a party for his daughter on the company dime. I'll tell them on the morning of the wedding, and I'm going to have a camera guy there to tape their reaction when they find out. When word hits the press, and we know it will, they're going to want video of it. And we'll own the rights."

"Wow." Ren coughed. "You're good."

I know.

Lunchtime break. Four men in dirty jeans worked on our freezer to get it up and running again, Zoe went out for a pedicure, and Ren and I checked out Sasha Worthington's wedding Web site just for kicks.

"The clock is ticking! In just a few months, I'll be a WIFE. That reminds me of the time I played Johnny Depp's wife in the movie . . . wait . . . that wasn't me. I only WISH I could play Johnny Depp's wife in a movie! ☺"

"Just in case Tim Burton is reading her wedding blog." I laughed, taking a big bite of my Chalupa.

"She's trying to get work through this thing." Ren laughed, picking the onions out of hers. She had a client meeting in a half hour.

"Donnie and I went to try on wedding rings today, and the bling is the thing!"

Does anyone say "bling" anymore? I thought that was passe.

"We'll have matching wedding bands, and mine will have fourteen carats of the pointy diamonds."

" 'Pointy' diamonds?" Ren wondered.

"Marquise. She probably couldn't spell it."

"And to thank you all for being my Number One fans—"

"That makes no sense."

"You expect logic from this girl?"

"The first 1000 people to buy my new CD will be invited to my post-wedding bash at Roseland. So come and eat cake with me!"

This was just painful to even look at, but we couldn't tear our eyes away. And it got better.

"And Donnie's new CD drops next week, so the first 10,000 people to order that magnificent piece of work by my loving sex god will get an autographed picture of moi. Kisses! Love, Sasha."

"Well, at least he's not using her." I laughed and shut down the site.

My cell phone, on vibrate, danced on the table. With the

freezer workmen here, any work talk was strictly forbidden. Not just for Celia and Kick's wedding, but for all of them. We had other celebrity events, some A-list, some B- and C-list, also events that would make the society pages, the daughters and sons of the fabulously nonfamous. We'd had incidents in the past of paparazzi getting in here, posing as delivery people, computer fix-it guys, even a very shrewd pair of potential bride and groom clients who actually were not engaged at all but worked for a British tabloid. They left a bug in one of our plants to get the inside scoop on our client list. Yes, part of my job was inspecting the potted plants and popping open the phone to check for listening devices. At one point, Zoe wanted me to throw out all of our pens every night and stock up with new ones in the morning. CIA spies used pen cameras, after all. Now we circle each of our pens with yellow tape and only use those.

We were no strangers to taking extra security measures around here. We shredded everything. We erased computer disks with magnets. We had about fifty levels of firewall on our computers. It was all necessity. The media got a huge sum of money when they got inside scoop on our most private events, so they kept coming up with new methods. One of those freezer fix-it guys could have been paid on his way in here for anything that he overheard.

The cell phone call was not work-related, though. It was Russell. I smiled and picked it up. "On a lunch break?"

"Running to the market," he said. "Seems I bought the wrong kind of wonton wrappers."

"There are different kinds?"

"The client says so. She refused my dinner shipment because the wontons are too thick."

I rolled my eyes. Russell probably had it worse than we did. We got diva behavior from many of our brides, but these were people Russell had to *feed* every day. *This chunky peanut butter is too chunky . . . I'm not paying. The tuna tartare was too tartare . . . so I'm not paying.*

"Well, how dare you serve her thick wontons!" I mock-scolded him, and Ren nodded because she figured out who was on the phone.

"Next, she'll want left-handed chopsticks," he joked, but I could hear his frustration underneath his laugh. This client was a handful. "Hey, when do you leave for California?"

"Tomorrow night. Why?" *He has a plan.*

"I have a plan," he announced. "See if Zoe will let you out of there at lunchtime, and we'll meet down at Dolphin Dance so we can have the place to ourselves for a few hours."

"Ooooooh, that sounds *nice.*" I could easily switch my plane tickets to fly out of Philadelphia, then be closer to Dolphin Dance when I got back on Friday. "I'll be there at two tomorrow."

Time alone with him at Dolphin Dance. No Emma. Five hours alone with him in the house. We can walk around naked. We can lie in front of the fireplace in the middle of the living room. We can be as loud as we want, as often as we want. Which lingerie should I bring?

And if I go to bed early tonight, tomorrow comes even faster.

Chapter 33

Russell and I drove up into the crunchy seashell driveway pretty much at the same time. At noon. I was pretty much worthless at work, so I faked a migraine and took off early. He was planning to get here early to surprise me, but I ruined that.

But the real surprise came when we saw Pete's car in the driveway, his big black SUV parked crookedly. And a little white car next to it. Staci's car. We knew it from the vanity plates: STACIRX. As in "Staci Rocks," not Staci is a pharmacist.

Russell climbed out of his car the same way I did. In shock. Nauseous. I switched to anger before he did. There was no what-should-we-do? discussion about the nuances of friend integrity. Did you tell or not tell? Did you get involved or not? There was no fear of walking into that house and getting an unwelcome image seared onto the backs of our eyelids forever. I had no worries about catching them in the act. I had my cell phone out to get the picture as proof for Ren. She'd never fully believe us with just a story, as much as she trusted us. I was just glad it was us catching Pete and Staci and not Ren. Seeing a blurry cell phone photo was going to be hard enough for her.

I had my key in the door and opened it slowly, quietly. I wanted to hear before I saw. Russell was right behind me, and I hated this for him, too. There was no way he wasn't re-playing his own memories right now, remembering when he caught his ex-wife in the same selfish stupidity. Pete had screwed us all. And I remember thinking, *What a shame we'll have to burn all the sheets in the house.* Staci was the type of girl who made you want to do that kind of thing.

A giggle from upstairs. I took the stairs slowly, knowing exactly which ones to step on in the far right corners. The middles of some of the stairs squeaked. Russell followed my footsteps.

"Gentle, Pete, you'll hurt the baby," she squealed, and I al-most lost my footing on the stairs. Russell grabbed me at my lower back, steadied me. I turned to him, my face in a red fury and mouthed "She's pregnant?" Russell's mouth hung open. This was *not* what he had in mind.

At the top of the steps, I paused. Which room were they in? *Come on, bimbo, speak again.*

No luck. Instead, we heard grunting from Pete, along with some very cheesy porno talk. I doubted he talked this way with Ren. *Oh, God, I'm about to throw open a door and see my best friend's husband naked, doing the most hideous woman on earth.* My hand was on the doorknob, and I'm sure I was imagining it, but the doorknob felt hot to the touch. I hoped the room was on fire. In a heartbeat, I twisted open the knob and threw open the door, clicked cell phone shot after cell phone shot as the shock registered on their faces. Pete practically threw her across the room, and she landed on the floor with a hard thud. Worrying only about himself, he gathered the sheets around him as I called him every name in the book. "Not so worried about hurting the *baby*, are you, Pete? Maybe you should see if *Staci* is okay, huh, Pete? What a good *father* you are, Pete!"

He held up his hand against my cell phone clicks. *Covering your face at this point does nothing for you. And adjust the sheets a little better, will you?*

"Jesus, Pete, are you out of your mind?" Russell spoke, pulling me gently back by the shoulder. "With *that?*" He gestured toward Staci, who looked surprisingly fine about just being discovered. I was sure she was used to it. Probably a little disappointed that it wasn't the wife this time. She was the type to call the wife, to show up and ring the bell at family dinnertime and tell the whole family.

Pete just lay there, holding his face in his hands, his bare butt sticking out, murmuring something about not meaning to, and she came on to him. He didn't know she was going to be here, she must have followed him from his house, he was just checking the water heater, and it just kind of happened. And then he grew silent. Probably hating the sound of his own voice. He pressed his face into the pillow, and I hoped he'd snuff himself out that way. His shoulders started to bounce up and down a little bit, then more. He was crying.

"How *could* you?" I yelled. "You have a wife and a baby." Just pure disgust was what I felt for him. He was not a man at all.

He pulled his face up out of the pillow and looked at us, trying to think of something—anything—to grasp on to to save his skin. The wheels were turning, but he had nothing. Lacking a good explanation, and further displaying his lack of loyalty in any area of his life, he decided to throw his buddy into the fire. "Hey, it's Chip's kid," he choked out between tears, and Russell and I just recoiled. Did he think we were that easily distracted? That we would sit down on the bed and nod along with him, concerning ourselves with "What will poor Chip do about this fiasco?" Um no, Pete. This one was all you. But he had managed to add another layer to my repulsion.

Pete and Chip would be taking paternity tests. Our circle

of friends had just turned into something I clicked past on daytime TV. Pete had brought this level of shame to our circle of friends. He'd classed us down. And we were all sick enough about Staci eating off the dinner plates.

She had nothing to say, just sat there with a sheet held up badly against her chest, and I swore she dropped it a little to give Russell a show. He wouldn't even look at her. His black gaze of hatred fell squarely on Pete. That Staci chick didn't exist to us. We reserved our loathing for Pete.

"Don't tell Ren, please . . . ," he whimpered, crying into his pillow. "I'll do anything."

"You already established that, Pete," I spat. "You'll. Do. Anything."

"Staci, get your clothes on and get out of my friend Renata's house," Russell ordered without actually looking at her. "We'll see you in court."

And not the Style Court, I wanted to say, but mocking her now was just going to make me look small and foolish.

"Court?" she blinked. "What do you mean, court? Hey, the coke's not mine."

Coke? Sure enough, there on the bedside table . . .

"Ren, it's Mylie," I said into the phone, gripping it so tightly my knuckles hurt. "I've spoken to Zoe, and you and the baby are coming out to California and I'll meet up with you there. Drop everything right now, go home and pack, and be at the airport in three hours. I have tickets waiting for you at the American Airlines counter."

"Mylie, is everything okay?" Ren could hear it in my voice. This wasn't a Yay! You're-coming-with-me-to-California! call. It was so far from that. We'd planned it in moments, made Pete sit there while we made the calls. We took his cell phone so that he couldn't reach Ren. Russell was watching him right now while I made my call in the office.

"It's all going to be okay," I breathed, and Ren assumed

we just had some trouble with the wedding, that I needed her to come save the day again. I was fine with her thinking I was inept at work right now. I was definitely not inept at saving her.

"I just have to call Pete and let him know," Ren said innocently, and it broke my heart.

"Pete's here with us, Ren. He knows."

And she was quiet. She knew, too.

"Ren?"

"Was he at the house?" she asked, her voice shaking.

"Yes."

"With *her*?"

How could I answer? I didn't want to tell her over the phone. I didn't want her driving dangerously, hurt to the core by a blindside of betrayal. I didn't want baby James in danger. I didn't want her refusing to come to California with me, preferring instead to confront Pete when he got home. I didn't want her dealing with this while I was across the country.

"Mylie, he was with her, wasn't he?" Ren sighed. She already knew. "She's been calling my house the past few days, leaving messages for him on our voice mail, making it as obvious as possible."

I closed my eyes. We shouldn't have let Staci out of the house. It would have been a service to all married women in the tri-state area to bury the sociopathic bimbo in the backyard. She just wanted to cause pain everywhere she went.

"Mylie?"

"Yes, Ren, he was here with her," I said, then swallowed hard, trying not to cry.

"Good," she said. "I'm finally free of him."

It may have been harder on the two of us, Russell and I, than it was on Ren. I'd had no idea they were unhappy, but I did remember Ren flipping him off at Dolphin Dance just the weekend before. I did remember Ren stabbing the salad while Staci riffled through Ren's refrigerator.

"Is she okay?" Russell asked me, his arms crossed over his chest. Closed off. Pete's indiscretion had torn open an old wound for my boyfriend as well. Fascinating how many people they hurt, and in so many different ways.

"She seems . . . relieved." I shrugged. "She knew already. Staci left messages for Pete."

Russell winced.

"She's packing now and getting the baby," I said, my eyes filling with tears. The sobs were coming. "Follow this sick son of a bitch home, watch while he gets his things, and put him in a hotel. Take his keys, and go to the house and have the locks changed. I'll make sure the cops watch the house while Ren's away."

Russell nodded. Seemed my event planning background enabled me to choke back the sobs long enough to cover the Crisis Mode To-Do list. Then I fell apart, and Russell held me, rocking me back and forth, kissing my temples and my forehead while Pete watched from his chair. *Your whole life is over, buddy.*

Chapter 34

I took an earlier flight to California, and waited there in the terminal for the fifty minutes until Renata's flight would land. I felt dizzy from not eating, having no appetite after that scene, so I bought a baked potato and pretty much stabbed at it with a little plastic fork as the time ticked on slowly, so slowly.

I thought about Pete, about how he seemed to be the greatest guy in the world, such a great husband and father. So good to everyone else's kids, the friendliest guy in the room, the gentleman host who poured your wine. And inside . . . inside was a guy who used his wife's bed and breakfast during the week to do coke and have sex with his buddy's girlfriend-of-the-moment who broke up *his* marriage as well.

Was she going to move through our entire group? Had she already gotten to Glenn? Were we surrounded by a bunch of idiots?

I'd never understand why men went for women like Staci. Was it a porn thing? Like she was a character that stepped out of their TV screen? She had no redeemable qualities, no kindness, no intellect. And she was cruel. Anyone who would call up the wife just wanted to destroy people. Pete *knew* Staci did that to Chip's wife. He *knew* she'd do it to Ren.

Which made him a big, giant loser. In my book, he was a fail-ure of a man. In every way.

"Hey you." Ren appeared behind me, baby James sleeping against her chest. I jumped up and hugged her as best I could. I was the one in tears, and she smiled peacefully. "No, no, don't you waste your tears on him."

Wait, I'm supposed to be saying that to her.

"He's not worth it."

Again, I'm supposed to be saying that to her.

"We're going to be fine without him." Ren shrugged. "Ac-tually, better now. With infidelity in the divorce, it just makes life easier on me in the future. He doesn't get the house or James. He doesn't get Dolphin Dance." She winked. "He doesn't get anything at all."

"She's pregnant, Ren," I whispered, and she just laughed. "What? Why are you laughing?"

"She tells *everyone* that, I hear." Ren smiled. "She told Chip that and it turns out she wasn't. It's just how she gets her hooks in for a while."

That's disgusting.

"Pete's an idiot." She laughed. "And I'm now free of the idiot."

A smile grew on my face. I should have known that Ren would be strong about it. And also that she'd ask the next question.

"How's Russell doing with this?" she asked. She knew him well. "That can't have been easy."

I sighed. "He's a little quiet."

"Yeah, bad memories." Ren nodded. "But don't even think he's going to bolt or anything. He really cares about you, and he knows you're not like Melissa."

I nodded. *She knows me well.*

"Just let him absorb this for a while, don't worry if he's quiet. It's a good thing we're in California for a few days, both of us far away from everything. Let the men think about what they currently have." She winked. "For Russell, it's everything. And for Pete, it's nothing. Who says there's no justice in the world?"

There definitely was justice in the world. It just took its time sometimes.

"Now shake this off, and let's get to the hotel." Ren bounced the baby as he started to wake, making a face like he wanted to cry but no sound coming out.

"We're not going to a hotel." I smiled. "We're staying at the clients' place."

Ren wanted to yell, to celebrate, but we had that pesky little confidentiality thing to be *really* careful about in public.

Ren, of course, compared each of the bed and breakfasts we passed to her own. "Did I mention that Dolphin Dance is *mine?*" she said about five times with pure glee, and I high-fived her each time. The house was in her name.

"Now, when we get there, they're going to put you through a lot of security," I warned her, but they pretty much just waved us in through the gates. I guess they figured if Ren was with me, she was okay. No retina scan for her.

"Oh . . . my . . ." Ren leaned forward in her seat to take in the massive estate, the trees on either side of us, and today the collection of amazing cars in the driveway. No minivans in this league. What was going on at the house?

"Miss Mylie, Miss Renata." The suited assistants opened our car doors for us and knew enough to let us get our own bags. Ren raised an eyebrow at that, but I shook my head that it was fine. "The ladies are inside."

I smiled, knowing the thrill Renata would get from *this* surprise.

"Mylie!" Celia came over and hugged me, then hugged Renata. "Renata, how are you?" It was a kind "How are you?" not a sorry-your-husband-was-banging-a-bimbo kind of pity-soaked "How are you?" "Sorry we started without you." She waved us to follow her through the house and out to the back terrace.

"Without us?" I laughed. "You're the guest of honor!"

It was Celia's bridal shower. I'd arranged it from New York, and everything was exactly as planned. Tables set with light lavender tablecloths, tall white floral centerpieces with lilacs, servers strolling around offering the ladies hors d'oeu-vres from silver platters, waiters with champagne and berries. By the pool, massage therapists and pedicurists worked on the guests, and I did not insult them—or go too trendy—with the wandering Botox minstrel.

"Oh, my God, Mylie, that's—" Ren started to gush, then stopped herself. Be professional.

Celia hugged her with an arm around her shoulders. "Go ahead and mingle, Renata. My friends are your friends. We'll work after the party . . . so don't drink too much."

Having baby James strapped to her chest made Renata the hit of the party. Her favorite stars were there, all coming over to *her* to say hello and admire baby James. A waiter handed her a champagne flute and dropped in three raspberries with tongs. For all impressions, it looked very much like Renata was the star of the party, the guest of honor. I stood back with Celia and watched, smiling like the best friend that I was.

"How's she doing?" Celia looked concerned for Renata, having liked her so much at Dolphin Dance.

"She's fine." I smiled. "Glad to be rid of him."

Celia whistled. "I'd have killed him on the spot."

"I really wanted to, but my boyfriend was there."

"So if you joined together, it would have been quicker." Celia laughed, and we walked forward to join in the celebra-tion and accept our champagne flutes with smiles from the waiters. They, too, weren't told whose event they'd be work-ing, so I noticed them noticing every famous guest and trying hard not to favor them with oversolicitous service, too many hors d'oeuvres offerings, at the expense of Celia's friends and family.

And then it was time for Kick's first surprise. . . .

A clinking of a knife against a champagne flute, and all eyes searched to find its source. Kick stood at the top of the terrace stairs, smiling down at Celia. "Ladies, I'm sorry to crash your party. . . ."

A smattering of "Please do!" and "Join us!" shouts from the champagne-soaked ladies.

"I have a very special gift for Celia . . . ," he went on, keeping his position at the top of the stairs. "Actually, this is the first of *twelve* special somethings leading up to our wedding day. . . ."

The ladies approved, the nearest touching Celia's arm or hand, perhaps wishing for some of her otherworldly luck to rub off on them. People got very weird about touching brides-to-be for their luck. It was an ancient, hardwired thing.

"So today is surprise number one." Kick beamed. "When Celia was a little girl, she had a best friend . . ."

I watched Celia's face, not Kick, wanting to see the moment when confusion gave way to knowingness.

"And the best friend's family moved away when Celia was young . . ."

There. Celia's eyes began to water.

"They lost touch, and Celia has always talked about wanting to find this friend, wanting to touch base again, but we just couldn't find her."

The ladies knew what was coming. Excited smiles all around.

"Our wedding coordinator, Mylie Ford, found her. Take a bow, Mylie!" Now all eyes were on me, and for some strange reason I did an awkward little curtsy and waved at the guests . . . who would all be booking me for their parties, I hoped.

"Ladies . . . Celia . . . here is Evelyn Greenberg!" The door opened behind him, and Evelyn ran past Kick, right to Celia. They smashed together in a hug, shaking each other, stepping back with arms still locked, looking at each other, touching each other's faces, crying, incoherent with partial sentences, and Celia led her away by the hand to the far edge of the lawn, both of them stumbling as they ran. They needed a moment alone to absorb the reality of being together again after sixteen years apart.

I looked up at Kick, who had teary eyes of his own, and he blew a kiss down to me, mouthing the word *Thanks*.

That was a real man.

And Renata came to me, handing off the baby to someone standing nearby, so she could hug me fully and cry a few tears of her own. "Thank you, Mylie. Thank you so much."

Celia hadn't wanted any shower games, so we got right to the cake. A two-tiered confection with chocolate mousse filling, a raspberry sauce on the side. The ladies dug in with a fervor, *oooh*ing and *ahh*ing and demanding the baker's name. It was a new pastry chef, a friend of Russell's, who would be on everyone's speed dial by the end of the day. Celia sat next to Evelyn and asked Renata to sit on her other side. We'd sold the rights to Celia's bridal shower to *InStyle*, so the photographer was given one hour to snap the photos she wanted, and I made sure that Renata would be in the big-time pictures, the ones that would make it to print. It could have been me, if I'd kept the seating arrangement Celia wanted, but I wanted Renata to be the person of greatness she was, and have it shown to the world. *Here, Staci. Here, Pete. See where the wife is now.*

I also wanted it for baby James. Someday he'd look at these pictures, of himself held by Celia Tyranova and the other big stars, and he'd love his mother even more.

Filled to seams-bursting with chocolate cake, and my

pockets lighter from handing out the baker's very clever little business card in the shape of a cupcake, I wandered with Renata to the massage area. We stuck our faces into the soft, thick breathing slots and let the handsome, muscled massage therapists work the kinks out of our shoulders. "Wow, it's like you have extra bone," one of them said of the knots in my neck and shoulders, and Ren and I giggled.

"This is the life." Ren sighed, letting go of a lot more than muscle tension. "Can we keep Celia and Kick after the wedding?" she joked.

"I imagine so." I exhaled against an elbow digging into my shoulder blade. I hated to think we'd be tossed after the big day. I hadn't even thought into the future, just enjoyed the friendship while it was here. I'd never been friends with clients before, never heard anything about their lives, was never welcomed into their homes like this.

"Chopper," Ren said, and I thought she said "Chipper," as in the poor, pitiable fool who brought Staci into our lives like a cancer. "Overhead . . . helicopters . . . paparazzi."

"Damn," I yelped, but not from the inevitable helicopters, which too many of our brides were way too excited about on their wedding days. If helicopters hovered in dangerous groups over your back lawn, you knew you were on the A-list. Celia looked over, shrugged at me, and closed her eyes into the foot massage she was getting with Evelyn at her side. She munched on a pineapple ring and admired the reflexology effect.

"Right now, I'm clearing your spleen," the heavily accented foot massage therapist told her, and she giggled. "This toe is connected to your heart."

We decided, wisely, to interrupt her. With my face pressed into the massage table, the air pushed out of me by a rough knuckle drag up my spine, I spoke to her. "So, Celia . . . are you aware that Kick worked *really* hard to find Evelyn?"

Evelyn, deeply blissed out with her foot in the hands of a

massage therapist who you could just tell was going to be a major star someday when his big break hit, wanted to know the story. "I can't believe it. . . ." She smiled. "Kick *Lyons* was trying to find me."

Celia laughed. "I can't believe he remembered. We've talked about it so many times, but it never occurred to me that he really understood how much it meant to me to find you."

"How *did* you find me, Celia?" Evelyn, with puffy eyes from all the crying, pulled her matte brown hair back over her ears and seemed concerned about her smile lines, her crow's feet. She kept moving her hands up to cover parts of her face while she spoke.

"You'll never believe it." I smiled. "But I found you on Match.com."

Evelyn's face paled. "Oh, my," she breathed. "I'm so embarrassed!"

"Don't be," I wanted to assure her, but grunted against an assault on my kidney area. This was supposed to be relaxing? I'd be better off walking into a kid's karate camp and asking them to beat the crap out of me. "I was on there."

"How was it? Did you find anyone?"

"No," came another grunt from me. "But I've heard that lots of people—"

"Yeah, I know." Evelyn brought her fingers to the dark circles under her eyes. "Some people meet their future husbands on there. Whatever." Ah, the disgust of a few bad on-line dates. "I'd rather camp out in the frozen foods section at the supermarket and wait for some guy who needs a Hot Pocket."

We laughed, imagining the lounge chair, a cooler, a little side table with her business cards on it. It was no more of a gamble than signing on to a singles site.

"I always followed your career, Celia," Evelyn confessed. "I'd get in my pajamas when the Oscars were on, eat some cookie dough, and just wait to see you in your dress." It was charming, not creepy. "And I'd tell the dog, 'I used to know her!'"

Celia smiled. "Well, you're coming with me to the Sundance Film Festival. We're not letting you watch another big event at home in your pajamas with cookie dough and a dog."

"Really?" Evelyn squealed. "Oh, Celia, I'm so happy for your life. You're so lucky."

"Evelyn, let's get to the good stuff," Renata said from her face cushion. "What was Celia like when she was a little girl?"

Evelyn smiled. "She was quiet, a reader. She was always sketching in a notebook, always dreaming."

"Yeah, my parents thought I was developmentally disabled." Celia laughed. "They brought me to therapy, and it just turned out that I knew I wanted to act, so I was observing everyone around me, mastering their facial expressions, their accents. A six-year-old kid who just sits under a tree and takes notes about what people are doing . . . I guess that can raise some concerns."

"We used to climb out of our windows and go out and look at the stars." Evelyn nodded, now self-conscious about her hair, pulling it away from her face. "We'd walk all night, talk about running away. We'd climb trees and write stories, act out plays. Oh, Celia, do you remember the Chipmunks song we did a routine to?"

Celia feigned not remembering, with a twinkle in her eye. She was *not* going to reenact the Chipmunks song. It sounded like they were perfect little best friends, quietly creative, doomed to separate.

"And you moved away." Celia blinked her wet eyelashes. "I remember standing on the curb, waving to you as the truck pulled away."

"I remember, too." Evelyn looked down. It was the worst day of a little girl's life.

"But you're here now . . . *good God!* Stop it!" I jumped up from the massage table. "Do I look like your ex-wife or something?" I snapped at the massage guy. Clearly, Renata had gotten the better man, since she appeared to be sleeping right now, with little angel wing flutters of fingers over her back and shoulders. Her back rose and fell with great, deep, peaceful breaths. Every now and then we heard an *mmmm* come out of her closed mouth.

"You've accomplished so much, Celia, I'm so proud of you," Evelyn said, and then went on with the litany of her life. A failed marriage. A failed business venture with a tanning salon. Now a business raising pedigree puppies. In Kentucky. "It's a good life, and I'm not embarrassed at all," she said, her hand moving up to her mouth. "Really . . . I'm not embarrassed."

We all sat in awkward silence. Evelyn Greenberg had changed a lot since childhood. So had Celia. It was an unspoken thought bubble between us all. *Please Evelyn, pull it together.*

"Evelyn." Celia placed her hand on her friend's. "You were my best friend, and I've missed you for so long. And now you're here. That's all I care about. So everything in the middle doesn't count. Okay?"

"Okay." Evelyn blushed and took a deep, peaceful breath. Unfortunately, it was really bad timing for Kick to present Surprise #2: the $750,000 necklace in a red velvet box. Evelyn's eyes turned from soft acceptance and comfort . . . to sea green jealousy. That got greener and greener and greener then blacker and blacker with each extravagant shower gift the bride-to-be opened. Cashmere blankets. Vera Wang formal place settings, the whole set. La Perla lingerie. Even the blender seemed to tick Evelyn off. Celia would probably never see her again after this.

Celia handed out the favor boxes to each of her guests as they headed for their cars. We'd packaged up fluffy sage green

Karen Neuberger socks, monogrammed spa robes, white tea body lotions and bubble baths, lip glosses, cuticle creams, packets of hot chocolate and wide-rimmed coffee mugs, Bliss Trips music CDs, plus a selection of paperback novels in our "Take a Day Off" care packages. Back at the office, I'd wrapped each box with sage green and lavender print wrapping paper, big lavender bows, and attached a poem written by Celia, which we'd printed on lavender card stock.

Renata and I stood back from Celia's favor-bestowing lineup, staying subtle about the business end. Most of her guests, the famous and nonfamous, had approached us earlier for our business cards, but some still walked up to us now to compliment us on the day and tell us about the events coming up in their lives. And of course, some of the random Snooties name-dropped Colin Cowie and Preston Bailey as the designers for their upcoming weddings and baby showers. There were always a few in every crowd who wanted to test you, put you in your place, remark that no one will ever be as big as Colin and Preston. We just smiled and happily remarked that we were happy with third place, which really annoyed the Snooties.

And of course, there were also the faux-pearl-wearing Snooties who trash-talked Celia and Kick even as they walked through their living room, insulting their décor, criticizing their latest magazine covers and movies, then flicked a switch to big, fake smiles as they hugged Celia and thanked her for a *lovely* party. That was the great thing about being an observer, almost invisible to the guests. You heard a *lot*.

Evelyn Greenberg was close to the last to leave. Celia had asked her to stay, and she nervously walked around the yard, touching the landscaping, running her hand along the tablecloths. I nudged security to watch her, actually. She was definitely the steal-an-ashtray-and-sell-it-on-eBay type. Finally, noticing that Celia's security force—women dressed in floral sundresses and floppy hats to mix in with the guests—was noticing her, Evelyn practically ran out of there with a quick kiss to a stunned Celia and a promise to call or write or e-mail sometime.

"I'm sorry, hon." Kick appeared behind her, having watched the party on their security cam from the comfort and safety of his TV room. "Surprise #1 was a big disappointment, huh?"

Celia smiled and hugged him. "Not at all."

"That's why I busted out Surprise #2 so fast." He laughed. "They're in the safe, by the way."

"They are?" She blinked. "But I put them—"

"No, your friend was eyeing the velvet box." Kick winced a little bit. Good old Evelyn was going to lift the jewels. "So much for old friends."

"Still, it was good to see her," Celia assured him. "Makes me realize how far I've come." She gave him a squeeze, then turned to us. "Mylie, Renata, thank you. The party was fantastic."

We grinned and assured her it wasn't an effort at all. We were glad to do it.

On my hip, my pager went off. Text message. GREETINGS FROM OVERHEAD. THANKS FOR LEADING ME TO THE PARTY. BRYAN.

I rolled my eyes and kept it secret.

Then another one. YOU LOOK GREAT, BY THE WAY.

Apparently, pigs can fly.

"Ah, three women in my bed." Kick strolled through as Celia, Ren, and I took our places on the bed, where Celia wanted to lie back and work. Ren and I sat at the foot of the bed while Celia set up a heating pad for her back and relaxed down into her pillows. She'd spent sixteen hours dangling from cables for her new movie, and her back knifed her with pain.

"You wish." Celia winked at him. He grabbed a change of clothes from his dresser and waved as he left the room.

"We'll get to you later, Kick," Ren shouted out, meaning we'd talk with him about the wedding plans.

But he joked back to us with, "Promises, promises."

I couldn't help but look around. This was Celia and Kick's bedroom, the one room they wouldn't show us on the original tour. A massive poster bed. Big windows overlooking the garden with a glass-topped circular table and two cushioned chairs, plants on either side of the window. Big mahogany dressers, six of them. A domed ceiling, similar to the one in Kick's chapel but without the gold accents. And the softest comforter I'd ever felt. Mountains of pillows. Great lighting. And a dish of Mounds bars on the bedside table.

"Kick designed it." Celia noticed me admiring the place, and I prayed she'd read my mind again. "Want to see the closet?" She did.

I was a little too eager, springing from the bed, all but clapping my hands and jumping for joy. Renata suppressed a smirk, having heard from me all about the original tour and how I hoped to get a peek at the inner sanctum of Celia's fashion and shoe collection. The last time I set my hand on a doorknob, it felt hot and there was something awful behind it. This time, it felt cool and I knew there was something amazing behind it. I felt like Dorothy in *The Wizard of Oz*, opening the door to a colorful new world.

"Oh, my God," I exhaled. This was not a closet. It was a *wing*. Sectioned areas held all of her dresses, suits, jeans, sweaters, with about three inches between each item.

"No wire hangers," Ren joked, and we could hear Celia laugh from her spot on the bed.

A full wall held shoes of every color and style, Celia's on the top shelves and Kick's on the bottom. Ren and I both noticed that he had more shoes than she did.

Out of reverence for the collection, like we were in a museum, we touched nothing. We barely even breathed.

Kick's suits and pants and shirts took up the opposite wall, and we noticed a basket with black handwriting "For Goodwill." Piles of clothes overflowed from its edges, and I liked Celia and Kick even more.

"The one from the Golden Globes is hanging on the back of the door," Celia announced. "Want to try it on?"

Ren and I looked at each other, then at the red halter-top sheath on the hook. We started pushing each other in a silent "You do it!", "No, *you* do it!" little girl argument. I'd given Ren the photo spread in *InStyle*, so I was going to take Celia up on the offer of trying on the Dress Seen Round the World.

Ren walked out of the closet to join Celia, and I whipped off my shirt and skirt, knowing full well that there were security cameras everywhere in this house. Kick was probably eating Chee-tos and watching me right now. I stepped into the red dress, my pulse racing, and zipped it up. All I heard was my own breathing. I was wearing The Dress. I was a little too big up top, so I did half spill out of the halter, but the waist fit. I held the skirt up, as Celia was about four inches taller than me, and walked out to show the girls.

"Lovely." Celia clapped. "But you're missing something."

She sat up and flipped around onto her knees. She pressed against a panel on the wall behind her, and it loosened. She pried it open, and even though she tried to be discreet, I could see that it was filled with shiny things. Lots of them. When she drew her hand back out, she had her Golden Globe award in it. The one she accepted in *this dress*. "Here!"

She handed it to me, and I know I heard myself mumbling something in my numb state. *This must be how it feels when you win one. No wonder some people completely lose it on stage.*

It was heavy. And shiny. I handed it right off to Ren so that she could feel it, too, then ran to get out of the dress before I sweated right through it.

*   *   *

"And now for your song playlist." I looked at my clip-board, with about two-thirds of our tasks checked off. Celia flipped through some papers, all on pink legal-sized, then pulled out a page in Kick's handwriting.

"We worked on this last night," Celia announced, feeling like she needed to assure us of Kick's involvement since he hadn't come up to join us. "Here are the songs we want . . . and on the back are the songs we *don't* want." I always loved the Do Not Play list. They were songs that reminded the cou-ple of their previous partners, their previous marriages some-times, the soundtrack of passionate nights with forgettable flings, and overplayed pop stars. Line dances. In Celia's handwriting: "NO CHICKEN DANCE. NO MACARENA. NO LINE DANCE OF ANY KIND. PERIOD."

I read through the other No Plays: "Unchained Melody," "Living on a Prayer," "Love in an Elevator." My guess was that the last one was Kick's cross-off, since he'd had a tabloid report that he had sex in a glass elevator in Vegas with a stripper. No need to remind everyone at the wedding about that. True or not.

I flipped the page over to see their picks for the special dances. Kick had written in "When I Fall in Love" for their first dance, and I smiled a little to myself knowing that one of Kick's surprises was flying in Chris Botti to play that song himself. Celia would dance with her father to "What a Won-derful World" by Louis Armstrong, and Kick would dance with his mother to Mariah Carey's "Hero." Nice choices. I was glad they went traditional and didn't try to grab spot-lights with irreverent selections. I once had a bride who wanted to dance with her father to Peter Gabriel's "Sledge-hammer." No one in the room could make sense of the choice, and it just seemed icky at the time. And don't even get me started about the groom who danced way too closely with his mother to "All By Myself." Even the bride seemed mortified.

Celia and Kick's playlist was indeed complete, and Ren scanned it as well. Her eyes resting, I knew, on "At Last," which was her and Pete's wedding song. Her armor was thick, but not that thick. She cleared her throat and passed the paper back to me.

"I have an idea." Celia hugged her folder against her chest. Somehow, I knew what was coming. "Since Kick has all these surprises in store for me . . . I'd like to plan a few more surprises for him."

Ren and I beamed. Somehow, we didn't care that extra surprises meant extra work for us.

"I want to get Chris Botti to play our wedding song *live*." She wrinkled her nose. "Do you think you can make that happen?"

Ren and I sat with our mouths hanging open. Turned out it wouldn't be extra work.

"It's too much?" Celia looked disappointed.

"No, no." I smiled. "We can make that happen."

"Good. Kick's going to flip out." She clapped her hands and kicked her feet, then winced with her back pain.

"Now, about the doves," I went on, deftly switching the subject before our faces gave it all away.

"How's she doing?" Russell asked about Ren.

"She's fine, Russell, just fine." I squeezed the phone between my ear and my shoulder as I tried to get into my bathing suit. Phase Two of our planning session would be in the hot tub. "There was a party here, and she had a blast."

"Good, she deserves it." He sighed.

"How's the Ape from Hell?"

He knew who I meant. "Checked in to a dive hotel. I took his credit cards for Ren's sake. He's a hollow man right now."

"Good." I struggled with my bikini bottoms. They'd rolled into a tight bunch.

"What are you doing?" He laughed. "Sounds like you're dragging something heavy around."

"Um, thank you, Mr. Sensitive. I'm getting into my bathing suit." I laughed.

"Ouch. Sorry. Bad choice of words. You're definitely not dragging anything heavy around." Russell paused a moment. "I think I'll change the subject."

"Yes, please." I smiled.

"Bathing suit, huh?"

"Yup."

"What color?"

"Baby blue."

"Bikini? Gimme the visual . . ."

"Strapless top, Brazilian bottom." I changed the bottom because "hi-cut, full-coverage bottom" just wasn't the effect I was going after.

"Going swimming with the girls?" *Uh oh. The who-are-you-with? question.* I had to expect it, but still hated the paper-cut effect on our relationship. It was a small presence, but you knew it was there. Russell had armor of his own, and like Ren he had tiny fissures in it that cracked a little more when bad reminders arose. He wanted to trust me. But once you'd been blindsided, that wound never healed. Never. I didn't care what the self-help books said. It might get small and pink, rather than bleeding red, but it was there.

"It's going to be me, Ren, Celia, and Kick in the hot tub," I gave him the truth. "Celia's back hurts from being held up on a wire for a movie shoot, and the heating pad wasn't doing it. So we decided to take the meeting to the hot tub."

Maybe I should have confessed to the hi-cut, full-coverage bottoms I was actually wearing.

"I'm staying at Ren and Pete's for a few days, just to keep an eye on the place," he said, and I wished I could be there.

He went through an ordeal today, too, and here I was comforting Ren on one coast when I really wanted to be comforting my boyfriend on the other coast. While I took a meeting in a hot tub, he would be wandering around Ren's place with a beer in his hand, thinking. Just thinking. Did I hug him well enough before I left?

"Russell?"

"Yes?"

"You're a phenomenal man, you know that?"

He laughed a little bit.

I took a breath. "You're the best thing that ever happened to me." I wanted to tell him I loved him. I didn't mind being the first to say it. But I didn't want it to be over the phone.

"Thanks, Mylie," came his reply. Not the tone or response I'd hoped for. I closed my eyes. Ren told me to give him time, not to worry if he got quiet. But if he went . . . if he ran . . . if Pete ruined this for us . . . "You're phenomenal, too," came his reply.

More! Say more!

"I'd better go." He sounded deflated. He had, after all, spent most of his day with Pete. I had to force myself to chalk it up to his just being tired, not take it personally. I wasn't going to lose my man to bad memories. I just wasn't. And I couldn't let him sit in Ren's house alone, with a picture show flashing in his head of all that we'd seen that day, and all that he'd seen in the past.

So I said it.

"Russell, I'm in love with you."

Silence.

"I am. I love you," I breathed.

Silence. The clink of a bottle being set down on a counter. I imagined him standing there, running his hands through his hair. I hoped he was smiling.

"Russell?" I tried. "Say something . . ."

Ren should have been here to punch me in the face, get me

to stop. She should have been able to flip time back and punish me for not taking her advice to just let him be quiet and think.

"Me, too," came his quiet reply. "I'll see you when you get back, okay?"

"Okay," I exhaled. *He said, "Me, too."* I'd have analyzed that a thousand different ways in a sleepless, fitful night, but then I heard him say something to Emma. Ah, she was with him. He couldn't speak freely. "Me, too" was the best he could do.

Ren was not pleased.

"Are you out of your mind?" She tugged at her own hicut, full-bottom-coverage bathing suit. "The guy goes through a nightmare, he has to cart Pete off to a hotel, he's replaying a horror show of reminders about Melissa, Emma is with him, and you drop the *L* word over the phone because *you* need reassurance. God, Mylie."

"It's fine." I shrugged.

"You can't push him like that, so ease up, okay?" Ren put her hand on my arm, motherly warmth. "Seriously. Just let him have time to think. Control yourself."

"You're quiet," Kick noticed as the four of us talked ideas in the hot tub. From very far apart. It was one of those enormous hot tubs with full lie-down areas and enough room in the center for a dozen more people. Our drinks sat in cooling cup holders on the outside rim of the hot tub, and the lights underneath changed from blue to green to yellow and then back to blue.

"Just taking everything in," I lied. "Just listening."

"Yeah, for a change." Ren laughed, sipping her daiquiri. "Someone dropped the *L* word over the phone to her boyfriend a *leeee*ttle too early."

Kick laughed and splashed me, of course getting my clip-board wet. "Nice job, ScrewUp." Ah, I'd earned the nick-name again.

"Kick!" Celia warned him with a raised eyebrow. Then to me, "Don't worry about it, sweetie. If he's the right guy, you could say it any time, any place, and everything would be fine."

If he's the right guy.

"How did you say it?" Ren asked Kick, getting a leeeetle too drunk on her daiquiri.

Kick smiled at Celia, and she blushed. "You tell it better," he said to her, knowing this was definitely her story to tell.

She readied herself, took a sip from her drink, and then gave us the "ready?" look. "Okay, we were on-set in Egypt."

Already her story was better than mine.

"And Kick got a *really* bad case of food poisoning." Celia giggled. "He was laid out, sicker than you could imagine."

He nodded.

"This was supposed to be *the* night, you know?" She poked me in the arm. "And you wouldn't believe the sounds coming from the bathroom!"

"Celia!" He laughed.

"He was moaning . . . just miserable . . . and then he got really, really quiet. I was afraid we'd need a medic, but then he came crawling out of the bathroom for a bottle of water. I gave him mine, and I sat with him and held him until he fell asleep on my lap. My legs were numb from the weight of him, but there was no way I was going to dump him off of me. So I just kissed his forehead . . . and looked at his eye-lashes . . . his lips. And it hit me . . . I want this person's hap-piness more than my own. So, thinking he was asleep, I just whispered it in his ear . . . 'I love you.'"

"And I wasn't really asleep," Kick took over. "I just didn't want to open my eyes because she might make me get off of her. So I said it right back to her."

"Then we called the medics to hook him up with an IV and give him some antibiotics." Celia laughed.

So Celia said it first, too. At a rough time for him. *If he's the right guy . . .*

"Wow, that's some story." Ren shook her head, and by the droop of her eyes, it was time to cut her off of daiquiries. "Pete just said 'I know,' when I said it to him." And she was out. Passed out. Kick got her by the chin before she went under the water, then lifted her up, and we followed as he brought her inside. Celia and I changed her into dry clothes while Kick set up the trash can next to the bed, then placed water and crackers within reach. One of their staff motioned that the baby was sleeping fine, and that she would stay the night to be with him. She'd go to the store for formula if she had to. Celia thanked her, and once Ren was secured in her bed, Celia, Kick, and I went downstairs to the television room.

Like college roommates, we ordered in a pizza, cracked open some beers, and watched television until we fell asleep on the couches.

Chapter 35

"Good morning." Ren looked rather fresh and clean, not at all hung over, carrying baby James in one arm as she joined us out on the terrace for breakfast.

"Good morning." Celia poured her some coffee and motioned for her to join us. The table was set with eggs Benedict, sausage, bacon, whole wheat toast, cantaloupe slices mixed with blueberries, and smoked salmon. "Hungry?"

"Famished." Ren sat down, adjusted the baby on her lap, and dug in. In this good company, there was no need to apologize for passing out in their hot tub.

"Did he call?" I asked, seeing her cell phone tucked into her pants.

"About fifty times," she said without emotion. "He cries more than the baby does."

I'd never seen baby James cry, actually. All the kid did was sleep.

"What are you going to do?" Celia asked, buttering her toast. No sausage or Hollandaise sauce for her.

"What I should have done the last time," Ren answered.

There was a last time?

"So what are we doing today?" she asked, excited to get back to work. This was, after all, Ren's first real exposure to our biggest clients in *their* environment. She hadn't had the time I had to get used to Celia and Kick, to forget the magnitude of their celebrity and see them as real people. She probably imagined a *Pretty Woman* type shopping spree, while I knew that Celia preferred The Gap, or that she just told her bodyguards to order whatever she saw in a store window. Ren didn't know there wasn't a whole lot of hitting the town going on. Celia and Kick were homebodies by necessity. Especially with the wedding coming up so quickly.

It was just going to be all work today. We had a lot of the little things to do. Choose the favors, design the labels, design the menu cards, choose the items in the guest welcome baskets for those staying in hotels, choose garnishes for the food stations, design the monogram, finalize the groom's cake order, design the sashes for the flowergirls, design the floral wreaths for the flowergirls, and sneak off with Kick at some point during the day—probably during Celia's yoga class—to work on the next handful of surprises he had in mind.

As much as we'd all have loved to fly Ren to Vegas for a few days of wildness, we had a *lot* to do.

Chapter 36

"I'm glad you called," I whispered, slipping through the wispy window curtains and out onto the terrace, pulling the sliding glass door closed behind me as soundlessly as possible. Ren and the baby were sleeping in my room this night. We'd had a girls' slumber party with Celia, complete with toenail painting, eating cookie dough, and watching *Sex and The City* DVDs. Celia may have been enjoying us more than we were thrilled to be with her.

"Are you guys getting a lot done?" Russell asked. *Ah, polite smalltalk. That's how you know the big stuff is coming. We have a lot to talk about.*

"We're way ahead of schedule." I nodded, as if he could see me. It was cool outside, and the tiles felt cold and damp beneath my bare feet. I leaned against the railing, looking out over the moonlit garden, up at the sky full of stars. *I wish you were here, Russell.*

"Good to hear, good to hear," he said. It was late there, 4:00 A.M. "I'm glad it's all going well." He paused. *Come on, say something . . .* "How's Ren doing?"

"She's fine. We had a girls' night . . . junk food, toenail painting, hot chocolate."

"Hot chocolate?" He laughed. "Wow, I wasn't imagining you hanging out in Starsville and having a slumber party."

"What were you imagining?" I tried to be playful, and it seemed like I was drawing him in.

"I thought you'd be out partying." *Like Melissa.* This was bad. I had ghosts to slay.

"No, Celia and Kick aren't like that." Would he believe we spent an hour in Kick's chapel earlier today?

"So are you touring? Going to the wineries?"

Enough of this. "No, we're working. Lots of little details to cover, and Kick has some surprises for Celia that we have to work out. I'm not hitting the clubs or anything like that." *And I'm not banging the pool boy or the landscaper during my lunch breaks.*

"Oh," was all he said. "Yeah, I'm working a lot, too."

Where was the fire between us? The spark? Did Pete snuff out the electricity between us? I'd had better conversations with my gynecologist. I took a deep breath and dove. . . .

"Russell, are you bothered by what I said this morning?" I kept my tone soft, even though inside—after stewing about it all day—I wanted to pressure him into . . . into . . . making *me* feel better. I felt sick. Sick enough from all that cookie dough, but hollow sick from the long wait, the uncertainty, the sound of the wind whistling through the holes I imagined in the relationship.

"Not . . . *bothered,*" he said, and there was that whistling noise again. Until he paused . . . thought . . . "I wasn't expecting it."

I opened my mouth to talk, but he went on. Which was what I'd been hoping for all day. *Open up to me, Russell. Please open up to me. I'm not Melissa.*

"It just felt like it was the wrong reason to say it," he said softly.

What?

"Like you said it because you felt you had to."

The words hung between us, filling up every inch of every

mile between our separate coasts. I loved him for his wisdom, and his wisdom had pointed a great, big spotlight on
me.

"You only said it because you were scared," he went on.
"I've done that, too."

"Russell—" I had to stop this. I didn't like where it was
going, and that whistling noise . . . It was gale force winds
now. A hurricane was ripping through us.

"Saying 'I love you' isn't a tourniquet on a bleeding
wound, Mylie," he paused. He'd practiced this conversation
in his mind. "You don't pull that out for the first time as a
rescue."

I closed my eyes, the cold night air feeling colder on the
streaks of my cheeks and jaw where the first tears slid down
slowly. This would be a great time for a *But* . . . as in "But
I'm glad you did" or "But as long as it's out there, I love you
with all my heart." Turned out the only *But* was the one I'd
just fallen on. Because I didn't listen to Ren.

"Right now, I'm going to need . . ."

*Don't say "some space." Don't say "some space" or
"some time" or "to be by myself for a while." Don't say it.*

"A little bit of time." He confirmed my worst fears. "This
is moving too fast, and even you know that I'm scarred by
what happened to me in my past. That's why you did it." He
sounded a little harsh on that one. "That's why you said it."

"Russell, don't do this."

"I have to, Mylie," he said, swallowing back any emotion.
I heard none. "Emma is having a tough time—"

Emma?!

"And what just happened with Pete . . . when I'd planned
a romantic day for us at the house . . . what a blindside it
was. Everything came rushing back, and I just want to take
some time to think. And I want to be completely open with
you about what I need."

I exhaled, pushed my hair back over my cold-numb ears. "Don't make me pay for what Pete did," I half begged, my voice catching. "Don't add me to his victim list."

"It's not—"

"Yes, it is!" I shouted, too upset now to do the whole stay-calm, stay-soft, don't-make-him-defensive thing. "You planned a romantic day for us! You were happy! You were ready to make love with me all day before I got on a plane! You had no fears, no concerns, you didn't need time and space!"

"Mylie—"

"Seeing Pete like that shook me up, too," I cried. "He's a shallow, sick bastard, and he hurt Renata very badly. Now it's *you* hurting me on his behalf."

Harsh, but true. I felt, wrong or not, that he was using Pete's hellish behavior as the perfect excuse to wimp out and run from a good thing that *he* had been leading, by the way. *He* planned the day at Dolphin Dance. Now he was blaming Pete and Emma. And me, for choosing the wrong time . . . to be honest. It wasn't what I said, it was *when* I said it? *That's complete crap.*

"If it's the right person, it doesn't matter when you say it," I argued, fully realizing I was arguing, which I surely would regret later. But I had been spring-loaded all day. I had the courage to say the words. And now it was the wrong thing?

"It's not that you said it," he whispered. "Don't focus on that."

"I'm talking to a wall here," I barked. "You already made up your mind, didn't you? This is what you want?"

He didn't answer.

"This is what you want?" It came out softer, broken-hearted.

"Mylie, I'm not breaking up with you." He was a little edgy now. "I'm just telling you that I need some time to clear my head."

Inside, I heard Ren's voice. *Just give him time.*

"I'm not trying to hurt you; I'm trying to be honest with you about where I am." He sounded so tender, even in the midst of saying things I absolutely hated.

And I remembered something else Ren said . . . about Pete . . . *It would be unloving to ask someone to do something they're not capable of doing.* I tacked on a *right now* just to make it apply to us.

"Mylie?" He didn't like the silence either. "Mylie, I've been walking all night thinking about this."

While I was painting Celia Tyranova's toenails, my boyfriend was walking the streets of the city, tormented over the risk to love again.

"What do you want me to do?" I whimpered. "I hate this."

"Me, too."

Yeah, I remember the last time you said those words. You made me think you were saying 'I love you.' What could you actually mean with them this time?

"I meant what I said, Russell. It wasn't a tourniquet on a bleeding wound." I lifted my chin, tried to keep the sobs back. "It was real."

Nothing.

"I meant it." I pulled my arms around myself, fighting off the chill of the night air and a wave of nausea at the same time. While my body was cold, my face was hot. "And because I meant it . . . take all the time you need."

Nothing from him. Why couldn't we have Jetsons-style big screen video phones? I was missing out on that ninety percent of communication that was nonverbal. I couldn't see his eyes. I couldn't see if he was slumped or pacing or leaning against his counter or lying on his bed with his hand on his stomach, it moving up and down with his breathing. I had no visual.

"Thanks, Mylie," he breathed. "I know it's not . . . I know it isn't . . . it's just what I need right now."

Ren's words again . . . *just give him time to think.*

He was asking for what he needed. Because I had pushed him. I had.

I'd be a bitch not to grant him this.

"It's okay, Russell. It's what you need," I breathed.

"When will you be home?" he asked.

"Two days." My voice was flat.

"I'll call you then," he promised. "We'll talk then."

After we hung up, I was more baffled than ever. What were we? We weren't broken up, but we had three-quarters of the breakup conversation. What we'd agreed to was an even more terrifying limbo for me while he thought about his options.

I thought of Celia's words . . . *if he's the right man.*

Maybe he's not.

It wasn't Pete's fault. Russell's doubts were in there all the time. He did the best he could. I knew he was a man with deep wounds, and I just didn't think I could ever slay those ghosts. Not with Emma fighting me every step of the way on top of all of that.

I had to let Russell slay his own ghosts. I had to unclutch and trust. I had to trust.

"What are you doing in here?" A voice in the darkness, far back from the candle altar. I couldn't sleep, so I had gone down to Kick's chapel. Maybe the ability to shut up and trust would seep into me there. Maybe I'd absorb the skills I needed to absorb if I just sat there for a while.

"Thinking," I whispered.

It was Celia who sat down next to me, her hand on mine. "What's wrong, sweetie?"

"He asked for time . . . ," was all I could say before the tears really started, and I hated to disturb the quiet and calm of the chapel with my collapse.

"Oh, sweetie." Celia draped her arm over my shoulders.

"I know it's hard to do . . . especially when you care for him so much. But you have to let him do this."

"I know," I sniffled.

"Sometimes the bravest thing to do, the thing you'll be most proud of yourself for doing . . . is *nothing*," Celia promised. "Believe me. Hey, we just went over the wedding ceremony, didn't we?" She smiled and poked me in the shoulder. "Faith, hope, and love, right? You've got the love part down. Now all you need is the faith and the hope part."

I wiped at my nose. The faith and the hope part. It was what I was here to absorb. Maybe I'd absorb it from her.

Chapter 37

The key was staying busy. It always had been. Put your head down and work. Get lost in the details. Get so in the zone that entire days flew by, the hours disappeared, you didn't even notice the sunshine outside the window. The mind could only focus on one thing at once.

"Mylie, take a break, will you?" Renata warned me, holding a Starbucks up to her lips and wiggling it as an incentive for me to take a coffee break. No, I had three dozen large silk flags to cut, hem, and hand-sew hundreds of Swarovski crystals onto. I had taken the job away from Ren, preferring to do it myself. Same with the menu cards and the sashes for the flowergirls, the banners for the trumpeters, and just about everything else. Ren had other weddings to work on, after all. I could handle it.

"I'm fine," I said, a bad time to move my arm and scatter crystals across the table after I'd counted them out perfectly.

"Don't make me take you to the spa room," Ren joked, and when I looked up, I saw that she wore a smirk, a half smile that was also a warning. Yes, I was treading dangerously on Zoe territory here. I'm sure if I looked in the mirror, my eyes would be bugged out, my face pale from shallow breathing. And I was sure my lipstick would be off-kilter.

"Okay, coffee sounds good," I agreed, pushing myself

back from the counter so that my roller chair made a rough grinding sound on the floor. I looked to our dry erase progress board. I'd done a week's worth of work in three days. Who said panic wasn't productive? I had been falling behind when I was blissed out with Russell, right? So this was much better. I had a laser focus on my better responsibilities.

I poured only about a third of a cup of coffee. It was all I needed. Ren watched my every move. The way we watch Zoe.

"I think you're overreacting," Ren exhaled. "All he said was he needed time . . . which you knew already."

"I'm not reacting to anything," I said through a tight, fake smile and got right back to my crystal beads. Octagonal-shaped with a pinpoint hole in the middle.

"Mylie . . ."

"I'm going to lose him because of the horrible, terrible, evil things that *other* people have done." I pressed my hands into the table like I was trying to make an impression in wet cement. Pete. Staci. Melissa. Even Emma. "What they've done and what they've said absolutely haunt Russell. And I'm standing here with nothing but love for the man. . . ."

"I know that." Ren came over to hug me. "And so does he."

"So why . . ." I couldn't finish the sentence.

"Just give it time." She hugged me and rocked me. "I know it sucks right now, but it's all going to be okay."

"What happened now?" Zoe's voice always entered the room before she did. Today she had her hair pulled back into a low ponytail, not her usual tight chignon that did the work of a facelift with its severe pull on her temples. She looked softer around the eyes, pinker at the cheeks. "Whatever man troubles you two have, put them on the wayside," she announced. "We have a big fish."

* * *

Zoe accepted Sasha Worthington's wedding.

Sasha and Donnie would be here in an hour.

"It's too much, Zoe," Ren pleaded. "We have so many going on, and with Celia and Kick's—"

"Nonsense, nonsense." Zoe waved it off with a manicured hand and big, chunky diamond rings that she bought for herself. It was the promise she made to herself a long time ago. For each big fish, she got a sparkler. The woman had a collection in a bank vault. She'd give them to her daughter someday . . . when she found her.

Zoe's daughter had been abducted when she was twelve, and never found. So that was why she would spin out sometimes. Her mind, in every moment, was fighting down inhumanly difficult memories. She could function. She could excel with tremendous talent and vision. She could be happy. But every now and then the thoughts burrowed up to haunt her, brought on by a phrase or a song, a smell or the sight of waffles with syrup on them, or a bride who looked like Patricia looked. But Zoe always knew, didn't hope, always knew, that one day Patricia would walk through those doors, and Zoe would have everything ready for her. I'd have to be sedated once in a while, too, if I'd been through that.

"Look at the board." Zoe pointed to the dry erase board, at all of the tasks I had crossed off in the past few days. It seemed my superefficiency had screwed us. "If I thought you two couldn't handle this wedding, I'd never have taken it."

Oh, yes, you would have.

"We're all set with the Chance wedding, the McGregor wedding, and we're just waiting for a confirm from Senator Li's son." Zoe ticked off our status check. It was true. We did have the time.

"We need to be bigger slackers." Ren nudged me, and Zoe did not look pleased.

"But wait." I rubbed my chin. "Sasha already has a wedding coordinator."

"Fired him."

"She *fired* him?" Ren gulped her coffee, burning her throat, I'm sure. "Didn't she fire someone else just a few weeks ago?"

"Zoe, we can't get on board as 'Sasha Worthington's third pick,'" I tried, hoping to appeal to the boss's ego. How would that look in the media? "Really . . ."

"It's done." Zoe shrugged. "It's a four-million-dollar wedding, and it's a rush job."

"Isn't her wedding in like two weeks?" Renata remembered the 'we're moving up our wedding!' announcement—with more 'naked under the sheets' photos—from the Web site, her face turning white. "Zoe, we can't possibly do this."

"Sasha has everything in line," Zoe reported. "All you have to do is make the calls and do the creation part. Really, this wedding will plan itself. And Sasha is such a *sweet* girl. You're going to love her."

Ren and I exchanged glances. "Zoe, she was here?"

"Yes," Zoe said. "I had a meeting with her last night."

I looked at the dry erase board. "Did she get in this room?"

"No," Zoe assured us. "We met in my office. I was with her the whole time."

Ren and I hesitated before any minor relief could set in.

"Will you two just relax?" Zoe clucked her tongue at us. "I have some pharmaceutical help in the other room if you need it."

I'd quit before I got to that point.

"Sasha and Donnie will be here within the hour, so make yourselves presentable," Zoe instructed, nodding with disdain at our working-hours jeans and sweatshirts. We had Donna Karan suits hanging on the hooks in the other room for quick changes before client calls, so it wouldn't take us long to appear presentable. And professional. We nodded, and Zoe clicked off on her high heels back to her office. Probably to line up Satan as our next client.

"Well, this should be fun." Ren laughed, her hands on her

hips, surveying our workspace for any little thing she could accomplish before Sasha Worthington sleazed her way into our building. We'd lock the door to this room. Privacy. Confidentiality agreement. Our sanity.

As I slipped into my brown skirt and jacket, affixing a brown clip in my hair, I smiled a little to myself. This *was* going to be fun.

We got Bridezillas here every day. We got filthy-rich, spoiled princesses, old money, new money, impossibly sweet celebrities, impossibly sociopathic celebrities with hard edges and bitter shells, the random alcoholic mother planning the whole thing while the bride was away at college overseas, people who threw things, people who cried, grooms-to-be who flirted with us. We'd seen everything. But we knew . . . we *knew* . . . that we had never seen anything even remotely like what Sasha Worthington was going to be to work with.

She showed up in a pink limousine. Nothing like a subtle entrance. A line of traffic followed closely behind her for blocks, since she was standing up out of the sunroof and waving to the crowd. Car horns blared. Little kids ran along the street. Annoyed-looking police officers attempted to wave the cars out of the line, deplugging traffic, but in a heartbeat the entire corner surrounding our office building was jammed with people. Not to be deterred by something as simple as a sidewalk, they spilled into the street. Sasha pulled her head inside the limousine, motored shut the sunroof, and waited. For more of a crowd to build. For the paparazzi to arrive. At the sign of the first hawk, she would step out of her car.

She was the anti-Celia.

Ren and I pressed our faces to the window to watch, not caring about being seen, since Zoe had had all of the windows to our offices treated with a special coating that allowed us to see out, but no one else to see in. Privacy. Confidentiality.

I'm guessing that Sasha won't be asking us to sign any confidentiality agreement. Nor would she hand us a scrambled cell phone or scan our retinas. She'd probably give us the number to the nearest billboard company and ask us to post her dress size on that. Or rather, what she'd be wearing *under* the dress, if anything.

Ren gave me a wink. She was as excited about this happy distraction as I was. The circus had come to town.

Sasha stepped out of her limousine wearing pink shorts and a too-tight white belly shirt with the words *Bride-to-Be* on it. I'd seen those in the classified sections of bridal magazines. Donnie stepped out after her in a pink pimp suit. Ah, she'd turned him on to the pink thing. And of course, her dyed-pink teacup poodle who in most pictures looked like a limp stuffed animal lying along her arm, probably praying for some PETA activist to come save it.

She waved at her crowd, signed autographs, posed with her hip jutted out, and changed positions five or six times for the flashing camera bulbs, then grabbed Donnie to kiss him passionately with her hand on his butt for good measure. *Every second is a show, folks.*

As they walked toward the building, we lost sight of them, busily wiping our breath marks off the windowpane.

"Ready?" Ren asked me, straightening her jacket. It was a little bit snug after the baby.

"Ready," I said, and it being the first time I'd smiled in days, really smiled, my cheeks ached.

"Mylie, Renata." Zoe had greeted her first, then led her into her office where we were waiting. We had locked the door to our workroom . . . and pushed a table with a plant on it in front of the door. "I'd like to introduce you to Miss Sasha Worthington and her fiancé Donnie."

I guessed he didn't merit a last name at this introduction. Very unlike Zoe. She didn't like him on sight. And neither did we. He had stoner eyes, half-lidded, looking around him but not really seeing anything, not even with it enough to shake our hands.

"Sasha." I extended my hand, only then noticing that she had altered her "Bride-to-Be" shirt with a sloppy black marker addition. It now read "Bride-to-Bed." *Eyes. Do not roll them.*

"You're . . ." She batted her eyelashes, which were some-how affixed with tiny, tiny pink dots on the ends of them.

"Mylie, and this is Renata," I said, stepping back and smiling, trying not to be too obvious about her rollerskating-in-the-1970s outfit. With pink hi-top sneakers. Obviously, she couldn't decide which retro look she was trying to inspire back into style.

"Welcome," Renata said sweetly, and I knew from the smile on her face that she was biting the insides of her cheeks. "Congratulations on your engagement."

Sasha jumped up and down, waving her ring hand at us. We'd never quite had that kind of display in our office. We'd never had a jumper. So Renata and I jumped up and down, too. Zoe was not amused. Donnie was fascinated with the screen saver on Zoe's computer. I know I heard a "whoa" come out of his mouth as he watched a rose bloom over and over and over, his jaw hanging open, his head drooping to one side.

Sasha's hair was white platinum blond now, with pink edges and a blast of yellow in the back, like she'd been tagged in a game of paintball, but it was intentional, and her arms were covered from wrist to elbow with jangly silver bracelets. And the Lance Armstrong yellow bracelet. And the red Kabbalah string. Just to fit in everywhere. Her belly piercing was a pink diamond, of course, and the top of a pink tattoo stuck out from the low-rise edge of her shorts. Raw and jagged-edged, it was a new tattoo, undoubtedly sporting Donnie's name. Or the title of her new CD. Or his.

She caught me looking at her stomach and did a belly dancer roll with it. *I have to learn how to do that.*

Zoe cleared her throat before there was any more of a dance-off, and produced a four-inch-thick folder. In hot pink. And all the papers inside of it were hot pink. It certainly wouldn't get lost in the shuffle. "Sasha's collected a whirlwind of details for us to follow up on. Everything is exactly how she and Donnie want it, and they don't want any compromise."

Well, who does?

"You'll be dealing directly with Sasha, not through her assistants," Zoe went on, spelling out the details of the agreement they'd struck the night before. "And Donnie's requested to be in charge of the bar menu."

Of course.

"She has a dress fitting at nine tonight. Mylie, you'll go with her. Renata, you'll be here for a conference call with the caterer."

Darn it! Renata gets first access to the all-pink-foods menu.

"Since the wedding is in just under two weeks, we have a lot to cover." Zoe stood tall, every now and then sneaking a glance at Donnie, who was sitting behind her desk pushing a pen around in a circle. *What is he on?* "Sasha, we're accessible 24-7, and I've given you all of our cell phone numbers. No time is the wrong time to call."

"Thank you, Zoe," Sasha interrupted her, bored with us already . . . and equally concerned about Donnie playing with the pen. He loved the red circle around the middle. "We'd just like to say that it's been a *dream* of ours to work with you!"

Yes, after you fired the first two planners.

"And we'd like you to come to the wedding!" she squealed. "Isn't that *divine?!*"

We all stood silent. If we had crickets, they'd be chirping. Of course the coordinators attended the wedding.

"We're going to have Red River Rock *Lob*ster. I *love* lobster!" she moaned. *What is SHE on?* "Everyone's going to be there, you know."

They'd responded to the invitations sent out by the first wedding coordinator, prefiring.

"And what kind of arrangements would you like us to make for the media?" Ren asked, quite daring of her, since we never, ever even hinted at media being at weddings. But with this girl, we just knew they'd be seated in the front rows at the ceremony, with the couples' families in the back somewhere.

"Arrangements?" Sasha blinked.

Too many syllables, Ren.

"Where would you like them set up, and what would you like us to serve them?" Ren held her hands behind her back, her fingers laced.

"You mean, like, drinks?" Sasha's eyes grew wide. She hadn't thought of that. "Ooooh, a bartender for the media? That would work!"

Zoe shot a glance at Ren. *Don't make extra work.*

"See what your publicist thinks about it, and we can even set something up where you and Donnie can bring them their champagne glasses to toast you." Ren smiled broadly, nodding for agreement on her great idea.

"I like her." Sasha nodded, mirroring Ren's head movements. "I want her to come to my gown fitting, not the other one."

I guess I'm "the other one."

"As you wish." Zoe twisted her ring on her finger, unsure of Ren's edge today. Would it be wise to send the sarcastic one to the fitting?

"Oh, and we'd like to double up on the press releases." Sasha nodded. "Our publicists have a few sets going out, and we want your office to send out additional sets. Sorta, kinda like leaking the details to the press."

Sorta, kinda.

"You know, like what kind of flowers we're using, and the balloons . . ."

Balloons? What was *in* that folder? I knew Ren and I would be flipping through it with margaritas in hand.

"Oh, and the pink doves." Sasha beamed. "With the glitter on them."

Uh oh.

"Sasha, you might want to rethink coloring the doves and applying anything that could be toxic to them," Zoe warned. At the word toxic, Donnie looked up from his pen.

Sasha pouted, stuck out her lower lip, looking way too much like Emma. Someone had said something that almost sounded like a no. "Um, the doves are part of our deal?" Now she was talking Valley Girl. *Pick a decade and stick with it, girlie.*

"We'll do our best." Zoe shrugged. "But we are bound by the rule of the state against any form of animal cruelty."

At that, I looked at the depressed teacup poodle in Sasha's arms. He blinked a little too slowly. *Forget them, what is the DOG on?*

"If it's possible, we'll do it for you," Zoe said, and I knew she wasn't going to fight that battle. Dyeing and sparkling doves.

"What we *can* do, if you're interested"—I stepped forward a little bit—"is use regular white doves for the release at the ceremony, and then arrange with the editors at *InStyle Weddings* and *People* to have them digitally color the doves *for* you."

"They can *do* that?" Sasha bent forward, blue eyes large, her hand coming up to her throat. "They can *color* the doves? And add sparklies?"

"And add sparklies," I promised. "I have friends in the art departments at both of those magazines who have friends in the art departments of all the other magazines, so we can get it done across the board. No arguing with the animal commission or PETA."

"Who's Peter?" Sasha asked, and Ren lost her balance a little bit. Either from the mention of her husband's name, or in shock at the sheer brain damage of this partied-too-hard-in-preschool chick standing before us.

"Never mind, we'll get it done." Zoe put an end to the discussion and began the goodbye process, shoving the big pink folder into my hands.

"Oh, and I want a *crown*." Sasha giggled as she and Donnie started to leave the office with Zoe. "A crown with pink diamonds from Germany. I heard they're the *best*. I heard that Kick Lyons is getting pink diamonds for Celia."

It was a test. She was looking for our reactions, for proof that we *were* indeed the operation doing the Celia/Kick wedding. At that moment, I knew. The girl just wanted to have the *same* wedding-planning team as Kick and Celia, and she tried to be subtle about it. We just blinked at her. *It's not like it's a state secret anymore.* I'd been on the cover of a tabloid with Kick, after all. Word was out that it was our gig, but no word would ever get out about the details.

"What? They're not pink?" she said innocently, then gave us a wave with her poodle-carrying arm and motioned with her head for Donnie to follow her. He banged his shoulder on the doorway on the way out.

We waited until they were in the elevator and at least a few floors down before we ripped into the pink folder. Zoe opened a cabinet under her desk and pulled out the margarita mix and three glasses.

"They've moved the location."
"That's *great*."
They were not going to be down the street from Kick and Celia anymore, preferring to move it to the other coast. So

Donnie could be closer to his dealer, probably. Now it was going to be at an estate in Rhode Island.

"Keep the wisecracking to a minimum, please," Zoe warned us as the pages revealed plans for a giant pink train on Sasha's dress, with the words *I'm So Happy* painted on it in watercolors. Her tiara, as stated, would have to be pink diamonds, and she wanted pink teardrop earrings to go with it. And her pink hi-tops because "Heels make me look slutty." But the nearly-naked pictures on her wedding Web site made her look demure.

She wanted the pianist to play "The Wedding March," and we were pleased to see something traditional, something we wouldn't have to cringe at while asking a professional to accommodate her. Ah, but there . . . right under it she wrote "and then have them switch to something hotter."

Can we get the rights to porn music? "Something hotter?" Zoe asked, then cracked us up with her oh-so-innocent, "You mean, like something from Jamaica?"

Sometimes there were just too many jokes you could make.

Sasha wanted her father to give her away, but only after being escorted down the aisle, five steps each, taken by her agent, her publicist, her stylist, her attorney, and her yoga instructor. In that order. *Will Donnie be escorted by his parole officer, his AA sponsor, his agent, his publicist, and his dealer?*

Sasha named names for her bridal party, and all were teen stars, her friends and rivals, former hair-pulling archenemies during the 3:00 A.M. hours at the clubs when one or the other talked to one or the other's boyfriend, then wrote a song about it. Every cover of *Teen* and *Tween* magazines showed huggy-face pictures of the girls, with captions ranging from "BFF—Best Friends Forever" to "Kiki Steals Kira's Man!" I doubted they were friends in reality, but rather that some calls were made by some publicists for everyone's benefit.

And tucked inside the folder . . . head shots from several modeling agencies. Sasha was hiring models to stand in her bridal party line as well. "So everyone will be beautiful," she wrote. Donnie's lineup included no scar-faced felons, but rather his own lineup of male models and his twin brother . . . probably because he looked like him.

"Good Lord." Ren whistled as she flipped through the male models' head shots. "Please tell me we get to audition these guys."

I laughed and leaned over to look at them as well. *That's right . . . she's a single woman now.*

"I just want to say 'Work it!' to one of them." Ren giggled. "Please, Zoe, please sign me up for this part."

"Not our call." Zoe shook her head, downing a sip of her margarita.

"Wait!" I picked up a head shot. "What the heck is this?"

Zoe leaned over. Turned the picture over. "Oh, my."

"*Priests* with modeling head shots?!" I laughed. "Are they kidding? They're casting for a good-looking priest?"

"He has to look good in the pictures, Mylie." Ren wagged her finger at me. *Bad Mylie.*

"I consider it a compliment that Sasha's allowing us all to attend the wedding." I laughed, and Ren did as well. Zoe didn't quite get it. The margarita mixes with her meds pretty quickly.

"Honeymoon's in St. Bart's," I found. "She's requested champagne, fresh flowers every day, vodka, Twinkies . . ." I read on through the list. *Ugh.*

"Please tell me we're not doing her bachelorette party." Ren shuddered. "I'll have to get some immunizations first."

"No, they're hiring specialists, bachelorette party planners," I found on another pink page.

"People do that?" Ren marveled. "*We* should do that."

"No way." Zoe frowned. "The wedding's the thing."

"Rings are bought and paid for, flowers are taken care

of . . ." I flipped through more pages. "They want the flowers *spray painted* pink?"

Zoe nodded.

"But they're already going to be pink!"

"She wants a certain shade of pink, so we have to spray paint them all. Plus streaks of gold spray paint."

"*What?!*"

"Streaks. Just randomly across the floral arrangements. Donnie likes graffiti."

We all nodded like that made sense.

"And the tablecloths will have gold streaks as well."

"Naturally."

"What else do we have here?" I flipped through the pink pages, cringing at the bad spelling, the smiley faces dotting each *i*. The lipstick kisses on the tops of each page. "Oh, this is fun. . . ."

"What have you got there?"

"Her *dog* is bringing a date." I laughed. "And we're designing a sweetheart table for the two dogs, a table cut down to three inches off the floor, with a matching tablecloth and gold-colored platters of sushi." The best part was . . . that wasn't the first time we'd been asked to do that. "That should cheer the poor little thing up a little bit." I smiled.

"I *know!* What is with that dog?" Ren laughed, then looked to her hip. Her cell phone was on vibrate. Her smile faded. "Speaking of dogs . . ."

It was Pete on the phone, and she took the call.

"What?" She flipped her phone open and stood with her hand on her hip. "Nope."

With a click, she shut the phone, shaking her head.

"Now where were we?"

"Their wedding vows . . ." I waved the page in my hand, holding it by the tiniest corner between two fingers, shaking my hips.

"Oh, this should be good!" Zoe laughed, clearly done in by half a margarita. "Read it out loud."

I cleared my throat. "I, Sasha, take you Donnie to be my dance partner for life. I promise to move with you, grind with you, shake it with you, no matter the beat of the music." I stuck out my tongue like I'd tasted something sour. "You make me . . . Oh, God."

"What?" Ren's eyes smiled again, the aftereffects of Pete's voice worn off.

"It's X-rated, girls."

"And people are upset about the bride and groom taking out ' 'til death do us part.' " Zoe sighed.

"Oh, they have that in here." I smiled, waving the paper again. "Kinda."

"What do you mean 'kinda.' " Ren wrinkled her nose.

"It says ' 'til death do us *party*.' "

A burst of laughter from both Ren and me, and Zoe just hung her head. Either from sadness about the lack of propriety in the vows, or from the margarita. Probably both.

"Back to the dog." Ren held her own sliver of pink paper. "While Sasha and her cohorts are getting hair and makeup done, one of us is to take the dog and his date to the doggie spa."

"No!"

"Oh, yes. Haircuts and dye touchups, nails painted and affixed with diamond glue-ons."

She has to glitter up some animal, after all.

"But before that, an aqua massage where the dog must be suspended in the water and massaged by no less than ten water jets," Ren read. "And something called an 'anal gland expression.' "

I wrinkled my nose with that one. "A colonic?"

"I have no idea." Ren shrugged.

"Well, you're about to find out!" I laughed.

"Zoe, I need a raise." She leaned over to Zoe, who was fast asleep.

Ren called me from the dress fitting, sending over cell phone photos of The Gown. The top was mostly see-through netting with the exception of heart-shaped fabric panels over her breasts, illusion netting down to her hips, then about a six-inch panel of fabric before a huge slit opening up in the front, with fabric draping like a curtain opening on a show. Seemed appropriate. The train did indeed sport the words *I'm So Happy* in glitter, which thankfully would be covered when we bustled her up. Unless she had something written in glitter on the underside to be revealed by the bustle, which wouldn't surprise me at all.

As I struggled to keep my eyes open during the caterer's endless lists of foods that could be dyed pink, a parade of text messages from Renata:

DRESS NEEDS TO BE LET OUT.

S. WANTS MORE PINK BOWS AT THE BOTTOM OF HER OPEN BACK.

KILL ME NOW.

I texted her right back.

PINK MASHED POTATO BAR, COORDINATED WITH BROWN SAUCES.

PINK WEDDING CAKE WITH BROWN AND PINK CANDY ACCENTS. SEVEN TIERS, WITH A BROWN AND PINK LOLLIPOP ON TOP.

KILL ME NOW.

My phone rang right then, and my dreams were answered. Not the kill-me-now dreams. The other ones. It was Russell.

"Hey," he said, a smile in his voice.

"Hi," I breathed, holding my cell phone with both hands, practically hugging it to my face. "Perfect timing."

"Am I saving you from something unpleasant?"

"Just listening in on a conference call." I stepped away from the speaker phone on the other line. They wouldn't miss me, and I wouldn't miss a detail when I asked them to fax their final choices later. "Everything on the menu must be pink. With brown accents."

Russell laughed, and I knew his chef's brain was whirring with possibilities.

"How's everything with you?" I asked, really meaning *are you done thinking yet?* But doing an excellent job of hiding it.

"It's all right," he said, and it wasn't one of those defeated sigh answers. More like a surprisingly all right. *Sounds encouraging.* "I wanted to invite you to something."

I'm not going back to Dolphin Dance on a weekday. Ever.

"Emma has a dance recital tomorrow night, and we'd love it if you would come."

I smiled. *Sounds even more encouraging.* "I finally get to see her dance?" I laughed.

"Yes . . . finally," he answered, laughing. "She and I have had some discussions lately."

"Such as . . . ?"

"Such as 'Daddy's happy with Mylie, so get over yourself.' " He smiled, I could tell, and I closed my eyes, drinking in every word of it. *Daddy's happy with Mylie.* "I told her that I had walked away from you because she was taking it so hard."

He was just protecting his daughter.

"And that I was very sad about that," he continued. "I know she hasn't impressed you at all, Mylie, but she has a very sweet heart."

I know that. I saw it in her eyes. On the first day.

"She apologized to me, and told me to call you." He laughed at the memory of it. "She even told me her ideas on what to say."

"Such as?"

"That you have pretty hair." He laughed. "And that . . .

and that you're nicer to me than . . . than her mom." Before I could respond to *that* one, he went on. "So she's making you a card right now, an invitation to her dance recital."

Thank you, thank you, thank you.

"And here's a little insider information. . . ." He covered the mouthpiece so his voice was breathy and quiet. "Emma loves daisies, so if you're planning on bringing a bouquet of any kind . . ."

"Gotcha. Thanks for the tip." I beamed. I could hear the conversation on the other phone line still going on as the chef conferenced with his assistant and with Sasha's assistant. They went on and on about which particular breads could best be made in pink without looking like lumps of flesh. "Anything else to give me an edge?"

"Yes," he said, and paused. "Emma *really* loved Celia's necklace, so if you could get that . . ."

I smiled. "Hey, if it would work, I'd fly out to California right now and get it. Celia would let me have it for this." I wasn't kidding. And something struck me. I had a fresh shipment of pink crystals for Sasha's napkins. She wanted the dinner napkins monogrammed in crystal, so I'd ordered three thousand of them overnight-shipped. *You see where I'm going with this, right?* "So now that I have Emma all taken care of in the 'I Love Mylie' campaign . . ." *What can I do about her father?*

"You've already done it," he confessed. "Thank you for giving me the time, Mylie. It wasn't easy to ask you for that."

"It wasn't easy to give it to you." I sighed. "I've missed you."

"I've missed you, too." *No "Me, too" this time.* "And you were right . . . what you said."

Which part?

"I was happy when I planned the day at Dolphin Dance. And I did use what Pete did as an excuse to . . . to wimp out."

I took no joy in being right. "It's okay, Russell. I made my own mistakes because of that, too. But that's behind us now."

"Yes, it is."

I could hear a *Yoo-hoo* and some whistling on the other phone line. I was busted. "Yikes, I've gotta run," I whispered into the phone. "Caught sleeping on the job."

"Talk to you later . . ."

Yes, you will. I'm coming to your place.

The caterer gave me a curt, "I hope we aren't boring you," wrist slap, which I did deserve, and I sipped on some coffee as they discussed how to work pink and brown into a salad.

Chapter 38

The cobblestones shone wet beneath my feet, glistening in the circles of light from the streetlamps. Fall was attempting to push its way in, with cooler air, a bit of a chill tonight. I held Emma's bouquet of daisies against my chest, almost hugging it to infuse it with the amount of love I felt for Russell, giving her some as well.

"Hello, Mylie," from behind me.

Bryan.

I instinctively flipped my car keys around in my hand, a jagged-edged key now between each of my fingers. In case I needed to stab him and get away fast. Plenty of people were on the street that night. I wasn't alone in a dark alley. I could get him with my high heel if I had to.

"Leave me alone, Bryan. I have no information for you."

All he said was "555-8754," Russell's cell phone number. "I think you can help me out." I hadn't noticed the hard features of his face before, his eyes like slits to me now. If I hadn't known his character, I'd describe this face before me as ratlike.

"He knows all about you. He wouldn't believe a word you said." I shrugged, acting as nonthreatened as possible. "So go find someone else to hustle."

Walking away with confidence in that moment . . . in heels . . . on cobblestones . . . was pretty tough to pull off. *The thing about finding the right man is how bad the wrong ones look compared to him.* A few blocks later, my smile was back.

"Mylie!" Suddenly, Emma was my new best friend. What more had Russell said to her? The former little demon ran at me in a pink leotard and pink tulle tutu, her hair drawn up in a classic ballet bun. Her little ballet slippers were scuffed on the sides, with green crayon marks on them. And the residue of unsuccessful stain remover.

"Emma!" I accepted a hug around my hips, surprised by the affection and checking my back for a kick-me sign on a Post-it. *Hey, first impressions last.* Her little friends, all bun-wearing cherubs in pink tutus, gathered around, looking at me.

"This is Mylie . . . she knows Kick Lyons." Emma nodded, and the short crowd *oooh*ed with fascination. "Tell them, Mylie. Tell them I met Kick Lyons. They don't believe me."

"It's true." I nodded, making eye contact with each one of them. "In fact, these flowers are from him and Celia." I handed her the bouquet of white daisies, mixed with yellow daisies, since Russell hadn't specified. She looked at me with such surprise, such warmth, and the little smile grew larger and larger. Her fingers clasped around the cellophane at the bottom, and she hugged the bouquet to her face. All of her little friends leaned in to smell them, too. She was a hero.

Russell looked on with amusement, leaning against the wall with his arms folded across his chest.

"Celia Tyranova?" one of the smallest girls called out. "Emma, you know Celia Tyranova?"

Emma just grinned and nodded.

"And guess what else?" I leaned down to Emma's ear and whispered.

"No way!" Emma jumped back, put her hands on her hips, and leaned over. She was a very dramatic little girl. "I'm going to Kick Lyons's wedding!"

Russell winked at me, nodding at my job well done.

"Am I going to be the flowergirl?" Emma tried, and my heart caught a little bit. There was no way I could swing that.

"No, not the flowergirl, Emma. But we're going to get you the prettiest dress ever, okay?" I tried, and it worked. All of the little ballet princesses around her smiled and jockeyed for position to stand next to Emma. They all wanted to be her best friend. "So go get ready for your recital now. I'm going to talk to your dad."

Emma and the girls raced off, screeching and doing spastic little ballet leaps, toes pointed as they'd been well taught. Quite pleased with myself, I walked slowly toward Russell, toward the hug I'd been waiting for for so long. "Nice work," he said as I walked into my place—*my* place—against his chest, and his arms wrapped around me. "Pimping out your celebrity friends to win over a six-year-old."

"You gotta do what you gotta do." I shrugged.

"Hey, it worked." He kissed me on the top of my head.

Yes, it did.

"Hello, you two." Renata's voice from behind me. When I turned, surprised to see her, I was even more surprised to see who she was standing with. I instantly recognized him from the head shots in Sasha's folder. She had called one of the male models. "This is Kyle. Kyle, my friends, Mylie and Russell."

We shook his hand, and he smiled a dazzling green-eyed smile, the dimple in his chin matching the one on his cheek. He stood over six-foot, broad-muscled shoulders that you could just tell through the dress shirt belonged to an equally impressive chest and abs. He was dressed far better than the ballet dancers' fathers, that was for sure.

"Hey, Mylie." Ren winked. "What's better than working a celebrity wedding?"

I blinked at her. Where was she going with this? "I don't know. What's better?"

"*Not* working one." She giggled.

She quit?!

"What?" *Please. Just give me five minutes with everything being okay. Just five minutes. Please.*

"Sasha Worthington canceled her wedding!" Ren punched me in the arm and shook her head.

My jaw fell open. After I sat through all that pink-and-brown-menu talk? How *could* she? "You're joking."

"Nope." Ren shook her head. "We just got the call. Seems there's more publicity in a canceled wedding than actually having one. Now Sasha's playing the poor, pitiable bride-to-not-be. She's on every news channel already, so they got the calls before we did."

"Unbelievable." I pushed a stray strand of hair behind my ear, shaking my head, the mental computer inside whirring with all of the details we'd worked on for Sasha. And Donnie, who may not ever have known that he was engaged in the first place.

"And she has a book coming out . . . a memoir of calling off her wedding." Ren nodded. "And they already have cover art. It's on her Web site."

So that meant this was the plan all along. We were just a tool of her trade. Sure, she shelled out five figures for our work, but she probably got seven figures for the book deal. *That* explained the lipstick kisses on every page of her pink wedding plans folder. What we'd been looking at was all going to be in the book. She was designing it as we went along, and she took her folder with her at . . . at the last meeting we had.

"And she's auctioning off her dress, the tiara, everything." Ren shrugged.

"How did I not see this coming?" I exhaled, pulling in closer to Russell, who rubbed my back to comfort me. Then left his hand at the small of my back. *Wait, did I ever tell him how I always wished a man would do that to me?*

The house lights flicked on and off, giving everyone the signal to take their seats, and we climbed behind the wall of parents with video cameras to find four chairs set together. The music started, the spotlights on in four equal and stationary positions, and Emma led the way, dancing her little heart out, sneaking in cute little waves to us when she was supposed to hold in a still position.

An hour or so later, after the finale and during the parents' reception, I pulled a square, flat box from my bag. Emma saw the gift wrapped with a bow and knew it was for her. Russell looked at me strangely, nodding at the box with a question in his eyes. "Emma, the flowers were from Kick and Celia . . . and this is from me."

Emma ripped into the wrapping paper, shredding it, almost dropping the box, and when she opened it, let out a scream that frightened the other parents. *Wait, did I just say "the other parents?"*

"Wow!" Emma picked up the pink-and-clear-crystal necklace and held it against her chest. It was an exact replica of the one that she'd stolen from my room, the one that Kick had designed especially for Celia. Emma now had the first faux-gem replica of Celia's wedding-day $750,000 necklace. She'd be the star of the playground. "Daddy, can we go to Taco Bell now? And can I wear my necklace?"

"What do you say first?" Russell warned, nodding toward me.

Emma smiled. "Thank you, Mylie."

"You're welcome."

"And you know what?" Emma went on, kicking her one foot into the other. "I liked you even before the flowers."

"You did?" Renata took over. "When did you start to like Mylie?" She winked at me. Obviously, she had insider information, too. Something good was coming.

"When she was at Dolphin Dance . . . the day she made my daddy smile again."

Chapter 39

"Take him away," I said to the Bruise Crew. "And do whatever you'd like with him."

The six Cro-Magnon in black suits and earpieces each had a hand on Bryan. One hand wrapping almost completely around his neck, others on his jacket, his arm, his hand . . . his camera. Bryan's ratlike eyes blinked hatred at me for singling him out. We left the other paparazzi sitting in their cars, ducking, cowering, on the hill overlooking Celia and Kick's estate. I had noticed their hiding spot during Celia's shower, had driven out there myself through the winding mountainous dirt roads to get my own view of what their telescopic lenses could capture. I knew he'd be there on the wedding day, so I grabbed the Bruise Crew for a little ride through the countryside. I promised them big-game hunting.

The other paparazzi must have been floored. There I was in my light green formal-length gown, in heels, hair done up, light green jewels around my neck, directing these six giants to drag one of their own out of his car. "But first." I stepped closer to Bryan, took the camera from one of the bruisers. "Let's capture this moment, shall we?" I snapped a few shots of Bryan in his captors' grip. "Something to show the kids someday." I winked. "Something to commemorate how you were the *only* one not to get shots of Kick and Celia's wedding."

"Bitch," Bryan spat at me, and I stepped aside. No need to get venom on my dress.

"No, not yet . . ." I smiled and pulled a radio from one of the Bruise Crew's belts. I held up a wait-a-second finger to Bryan and brought the walkie-talkie to my lips. "Celia, Kick, come on out."

All around us, the paparazzi sucked in their breath, hit each other aside, and ran for the edge of the road, snapping their six-figure shots. In the distance, visible from here but I'm sure phenomenal through their camera lenses, Celia and Kick stepped into a clearing on their property, far enough from the wedding site so as not to spoil the surprises for Celia, in their wedding clothes. They embraced, kissed, waved to the cameras, gave them every shot they possibly could have wanted minus a wardrobe malfunction. They did it as a favor to me, and as an "up yours" to Bryan. He was going to get nothing. Not one picture.

"*Now* I'm a bitch." I winked at Bryan and gave him a few gentle taps on his cheek. "Take him away, boys."

The guests were starting to arrive. We had one of those perfect September days with an all-blue sky, gorgeous warm air, no humidity. The perfect weather to be standing on the steps of the estate in my light green gown, greeting guests who arrived by limousine. The famous, the famous who were *really*, jaw-droppingly famous as to make me catch my breath a little bit, their adorably dressed children, and no pink-dyed teacup poodles. Sasha Worthington had tried to crash the wedding, but we saw her pink monstrosity of a dress a mile away and had her diverted. The security team blocked additional uninvited cars at the gate, so I was far removed from the scuffles and arguments that broke out, the hurled insults. Our first line of defense was flawless. No one would get onto the grounds without a white wristband, which we'd messengered out to the invited guests this morning.

A familiar car made its turn around the circular driveway. Russell and Emma had arrived. I smiled my greetings to the guests climbing the stairs at the moment, all admiring Kick and Celia's estate with genuine admiration, and walked calmly and slowly down to greet my favorite people, the ones who really made my breath catch. Russell stepped out of the car in a phenomenal suit, and Emma bounced out of the front seat in her pink dress, wearing the necklace I gave her. I touched her chin and smiled, giving her a wink before I kissed Russell hello.

"Wow, this place is something else." Russell whistled. "Can't wait to see how you've improved on perfection in there."

"Speaking of perfection . . . it's not fair to the groom for you to look so good." I ran my hand along his lapel, feeling the chest beneath it.

"And it's not fair to the bride for *you* to look so good," he replied, saving the chest-feeling part for later . . . I hoped.

"And it's not fair to the flowergirl—who*ever* she is—for *me* to look this good," Emma pronounced, making the other guests around us laugh. Emma pointed to her necklace and told them, "It's a copy of Celia's necklace. I have the only one."

"Uh oh." Russell beamed at his daughter. "What a little diva you're becoming." To me, "We have to keep her from running with this fast crowd."

"The flowergirl had better get her act together." I giggled. "Emma's going to steal the show."

"You're probably right." Russell kissed me again, and waved a goodbye-for-now so that I could get back to work. I had guests to greet, to direct to the gardens and the champagne. And I had to get inside and make sure my tall silk bearers were still in place, holding the white flags in perfect arches as the backdrop for the ceremony. My drummers had been warned not to practice while on the grounds, so their surprise entrance would knock Celia out of her shoes. And speaking of Celia, I had to get upstairs to see how she was doing. . . .

"Knock, knock." I opened the door to Celia's room. Her bridesmaids crowded the mirror in the next-door bathroom, so there was room to breathe around the bride. "How are you doing, Celia?"

She just smiled, standing by her window and watching the guests file in to their places, everyone shaking hands and greeting each other. The tall silks were in place, so Celia couldn't see the drum line behind them even from here. I was glad I had the forethought to set up the silk bearers early.

"I'm excited," she breathed, and I handed her a mint with all the unspoken familiarity of a good friend. "Not nervous at all."

"Good."

"I can't believe the day is finally here. It's like a dream." She took my hand. "Thank you, Mylie. I can't imagine any of this without you."

"You're very welcome." I hugged her, careful of her dress, her veil. "I have to tell you, from the bottom of my heart, that no other couple has ever meant more to me than you and Kick. Honestly. I didn't expect to find two such good friends here."

"We didn't expect that either." She laughed. "But life is funny that way, isn't it?"

"Absolutely. Where's Zoe?" Celia wrinkled her nose. "We haven't seen her all day. Is she okay?"

"Yes," I answered. "She's just running an errand, but she'll be here before the ceremony starts."

"Ah, another surprise from Kick?" Celia knew. "Who is she picking up at the airport?"

Distract her. Distract her now. "Kick asked me to give you this. . . ." I handed her an envelope, and she took it with her other hand over her heart. She stepped away to read his love letter in private, waving her hand in front of her eyes to keep the tears back. As she read, I looked down over the gardens, spotted Russell and Emma taking their prime seats on the aisle, fifth row back, a seat next to Russell saved for me. It would be the first time I ever sat amongst the guests. Normally, we had to watch from the wings, or from a balcony, or we were sent to a separate room with no view of the ceremony at all but rather a call on a cell phone when it was time for us to work again. Not so at this wedding.

A knock at the door. Celia's sisters and mother entered for some private time alone with her, so I went to visit the groom.

"Knock, knock. You decent?" I asked as I pushed open the door to his room. But he was not there. The groom was missing.

But not lost.

I knew just where to go. The chapel.

"Kick?" I pushed open the door and called to him. He was on his knees in front of the altar. "Kick, it's almost time."

He stood, brushed off his knees, and smiled at me. "Just saying thank you." He shrugged.

"I know." I patted his arm as he walked past me and out to take his place before the ceremony started.

"Thanks, Mylie." He gave me a quick kiss on the cheek before leaving, and I warmed at the thought of how happy this couple would be. Before I left the chapel, I prayed that the world they lived in, and the people in it, would never tear them apart. And then I said a quick thank you of my own.

I'll never forget the look on Celia's face when the light lavender flags dropped at their first kiss as husband and wife, and the uniformed drumline came forward in a strong and commanding march, perfectly in step, beating out that primal rhythm that gave me goose bumps the first time I heard them. Celia turned to the crowd, unbelievable joy on her face, in a "can you believe this?!" directed at her parents, who joined the crowd in applause, everyone's heads nodding with the music. Kick and Celia danced and clapped to the beat, and the drummers walked right up in front of the pair, bowing before them, then snapping upright and throwing their drumsticks to one another. Celia's arms went straight up in the air. She was *loving* this. Kick snuck a quick look out into the crowd, met my eyes, and gave me a wink and a salute. I nodded, and the drummers signaled for Kick and Celia to follow them back down the aisle.

The doves flew. White ones, of course. Five dozen.

Kick and Celia were married. They danced to Chris Botti's "When I Fall in Love" at the start of their reception, and it took an amusing few moments to explain to the crowd how both Kick and Celia had separately requested for us to fly in Mr. Botti as a surprise for the other. That was just how right they were for each other.

Kick held her in his arms, his one hand on the bare small of her back, his other hand in knightly embrace with hers out to the side, talking quietly with her as they danced, her eyes sparkling, him looking proud to have the wife he adored. We'd bustled her train so that it fell in cascades of layers, and still she looked small with the mounds of fabric behind her, crystals catching the spotlights, glowing in rainbow colors with her every move. The dress designer, her friend, stood by us, her hands clasped with fingertips pressed against her lips, happier—I could tell—for Celia than for the crush of publicity her gown would bring to her personally.

I scanned the room to be sure everything was in place. Over nine hundred guests sat at tables across the grounds, all eyes on Kick and Celia, which was unusual for a celebrity

wedding. Usually, half the crowd was there for business reasons, shaking hands and making deals even as the bride and
groom danced their first dance or cut the cake. But not at this
wedding. Celia and Kick captured every eye. You couldn't
look away. Not just because they were beautiful, but because
the moment was. That was what pure adoration looked like.

The song ended, and I looked to Russell. Ren stood next
to him with Kyle and Zoe, champagne glasses all in hand,
but his eyes were on me. That too was what pure adoration
looked like.

"Hey you." Celia and Kick were standing before me, on
their way to their sweetheart table for the first toast of the
evening. I walked with them. "You keep a great secret."
Celia wrinkled her nose at me. "No wonder you and Ren
were so quiet when I asked you to book Chris to play our
song."

"Celia, we've never had that happen before." I laughed,
hearing whispers as we walked along, guests knowing my
name and saying, "She planned the wedding." "We've never
had both the bride and groom request the same thing. Just
shows how perfect you are together."

"And it's time for Surprise #10 . . ." Kick announced, and
I looked to Celia for the first glimmers of excitement on her
face. I knew what #10 was. But I was wrong. They had gotten me. "It's for you, Mylie."

"What?" I coughed out the little sip of champagne I'd
managed to get down, never having the time or frame of
mind to enjoy either the food or drink at weddings.

Celia and Kick exchanged a look with each other; then
Celia told me, "We'd like for you and Russell, and Emma, to
stay at our place while we're on our honeymoon."

Everything went quiet for a second. The music. The chat-
ter of nine hundred guests, which could get pretty loud. The
clinking noises the servers made with their tongs on trays of
hors d'oeuvres. Everything went silent. And slowed down for

a moment, then sped back up to reality pace, and I was back in the present. "You're joking," it came out as a whisper.

Celia and Kick shook their heads no. "Seriously," Kick said, holding Celia's hand. Their rings were blinding. The replica of her mother's ring on her hand shone with little tiny diamond chips along a channel in the center. "We want you to stay here for the week, and not just to clean up from the wedding," he joked. "You gave us the wedding of our dreams, and it's something we really want to do for you. For all of you."

"I see the way he looks at you." Celia nudged me. "And I know what you went through to get to this point. So think of it as a vacation on us. Really, Mylie, we want you to have this."

So I got Surprise #10. It wasn't the new car Kick had claimed to have bought, and talked about endlessly. *He really is a good actor.*

Kick sang to her (Surprise #11, a surprisingly good rendition of "Amazed"), and then presented her with the keys to Surprise #12—a ski house he'd bought, redesigned, and decorated just for her. It would be their winter getaway.

Evelyn Greenberg got drunk and left early . . . without saying goodbye to Celia.

Zoe gave out a *lot* of business cards and accepted all compliments with a very gracious sharing of credit to me and to Renata, her "angels." Her lipstick was fine all day.

Ren danced with Kyle, the hunky male model who was relieved not to have to be in Donnie's bridal party. Together, they were working off her remaining baby weight. She looked ten years younger with the flush of attraction and mind-numbing new relationship happiness. He was, after all, ten years younger than she was.

Emma made fast friends with the little girls at the wedding, all of them taking the corner of the dance floor to share their best dancing school moves. Every now and then, she would wave to me and model her necklace with little flourishes and ballet leaps of happiness.

And I danced with Russell, who asked if I wanted all-pink food at our wedding.